HENRY

Book Three of
The Tudor Trilogy

By

TONY RICHES

ISBN-13: 978-1544762425
ISBN-10: 1544762429

BISAC: Fiction / Historical

Tony Riches is a full time writer and lives in
Pembrokeshire, West Wales UK. For more information
about Tony's other published work please see:

www.tonyriches.com

Also by Tony Riches

OWEN - BOOK ONE OF THE TUDOR
TRILOGY

JASPER – BOOK TWO OF THE TUDOR
TRILOGY

THE SECRET DIARY OF ELEANOR COBHAM

WARWICK: THE MAN BEHIND THE WARS
OF THE ROSES

QUEEN SACRIFICE

For my grandson
Brannon

Chapter One

August 1485

Henry had a secret, a chilling truth only he would ever know. He'd never wanted to be king. He once tried to tell his Uncle Jasper. Dismissing him with a laugh, Jasper risked their lives to make it happen, so Henry learnt to live with his secret, which troubled his waking thoughts and haunted his dreams.

He'd not believed it possible to become King of England. Too many stood in his path and others waited for their chance. Given the chance he would live out his days in the serene Brittany countryside. He remembered the sadness in the eyes of the beautiful Breton woman he would never see again.

Even as he marched with his rebel army to Bosworth, he'd made his peace with God. Despite his faith, he feared a painful death and prayed it would be quick. The best he'd hoped for was imprisonment. He had been a prisoner of sorts for most of his twenty-eight years, so it wouldn't have been so bad.

Now he held the gold circlet, he could see it wasn't a proper crown but a symbol of kingship, made to fit over a sallet helmet. His finger traced the fresh, jagged scar in the soft metal. The force of the blow unhorsed the former owner, his enemy, King Richard. Henry heard the king's defiant curse as he fell.

An eerie quiet marked their victory, punctuated only

by the groans of wounded and dying men. An English knight close to Henry called out, his powerful voice shattering the silence like the boom of a cannon.

'God save the King! God save King Henry!'

Henry turned to see his uncle join in with five thousand others. Jasper raised his sword high and shouted at the top of his voice. He no longer wore his helmet and tears glistened on his weary face.

'God save King Henry! God save King Henry!'

'God save King Henry! God save King Henry!'

Henry mounted his white charger and lifted the gold coronet in the air to a rousing cheer from the men. The sound echoed across the battlefield, startling black flapping crows from their gruesome task.

God did little to save the last king, his body slung naked over a horse, on its way to public display in Leicester. Henry said a silent prayer for guidance. He must rely on his faith even more now. He pushed his dark secret away, its power over him replaced by a new foreboding.

He'd won the crown by God's will, his uncle's unwavering loyalty and his mother's determination. Now men looked to him as their new king, yet he'd seen what happened to kings. He waited for the cheers to subside and recalled the words of his uncle during their long exile in Brittany.

'A king doesn't have to fight in wars. If you were king, you could bring peace to this country.'

He clung to that thought on the long march from Mill Bay in Wales. Henry doubted any king could end all wars but he could make his mother proud. First, he must deal with Richard's supporters. Many lay dead on Bosworth Field, their armour robbed by scavengers. Thousands surrendered, throwing down their weapons.

Others escaped in the confusion to fight another day.

Henry stared into the expectant faces of men who'd been ready to sacrifice their lives for him. Several bled from wounds in need of attention, all looked weary from fighting. He raised his eyes to the sky as bright summer sunshine streamed from behind a cloud—a good omen.

'We give thanks to God for our great victory this day.' He fought to keep emotion from his voice. He must appear strong, like a king.

Another cheer tore through the soldiers crowding around Henry. He glanced across to his uncle. Jasper nodded in approval, a grin transforming his lined, serious face for the first time since they sailed from France.

Henry knew this was his destiny. God had chosen this path for him. How else could they have won against such impossible odds? The thrilling thought surged through his mind, driving out doubts and fears. He raised the gold circlet in the air a second time.

'This is the day which the Lord has made. We will rejoice—and be glad in it!'

His voice carried the strength of his new conviction. Henry drew comfort from the words of the psalm, chosen for this moment long ago. Jasper made him shout it across the marshes from battlements of Château Suscinio. He'd called out the words over and again until he'd lost all trace of his French accent.

His powerful horse snorted with impatience and stamped a hoof on the hard ground. Henry muttered soothing words to settle his mount and took a firmer grip on the rein. He resisted the overwhelming urge to leave this place of death. There was much to do. He would reward the survivors but the dead would be on his conscience. May God have mercy on their souls.

Word of their victory travelled faster than Henry's army. The narrow streets of Coventry thronged with cheering crowds, welcoming their new king. Riding his charger, Henry thanked God the people were ready to accept him. The clatter of hooves competed with the rhythmic thump of a thousand marching boots drumming on cobble-stones. Cheers echoed from half-timbered buildings on either side. An attractive woman caught Henry's eye and waved to him from an open window.

'Long live King Henry!'

Men applauded and raised their hats in the air as the grand procession passed, calling out in deep voices.

'God bless the king!

Barefoot children squealed with excitement as they ran ahead, leading the way to the waiting reception. Henry noted the rich velvet robes and heavy gold chain of the mayor as the man bowed before him.

'Welcome to our fine city, Your Grace.'

Henry nodded in acknowledgement. The face of the mayor seemed ordinary enough, yet his glittering badge of office set him apart. Conscious of his own mismatched armour, lank hair under an old felt hat and faded, travel-worn cape, Henry added more items to his mental list.

Jasper spoke for them. 'We need lodgings for the king and his servants, as well as billets for our men.' His voice carried the new confidence of a victor and uncle of the king.

The mayor peered behind Jasper at the battle-weary soldiers. 'I wish to offer the use of my own house, my lord. Your knights will find a warm welcome in our hostelries—and your men may camp on the common for as long as you wish.'

Jasper smiled. 'Thank you, good sir. We appreciate your hospitality, which we will reward.'

Henry sat at the heavy oak desk in the study of the mayor, Master Robert Olney, who proved to be a wealthy wool merchant and a useful ally. It had been a long day and his candle burned down to a flickering stump. He rubbed his eyes and hesitated, quill in hand, as he reread the arrest warrant. Bishop Stillington tried to trick him into King Richard's hands.

Not being in a vengeful mood, Henry might have forgiven him. Then came news the corpulent bishop had been complicit in declaring Princess Elizabeth a bastard. Henry's brow furrowed as he marked the parchment with a bold letter H, underscored with a tapering stroke of black ink.

The next warrant proved more of a test of his resolve. Henry had agreed that Edward Plantagenet, Earl of Warwick, should be taken to the Tower of London. Ten years old, the boy's only crime was one of birth. Henry bit his lip and pushed the warrant to one side.

'Fetch my uncle, if you will?'

His servant bowed and left, closing the door behind him. Henry found himself alone for the first time he could remember. He'd learnt all he could from the men fleeing King Richard to join him in exile, yet the burden of his new responsibilities unsettled him. Clasping his hands together he prayed again for guidance. He repeated aloud the Latin words of the *Te Deum*, sung earlier that evening in celebration by black-garbed monks in the nearby Priory of St Mary.

'Te ergo quæsumus, tuis fámulis súbveni, quos pretióso sánguine redemísti...'

The door opened and Jasper entered, wearing a smart emerald green doublet Henry hadn't seen before. 'What is it?' He sounded short of breath.

Henry raised a calming hand. 'The hour is late and you look tired, uncle, but I need your opinion.'

Jasper noted the warrants on Henry's desk. 'Is there trouble?' A worried frown returned to his tanned brow.

'On what grounds do we imprison young Edward Plantagenet?'

Jasper sat in the spare chair and rubbed the stubble on his chin as he considered the question. He'd chosen to shave his beard on the journey from Wales. He looked younger clean-shaven, but a beard suited his uncle, and Henry guessed he was already growing it back.

'King Richard considered the young earl enough of a threat to declare him illegitimate.'

Henry allowed himself a smile. 'King Richard declared everyone illegitimate, other than himself. Young Edward is a cousin of Princess Elizabeth.'

Jasper returned his smile. 'Half of England is related to the Woodvilles one way or another.' His face became serious. 'We need time, Henry. Time to win over the doubters. We could say it is for young Edward's own safety?'

Henry picked up his quill and dipped it in Mayor Olney's inkpot before signing the warrant. 'We must ensure the boy is well treated—I wish no harm to him.'

'Then we must move with all speed,' Jasper sat back in his chair, 'before the Yorkists see a chance to take him.' He loosened the front of his doublet and stifled a yawn.

Henry realised he'd kept his ageing uncle up too late. 'We must ensure the safety of the princess, who is also at Sheriff Hutton Castle...'

'Princess Elizabeth is in the care of her mother—so the sooner you marry her the better.'

A twinkle of amusement flashed in his uncle's eye. 'Not until after the coronation, as we agreed.'

'As it should be. You are king in your own right, not by any marriage.'

Henry was heartened by Jasper's words. 'Thanks to you, Uncle. I will never forget all you've done for me, and I'm finally in a position to show my gratitude.'

Jasper poured himself a measure of red wine from the untouched jug on the mayor's desk and took an appreciative sip. 'What do you have in mind?'

'A dukedom. Sir Jasper Tudor, Duke of Bedford— and of course we will restore your title of Earl of Pembroke.'

Jasper smiled. 'I should like that.' He noticed the candle looked about to burn out and placed a fresh one in the silver holder, lighting it from the flickering stub. He gave a nod of satisfaction as a bright flame caught. 'It would be good to have my own income again.'

'I've also been thinking... it's time you found yourself a wife, Uncle.'

Jasper laughed, 'I've been a bachelor too long...' His voice softened a little at the thought.

'Too long for a rich, beautiful widow, half your age?'

'Most certainly, although...' Jasper took another sip of wine, 'you have someone in mind?'

'Lady Catherine Woodville.' Henry watched for Jasper's reaction. 'It's two years since Buckingham's execution, so she's no longer in mourning.' His tone became conspiratorial. 'I understand Catherine has the pleasing looks of all the Woodville women.' Henry leaned forward in his chair. 'You will help to unite Lancaster and York.' It sounded like an order.

Jasper grinned at Henry's new authority and drained his goblet of wine. 'I will give the matter serious consideration.'

They first heard of the sweating sickness from a merchant fleeing London. Henry's entourage had covered less than two-thirds of the hundred-mile journey south-east to the capital to make arrangements for Henry's coronation. The merchant held up a gloved hand and shouted to Jasper as they passed on the road, not recognising Henry as the king.

'London has a plague, my lord.'

Jasper cursed and called them to a halt, glancing back at Henry, his eyes full of concern, then studied the man's florid face. 'What are the signs?'

'They shiver, then burn with the fires of Hell.' The merchant scowled at a memory. 'They call it the sweat, my lord, because the fever is so sudden. I've heard young and old are dead in a day—so I'd say London is no place to be heading.'

'I thank you, sir, for your good advice.'

The merchant tipped his hat and continued on his way. A horse-drawn wagon, laden with his baggage, followed with his coterie of grim-faced servants, struggling to keep up.

Jasper rode to Henry and glanced back at the departing merchant. 'We'll stay clear of the city until this fever has passed.'

Henry felt a stab of concern to hear his uncle dismiss the deaths of innocent people, then realised he too must become hardened. They had been safe from plague in Brittany but he'd heard the stories and his mind raced with the consequences.

'They will say this plague is an omen...'

Jasper dismissed the idea. 'It will pass—but for now we must find a place of safety.'

Henry peered up the long road ahead. More wagons laden with as much as they could carry headed from the city. 'No.'

'The risk is too great, if what that man says is true.'

'We take many risks. What would the people say if we ran to safety now?'

Jasper seemed undecided. 'I could ride ahead, see for myself.'

Henry shook his head. 'You should be at my side when we enter London. Trust in the Lord, Uncle.'

The setting sun cast a warm glow over the city as they rode through the gate into Shoreditch. Word of their arrival drew curious crowds, despite the sickness. It seemed he'd won over the people by his presence at such a dangerous time for them all.

This time his proud mother led the reception, flanked by the murrey-cloaked aldermen of the city. She looked older than he remembered, yet her sharp eyes missed nothing.

'We thank God for your safe arrival.'

The pride Henry heard in his mother's voice triggered long-forgotten memories, threatening to choke his words. 'We are grateful for your presence here, Lady Mother,' he recognised Lord Stanley, standing a discreet distance behind his wife, 'and to my stepfather, for his loyal support.'

An elderly alderman wearing a gold chain of office

stepped forward. 'We bid you welcome on behalf of the Mayor of London, Your Grace.'

Henry raised a hand in acknowledgement. 'Where is the mayor?' He guessed the answer.

The alderman's face tensed. 'He has the sickness, Your Grace, along with many other good men and women of this city.'

'We will pray for their mortal souls—and mark this day with a special service of thanksgiving.'

A discordant fanfare of trumpeters sounded as they entered the grand cathedral of St Paul's. Henry led a slow procession through the gathered nobles, recognising loyal Lancastrians who'd shared his exile in Brittany and France.

Choirs sang the *Te Deum* and Dean William Worsley, who'd outlived two previous kings, read a fitting sermon, his deep voice echoing. Henry studied the austere figure of his mother at the front of the congregation with her husband, whose action saved the day at Bosworth Field. He would reward Lord Stanley with an earldom and make his mother a countess. He also planned to restore his mother's fortune and build her the finest house in London.

As they were leaving the service Henry's eyes met those of his future wife. Wearing a rich burgundy robe trimmed with black fur, Princess Elizabeth studied him with a confident, knowing gaze. He'd imagined her eyes would be sapphire blue yet, like her hair, glimpsed under her hood, they dazzled with the golden intensity of a rising sun. The back of Henry's neck tingled as he had a vision of his destiny.

At Elizabeth's side stood an older yet attractive woman who studied him with an appraising stare.

Henry realised this must be his future mother-in-law, York's queen, Lady Elizabeth Woodville. He sensed her sadness, yet a flash of ambition crossed her face at the sight of him.

Back in the relative privacy of the Palace of Westminster he lowered his voice so only Jasper could hear. 'I am minded to reward Lady Elizabeth's support by making her Queen Dowager.'

'A shrewd move—particularly if I'm to marry Lady Catherine.'

'Was Lady Catherine at St Paul's today?'

'I don't know—there were so many there I've never seen before. England has changed a great deal while we've been in Brittany.'

'We have a task ahead of us, Uncle, deciding whom we wish to have at court—and whom to watch out for.'

'Now the people of London have seen you, we must leave Westminster until the sweating fever has passed.'

'Delay my coronation?'

'I don't see we have any choice. The royal hunting lodge at Guildford Castle would serve until you've chosen your permanent residence.'

'Is it far from here?'

'Some thirty miles to the south-west.'

Henry nodded. 'A short rest would suit us all. You must get to know your future bride, and I wish to spend time with mine.' He sensed a frisson of anticipation as he recalled the face of Princess Elizabeth. 'We must also make sure the Woodvilles stay safe from this sweating sickness.'

The royal hunting lodge, with a high laurel hedge and deep, stagnant moat, offered privacy and would be easy to defend against unwelcome visitors. Successive kings had allowed Guildford Castle to fall into disrepair, yet maintained the lodge as a favourite refuge. Ancient tapestries of hunting scenes and stag horns decorated the walls and grand fireplaces provided warmth in winter.

Henry had the largest of four apartments, next to a private chapel. The lodge reminded Henry of his time at Forteresse de Largoët in Brittany. For a moment he wished he could return to the peaceful château with its endless woodlands, tranquil lake, no worries and no responsibilities. Then he remembered this was his destiny, the path chosen for him, and he must thank God for his good fortune.

He watched as his servants unpacked his personal chests. He'd arrived in Wales with little more than a travelling knight could carry, but now he must live like a king. At least he had the advantage of his recent experience of the French court, where they spared no expense on clothes.

A gold badge set with a large ruby adorned his new black cap, and he wore an ermine-trimmed robe of gold brocade. Even his new leather boots had fastenings of solid silver. Henry chose not to wear a sword, although the sharp Breton dagger at his belt served him well.

At first the threat of assassination caused him to wake at the slightest noise, and his Uncle Jasper with a dozen hand-picked soldiers acted as his bodyguard. Now he had fifty liveried yeomen, chosen and commanded by the Earl of Oxford. The rest of his mercenary army paid off and long gone, more than enough of his Welsh followers remained, looking for favours.

A servant disturbed Henry's thoughts to announce the arrival of Richard Foxe. Foxe proved astute and loyal during the last year of their exile and was now his personal secretary. As tall as Henry, equally devout, and looking older than his thirty-seven years, Foxe dressed as always in cleric's robes. His long face and sunken, clean-shaven cheeks belied his dour sense of humour.

'Good day, Your Grace. May God be with you.' His voice carried warm sincerity with his soft Lincolnshire accent.

'And with you, Master Foxe.' Henry studied the face of his loyal friend. 'You've made the arrangements?'

'Your enemies are deemed guilty of treason, Your Grace. We've drafted Acts of Attainder to seize the lands of those who escaped to sanctuary.'

'You've not wasted any time.'

Foxe allowed himself a rare smile. 'A good number now profess their loyalty to you.'

'As you predicted. And after my coronation we shall announce that any who swear fealty will be secure in their property and person.'

'Your coronation date has been set for the thirtieth day of October.' Foxe studied Henry with slate-grey eyes. 'Before the first sitting of Parliament. It will show you do not need their approval.'

'Or the hand of a York princess.'

'Indeed. The papal dispensation for your marriage could take several months.'

'See that it does—and in the meantime I wish the princess to visit me here. It's time I got to know the future Queen of England.'

'And your mother, Your Grace?'

'I am invited to visit her tomorrow—and you shall accompany me.' A thought occurred to Henry. 'What of my uncle?'

'Engaged to Lady Catherine—and not before time, if

I may say, Your Grace.'

'Good. You've done well, Foxe. I will reward you by restoring your appointment as Vicar of Stepney.'

'Thank you, Your Grace, it would mean a lot to me.'

As Richard Foxe left, Henry called for his servant to bring him a fresh quill and parchment. His plans were coming together well, thanks to men like Foxe. He dipped the quill in ink and began writing a list of state appointments, starting with his commander at Bosworth, Sir John de Vere, Earl of Oxford.

Henry's mother greeted them in a high-ceilinged room at Woking Manor, her home for the past nineteen years. A fur-trimmed, burgundy silk gown replaced her usual black dress and a glimpse of grey hair showed under her close-fitting hood.

'Welcome, Henry, and you Master Foxe.' She gestured for them to take a seat at the dark oak table, laden with the gleaming Beaufort silverware.

'Good day, Lady Mother.'

'Your stepfather asked me to convey his apologies. He is in Westminster, helping with the arrangements for your coronation.'

Henry noted the pride in her voice. 'I will need you both to move closer to London when the sickness has passed.'

'I have a manor house at Coldharbour, by the river in upper Thames Street. With a little work it could be a fine residence.'

Henry glanced around the sparsely furnished room. 'I shall see to it, Mother, and would you be kind enough to find rooms there for Princess Elizabeth?'

'I thought she was in the care of her mother?'

'She is,' Henry glanced at Foxe and looked back at

his mother, 'but you need time to know your future daughter-in-law, and I will be able to visit you both more often.'

Lady Margaret looked pleased at the prospect. 'You are right. I will treat her as my own daughter.'

The red dragon of Cadwallader, last King of the Britons, flew high above the hallowed nave of Westminster Abbey alongside the flag of St George. The air carried the exotic scent of incense, burning in silver censers suspended from chains. A hundred roses of Lancaster decorated the pews, and everywhere shone gold and silver portcullis badges of the Beauforts.

Henry wore a fine silk doublet in Tudor green and white under a long velvet cloak of royal purple, trimmed with cloth of gold. Flanked by the high-mitred bishops of Exeter and Ely, he stared ahead as they made their slow procession to the throne.

His mind turned to the many people who brought him to this day. The merchant, Thomas White of Tenby, who hid him in his cellar and helped him to escape York's army. Duke Francis of Brittany, who gave him sanctuary in exile for so many years. The young King Charles of France, who funded his invasion fleet. His Uncle Jasper, now Duke of Bedford, who carried his crown, and his stepfather, now Earl of Derby, who carried his sword of state.

A noisy crash followed by shouts of alarm marred the moment as scaffolding outside the abbey collapsed under the weight of cheering crowds. Henry thanked God when told none were injured, and took it as a good omen.

The elderly Thomas Bourchier, Archbishop of

Canterbury, who had crowned Richard king two years before, stumbled over his words when he realised the amended order of service still referred to the former king's supporters. Henry heard a sob break the reverent silence as his head was anointed. His mother, always so controlled, was overcome with emotion.

Henry bit his lip to focus his mind. He was doing God's will. The choir sang a hymn of praise as Henry stood tall, wearing his heavy new crown. He'd defied the odds to become King of England. He'd defeated his enemies, overcome his secret doubts and made his mother proud.

Chapter Two

January 1486

Henry lay back in his sumptuous, canopied bed and reached out a hand to caress the curves of the woman sleeping at his side. Her flawless skin felt like warm silk to his touch. She murmured as he stroked her long golden hair, and opened her eyes.

He studied her perfect features, trying to read her thoughts. In his twenty-eight years he'd kept the company of men and only slept with one other woman. Their ways were still something of a mystery to him. One he planned to take great pleasure understanding.

Wintry sleet pattered against the shuttered window and he heard the sharp cough of the guard outside his door. The sweating sickness seemed to have passed yet Henry remained vigilant. He could not afford to be unwell and made a mental note to have the coughing man seen by a physician.

At last she spoke, her voice soft. 'I fear our secret is out, Henry Tudor.'

'Which one would that be? That you've bewitched the King of England?'

She laughed, her eyes sparkling with delight. 'Your mother seems to suspect as much.'

'My lady mother wishes to see us wed. She never misses an opportunity to remind me of my promise.'

'She's right.' Elizabeth pulled back the coverlet. 'If

you delay much longer it will be too late to hide this—even under my new velvet gown.'

'You're with child?' Henry heard the wonder in his voice. 'It must be too early to tell?'

'A woman knows these things.' She sounded defensive. 'My mother had twelve children. She told me she knew for certain each time.'

'And you know?'

'You planned this, surely?'

He raised an eyebrow at the note of admonishment in her question. 'No. As God is my witness.' Henry caressed her with new tenderness. 'You think it is a son?'

'The next King of England.'

Henry sat up, his mind a whirl of new plans. His Uncle Jasper always told him his first duty as king was to produce an heir, a son to continue the Tudor line. Jasper was one of the few people who knew Henry already had a son in Brittany. He'd advised Henry to keep it secret from his mother, who would not approve.

'Years ago in Brittany I thought to name my first son Arthur.'

'King Arthur...' She sounded thoughtful. 'I expected you would wish to name him Henry?'

Henry smiled. 'We shall name our second son Henry.'

'And have you already named our daughters?'

'Margaret, after my mother, then Elizabeth, after yours.'

Elizabeth laughed and kissed him. 'I was right—you've planned everything!'

'Except for one detail. People will worry if the baby is born after eight months?'

Elizabeth pulled him close and kissed him again, this

time more slowly. 'Then we must marry as soon as we can.'

'Richard Foxe has finally secured the papal dispensation. There is no need to delay any further.'

He kissed her and she responded to his touch. Years later Henry recalled that kiss, the moment he fell in love with Elizabeth, his beautiful York princess.

Westminster Abbey glittered with the warm glow of a thousand candles as they said their vows. Elizabeth's gown of crimson satin rustled as she walked through the hushed guests to where Henry waited in cloth of gold and royal purple. Sapphires and emeralds woven into her hair, worn long and loose as a symbol of purity, sparkled in the light.

Archbishop Thomas Bourchier, now a frail eighty-two years old, asked the congregation to confess before God if there were any known impediments to the marriage. After a short silence he turned to Henry.

'Do you, Henry, take Elizabeth to be your wife?'

'I do.' His voice echoed in the high-vaulted abbey.

The archbishop continued. 'Do you, Elizabeth, take Henry to be your husband?'

Her reply echoed in the silence. 'I do.'

Archbishop Bourchier asked Henry to take Elizabeth's right hand in his and recite his vows before God and the people. Henry looked into Elizabeth's veiled eyes. He'd taken the trouble to learn the words of the solemn, scripted ritual yet now struggled to keep his voice steady.

'I take thee, Elizabeth, to my wedded wife, to have and to hold from this day forward, for better for worse, for richer, for poorer, in sickness and in health, until death us depart, if holy church it will ordain, and thereto I plight thee my troth.'

Elizabeth's reply echoed in the abbey. 'I take thee, Henry, to my wedded husband, to have and to hold, from this day forward, for better for worse, for richer, for poorer, in sickness and in health, to be blithe and bonair, meek and obedient, until death us depart, if holy church it will ordain, and thereto I plight thee my troth.'

Jasper passed the wedding ring to the archbishop, which he blessed and handed to Henry. He slid it over Elizabeth's thumb.

'In nomine Patris,' he placed it over her index finger, 'et Filii,' then on her middle finger, 'et Spiritu Sancti. With this ring I thee wed. This gold I thee give, with my body I thee worship and with this dowry I thee endow.'

The archbishop blessed their union and declared them man and wife. Henry lifted Elizabeth's gossamer veil and kissed her. As he did so, a weight lifted from his shoulders. He'd finally united Lancaster and York and would never have to face life alone again.

As Henry led her by the hand back down the knave to the tuneful music of Elizabeth's minstrels, he had his first look at the congregation. Jasper sat next to his wife, the new Duchess of Bedford, with the Dowager Queen Elizabeth. He glimpsed a satisfied expression on the face of his new mother-in-law before her usual composure returned.

His mother, dressed in her finery, sat with Earl Stanley, who'd stood in for Elizabeth's father. Once a favourite of King Edward, who made him Steward of the King's Household, Stanley had known Elizabeth since she was five years old.

They emerged through the great doorway to rousing cheers from crowds, which waited despite a bitter January wind. The sound lifted Henry's heart. He'd worried about how to win the affection of the people. Now he wondered if the cheers were for him or his York queen.

Henry had little appetite for the royal banquet, prepared regardless of expense. A pair of gilded swans formed the centrepiece, their long necks entwined in the shape of a heart. It seemed a good idea when Oxford suggested it yet now the display looked extravagant. He noted that the servants who carried it wore York murrey and blue and resolved to order new livery of Tudor green and white.

Jasper raised a shining silver goblet and grinned as he leaned across to congratulate them. 'To many happy and peaceful years.'

Henry stared into Elizabeth's bright amber eyes for a moment as he raised his own goblet in response. 'And to my beautiful new wife.'

Jasper smiled. 'Your grandfather would have been so proud to see what you've achieved.'

'I couldn't have done it without you, Uncle.'

Elizabeth raised her goblet. 'We both owe you a great debt, Sir Jasper.'

'If that's true, I am repaid in full by the sight of the two of you as husband and wife.'

At dusk the sky lit up with celebratory bonfires and fireworks, never seen before by the people of London. Great explosions thundered and echoed across the fast-flowing River Thames as rockets soared high into the air. Like bright comets, they flared and burst in a dazzling celebration of the union of Lancaster and York.

Henry shuddered as he recalled the thunder of

cannons at Bosworth and the inhuman screams of maimed soldiers. He said a silent prayer he would never resort to war again. As he watched the fireworks he knew, despite his hard won peace treaty, he still faced the risk of invasion from the Scots. He frowned at the thought of using his scarce resources to defend the North.

As fireworks boomed and crackled in a cascade of stars, Henry worried about news rebel Yorkists were preparing to return from sanctuary. He glanced to either side to ensure his ever-present Yeomen of the Guard were in place. He'd been generous with pardons and lenient with the Yorkist lords and prayed they would not give him cause to regret it.

A plan formed in his mind as another rocket flashed high across the night sky, its luminous path reflected in the dark swirling waters of the Thames. He should make a royal progress to York to win over the people of the North.

The plan had its dangers, yet was his duty as king. He would trust in his faith although he worried for his new wife and unborn child. Elizabeth must wait in the safety of Greenwich Palace and pray for his safe return. He hoped Yorkist rebels would treat their former princess with respect if he did not.

Elizabeth seemed unaware of the dark thoughts troubling him. 'Now we are married, I must ask you a great favour.'

He guessed she'd been waiting for this moment. 'What do you wish for?'

'You restored my mother's status as Queen Dowager, yet she has no income. She's sold most of her jewels...'

Relieved she asked for so little he took her hand in his. 'I will grant all that is due as your father's widow.'

Elizabeth squeezed his hand in thanks and looked as if she might ask for something else. Another firework boomed in the night sky overhead and the moment passed. He knew he must soon decide about her coronation and decided to speak to his mother.

Henry set off on his progress, his mood lifted by the bright March sunshine and cheering well-wishers. Jasper rode at his side and the Earl of Oxford carried their flowing banner of the red dragon and cross of St George. Henry's liveried yeomen followed with the knights and retainers of his household. Ten gold-painted wagons laden with servants and supplies, hauled by straining oxen, completed the grand procession.

At the end of February, they'd had to deal with riots in London, sparked by rumours of the murder of Edward Plantagenet in the Tower. Henry understood why people were suspicious. He'd found no evidence but believed Elizabeth's brothers, the two princes, might have been murdered by Richard's supporters.

The innocent Edward, though young and simple-minded, would always be a threat to peace. Henry had the boy marched through the streets to a service in St Paul's so all could see he remained safe and well. Only a few days before, one of the Yorkist leaders, Lord Lovell, emerged from hiding to raise support for a bid to rescue young Edward. Henry sent Jasper with men to arrest the rebels and heard nothing since.

Such incidents hardened Henry's resolve and, after covering more than twenty miles a day, they were passing the point of no return. Stopping to change from his travelling clothes into new cloth of gold and an ermine cape, Henry regretted allowing Jasper to ride ahead and prayed no harm had come to him.

He felt relief to see Jasper raise a hand to greet him. His uncle waited with a small army of retainers at Tadcaster Bridge, the main crossing of the River Wharfe some ten miles from York.

'Welcome, Your Grace!' Jasper grinned.

Henry raised his gloved hand in acknowledgement. 'Good to see you, Sir Jasper.'

Jasper approached and spoke so only Henry could hear. 'I offered Lovell's followers a pardon, which they were happy to accept.'

'Thank God. What became of Lovell?'

'Escaped. He's more slippery than an eel, that one—but I have men pursuing him, all the way to France if necessary.'

Henry cursed at the prospect of another rebel slipping through his hands. 'What's the mood in York?'

'They've prepared a reception for you. It seems you've not had a wasted journey.'

'All the same, tell your men to be vigilant.'

'Of course.' Jasper glanced round at the clatter of approaching hooves. 'Earl Henry Percy, with a good few men.'

Henry had already spotted the proud gold banner with its rampant blue lion. 'I arranged for Percy to meet us here with as many as he could muster.'

'A show of strength?' Jasper raised an eyebrow. 'I'm not sure I trust Percy, despite your faith in him, Henry.'

'I hope to send an important message by having so many of King Richard's men following us into York.'

A noisy pageant followed the service of thanksgiving at York Minster. Costumed performers represented each of the previous kings named Henry and acted out their great deeds. Musicians played and the people were in good spirits, dancing and drinking in celebration. The mayor and aldermen of York were effusive with their welcome, despite nervous glances at his armed guardsmen.

Cheering crowds filled the narrow streets of York, so the procession continued on foot. Henry noted the proliferation of his adopted emblem, red and white roses, symbols of the Virgin, representing sacrifice and purity. Freshly painted over doorways, the red rose now had a white rose in the centre, the Tudor rose, the unity of Lancaster and York.

Drummers beat a staccato rhythm and trumpets blasted, echoing from the houses on either side. Women waved from open windows and many voices chorused. 'Long live King Henry, long live King Henry!'

The attacker took them all by surprise, rushing from the crowd towards Henry with an angry cry of 'For York!'

Henry turned at the shout in time to see a raised dagger as the man charged at him. Sunlight flashed on Jasper's sword and the knife clattered to the cobbles. Two of Henry's burly yeomen dragged the wounded man away to meet the fate of all traitors.

The attack was over in seconds yet to Henry it felt as if time stood still. He raised his eyes to the heavens in thanks and took a deep breath before turning to his uncle.

'I owe you another debt.'

Jasper shook his head. 'I happened to be the closest.'

Henry glanced around. The narrow street with high, overhanging houses made the perfect spot for the attacker. It also meant there were few witnesses. He didn't wish his progress blighted by talk of attempted assassination.

'We should not condemn the whole of York for the act of one man.' He forced a smile, although he could be dead if not for Jasper's swift action.

Jasper sheathed his sword. 'I'll need to double your guard. There's no way of knowing if he acted alone.'

Henry studied the faces in the shocked crowd and wondered how many murderous assassins waited, prepared to give their lives to end his. The attack was too close, too easy. His heart pounded at the thought of what could have happened.

The sharp memory of the man raising his dagger troubled Henry as their progress continued south-west towards Bristol. Since the moment of his coronation he'd been certain this was God's plan, his destiny. The attack served as a warning—a reminder of his mortal vulnerability. He'd won the crown by ancient right of conquest and must fight to retain it.

The rider galloped straight for Jasper and spoke in an urgent tone, too low for Henry to hear. His uncle glanced across and Henry sensed the familiar frustration as he recognised the appraising look.

'What is it?' Henry heard the challenge in his voice.

Jasper turned in his saddle. 'Yorkist Rebels. Our men pursued their leaders but they've found sanctuary in a church near Abingdon.'

'Lovell's men?'

'Humphrey and Thomas Stafford. They planned to take advantage of your absence to raise an army against us.' Jasper gave a wry smile. 'They failed. It seems we're winning more support every day, Henry. You were right about the need for this progress.'

Henry agreed. 'It is the only way—but we must deal with these rebels.'

'There's nothing we can do about the Stafford brothers, for now at least.'

'We can't let them escape?'

'I'll order a watch kept over them. They can't stay in a church forever—and when they come out we'll be waiting for them.'

Henry struggled to control a surge of anger at Humphrey and Thomas Stafford's disloyalty. 'They must swear fealty—or face the consequences!'

'You wish to violate their right of sanctuary?'

'I do. Send men you can rely on.'

Jasper studied him before replying. 'Your grandfather used the right of sanctuary...'

'My grandfather wasn't plotting treason against the king!' Henry heard the edge to his voice and managed a smile. 'I will sleep more soundly knowing these rebels are in the Tower, not turning people against us.'

Henry knelt in prayer in the Venerable Chapel of Winchester Cathedral, his refuge during Elizabeth's confinement. Glad of the privacy of the small chapel, with its richly carved and coloured screen, he found the tranquil atmosphere helped him think.

He thanked God his first year as king could be counted as a success. Astute appointments of many of King Edward's former advisors meant he could rely on the support of Parliament and the church. He'd avoided rewarding nobles without good reason and reduced their power in the land.

He prayed for the fragile peace to continue. Yorkist rebels were silenced by the execution of Sir Humphrey

Stafford at Tyburn for treason. He'd pardoned Stafford's younger brother Thomas and hoped the rebels would understand his message. He continued to worry about the threat of insurrection. Lovell had yet to be captured and was thought to be raising an army in Flanders.

Richard Foxe appeased the troublesome Scots yet Henry kept his northern borders guarded. He planned to reward Foxe's loyalty by appointing him as Bishop of Exeter and Keeper of the Privy Seal. The income would make him a wealthy man, although Henry wondered what Foxe would do with the money, as he lived a simple life and still dressed as a cleric.

Henry prayed for the safe delivery of his child, the focus of his life. He worried about Elizabeth, so pale and tired as she reached full term. Her physician tried to set Henry's mind at rest but he'd read concern in the old man's eyes.

After his prayers Henry lit a candle in memory of the father he never knew and made his way to his chambers. He liked the slower pace of life in Winchester, the ancient capital of Alfred the Great, King of Wessex and the mythical King Arthur, chosen as the birthplace of the son he prayed for.

Richard Foxe greeted him as he entered. His dour secretary now had the duty of keeping watch over Elizabeth, confined at St Swithun's Priory in Winchester Close.

'How is my wife today?'

'She slept well, Your Grace, and took a little broth.' Foxe hesitated as he chose his words. 'Your mother overheard the Queen Dowager accusing her of interfering.'

'She confronted her?'

'No—but Lady Elizabeth has endured great hardship with much fortitude, Your Grace. After the child is born, she might retreat to an abbey?'

'My mother asked you to propose this?' He took Foxe's silence for confirmation. 'Elizabeth wished to have her mother in attendance. I was happy to agree.' Henry recalled Jasper's stories. 'My grandmother was cared for in Bermondsey Abbey. It's close enough for Elizabeth to visit her mother...'

'Yet far enough for Lady Margaret's peace of mind.'

Urgent knocking woke Henry from a troubled sleep. He immediately guessed the reason as he opened the door to see Richard Foxe with Thomas Swan, page of Elizabeth's chamber, water dripping from his hat and cloak. There was only one reason he'd be out in the rain at such a late hour.

'The baby?' He hardly dared to ask.

'Congratulations, Your Grace.' Foxe gave him a rare smile. 'You have a healthy son.'

Henry felt a weight lifted from him yet sensed Foxe held something back.

'And my wife?'

'She asks for you, Your Grace.'

Henry dressed in a hurry and followed Foxe and the page. In his haste he'd neglected to wear his cape. Rain soon soaked his doublet through to his undershirt, the cold shock helping to calm his mind as they made their way through the dark alleyway to the priory.

In keeping with tradition he'd been excluded from Elizabeth's confinement, yet he'd spared no expense. Fine silks and linens, brocade and cloth of gold, sweet-scented perfumes and precious rose oils ensured her comfort.

Elizabeth's shy young maidservant bowed to Henry and announced his arrival as he entered and removed his dripping hat. Elizabeth sat up in her bed, supported by silk cushions and surrounded by her sisters. Flickering candlelight reflected from the pale whiteness of her glistening brow. Her golden hair flowed over her shoulders and she cradled a tiny bundle.

For a second Henry felt like an intruder in her private sanctum, then she smiled at him in greeting.

'We have a son, Henry.'

'It is... a miracle.' His voice choked with emotion. His prayers had been answered and he sensed his life would never be the same again.

Henry's mother stepped from the shadows and placed her hand on his shoulder. 'We give thanks to God he is a healthy boy.'

Henry wiped a tear of happiness from his eye. 'My son, Arthur Tudor.'

Chapter Three

June 1487

Henry smiled as he studied his cards, a promising hand. The king of diamonds, ten of clubs and six of spades. He glanced at Elizabeth. As always, her face offered no clues. He'd played endless games of one-and-thirty during his long exile in Brittany, gambling for small silver coins with his guards.

Now he played for gold ryals, bearing the proud image of Elizabeth's father and his emblem of the shining sun. He made a mental note to have gold coins of his own minted with the scene of his grand coronation, a permanent reminder for those with short memories.

He'd taught Elizabeth to play and their card games brought them closer as she recovered her health. She'd burned with fever after Arthur's birth and tested his faith as he prepared to lose her. His prayers were answered at Michaelmas, nine days later, when the fever broke.

Elizabeth still suffered from dizzy spells and although she made light of it, Henry knew her illness sapped her energy. He thanked God for sparing her and for his healthy son. Young Arthur now thrived in the care of his nursemaids and the formidable Lady Governess of the Nursery.

By the feast of All Hallows, Henry judged Elizabeth to be well enough and finally acted on advice to move his court to Kenilworth Castle in Warwickshire. He enjoyed hunting stags in the four-thousand-acre deer parks and felt safe within the privacy of the great moated Pleasance.

Elizabeth fanned her playing cards as she made her decision. Discarding a seven of hearts, she dropped it next to the pack on the velvet covered table between them. Henry noted the briefest frown of displeasure as she took the top card.

'My ladies tell me London is full of rumours...' she glanced across at Henry, 'that young Edward Plantagenet has escaped to Dublin.'

'An impostor!' Henry raised his voice in irritation. 'Edward's safe in the Tower.' He discarded the six of spades and picked up the eight of diamonds from the top of the pack.

'You'll have to show him again—for the people to believe the truth?' Elizabeth laid down the four of clubs and picked up the next card.

Henry cursed inwardly as he exchanged his eight of diamonds for the three of spades. 'I'm more concerned with rumours of a rebel army gathering in Ireland. Now I have to pay men to watch the coast.' He glanced up at her. 'What will it take to end these Yorkist revolts?'

'My grandfather became Lord of Ireland. He had the measure of the Irish and won their trust, then my father had their loyalty...'

'There is my problem.' Henry interrupted. 'The Irish provide sanctuary to those who plot against me— against us, against our son Arthur...'

'Have faith, Henry.' Her voice softened. 'We have a truce with France and there is peace in the North...'

'A fragile peace. The King of Scotland has no control over his rebel lords—yet you are right. I lay awake at nights, worried I might lose you—or young Arthur. I must remember to place my trust in God.'

Elizabeth smiled as she tapped twice on the table and waited while he laid down the worthless three of spades. She looked up at him again, her eyes sparkling with mischief. 'Arthur grows stronger every day. He's a true Tudor, always seeking attention!'

Henry laughed. 'I'd still be hidden from the world in Brittany, if not for my uncle's ambition.' He picked up the knave of diamonds. A total of thirty and a possible match for Elizabeth's hand, if not a winning score.

She revealed her cards with a satisfied smile. 'Ace and two queens. One-and-thirty!'

'Another game?' He eyed the golden coins as they disappeared into her purse, forgetting his new wealth for a moment. He'd no wish to return to his troublesome court papers. They spent little enough time together without his mother or hers listening to their every word.

She shook her head and gathered up her cards, absent-mindedly shuffling them in her slender, gold-ringed fingers. 'It's time to visit Arthur. Will you accompany me?'

A knock on the door interrupted his answer. Richard Foxe entered and addressed Henry.

'The Earl of Bedford is here, Your Grace, with the Earl of Oxford. They say it is most urgent.'

Henry's deep sense of misgiving ruined his good spirits. His heavy chair scraped on the tiled floor as he stood. 'It seems I have matters of state to attend to, Elizabeth. I shall come with you next time.'

'I should like to know what troubles your uncle before I leave.'

'Of course.' He placed an affectionate hand on her

shoulder. 'I will see you off when you are ready.'

Jasper's expression looked grave as Henry and Foxe entered the room where he waited with John de Vere. The pungent aroma of horse sweat told Henry they'd been riding hard and he noted the dust of the road on their cloaks. Jasper wore his sword and his breastplate emblazoned with the fleur-de-lis. Henry recalled the artisan-crafted armour had been a gift from the young French king. He hadn't seen his uncle wearing it since their victory at Bosworth.

'An invasion is underway.' Jasper glanced at John. 'A rebel army has landed at Furness and marches for York. We must raise as many men as we can muster, as we've no idea of their strength.'

Henry gestured for them to be seated. 'We knew a rebellion was coming—but I prayed to God we could avoid a battle.'

John de Vere answered. 'If we act now it could be a short enough fight, Your Grace. We have to stamp out this... insurrection—before others join them and it turns to civil war.'

'He's right, Henry.' Jasper looked older, with deeper shadows under his eyes and hair turning grey where it showed under his cap. 'There is no time to waste on diplomacy.'

Richard Foxe narrowed his eyes. 'Once we have them, you can show the king's mercy to all but the leaders, Your Grace.'

Henry scowled. 'Who is behind this treason?'

Jasper spoke for them. 'That scoundrel Francis Lovell—and John de la Pole, with mercenaries paid for by Margaret of Burgundy.'

'I wish we'd caught Lovell when we had the chance,'

Henry studied his uncle's lined face, 'although I suspect there is more to it this time?'

'Our agents say the boy pretending to be Edward Plantagenet bears a likeness and has been crowned by the Irish.' Jasper shook his head. 'I doubt he even knows what it means—but he's being used to rally Yorkist support.'

Henry cursed with exasperation. 'We'll prove the boy's an impostor by parading Edward through the streets of London!'

'By then it might be too late, Your Grace.' Oxford scowled. 'More than two thousand rebels have already landed, with God knows how many more to follow.' He glanced at Jasper for confirmation. 'We cannot afford to let them reach York.'

Henry glanced from one to the other. 'I'm appointing you, John, as commander of the vanguard. You shall have the pick of our best men and do what you can to stop the rebel advance.' He smiled. 'If their mercenaries are anything like those we had at Bosworth they will not welcome the attention of your archers.'

He faced Jasper. 'You, Uncle, will command my army and raise as many as you can—regardless of the cost. Send a rider for Rhys ap Thomas to bring his Welshmen—and tell him they will be well rewarded. I'll ride with you as soon as I've said farewell to Elizabeth.' He turned to Richard Foxe. 'We will need special commissions of array—as well as the funds to support this army.'

Foxe gave a curt bow. 'The orders are already drafted, so I can make the arrangements right away, Your Grace.'

After they left Henry stood at the window and stared out over the tranquil countryside. Sheep grazed lush green castle lawns in bright summer sunshine. In the distance he heard the laughter of children playing and the midday bell of St Mary's Abbey chimed, calling the monks to prayer.

He closed his eyes and said his own silent prayer for guidance. He could have no better commanders than his uncle and Oxford, who fought with such distinction at Bosworth, but the impending battle loomed like a black thundercloud over the idyllic scene. More lives would be on his conscience. After all he'd achieved in the past two years, rebels once again threatened his crown, perhaps even his life, and that of his young son.

An unseasonably chill breeze tugged at the heavy canvas of Henry's tent, which doubled as his mobile command post. He watched as Jasper dipped a quill in ink and marked their location on a parchment map of the area with a neat cross, ten miles south of the market town of Newark in Nottinghamshire.

They had covered less ground than Henry expected, partly owing to the weight of the cannons and the need to stop in every town and village to recruit more men. The commissions of array arrived too late for many, so all able-bodied men were pressed into the king's service and armed with whatever came to hand.

The flap covering the entrance to their tent opened to admit Henry's guards, escorting the man they'd been waiting for. Henry felt a stab of misgiving as he recognised the red wyvern badge of Henry Clifford, his commander in the North. A bloodstained bandage covered the soldier's right hand and pain showed in his troubled expression.

Jasper had learnt of the man's arrival and suggested he should be questioned in front of Henry, who would remain incognito. They'd found men spoke less freely when they knew they were in the presence of the king. He gestured for the guard to leave them.

The soldier cleared his throat to speak as his anxious eyes flicked to Henry. He failed to recognise him and turned to Jasper.

'I've come from Tadcaster, sir, on orders from my Lord Clifford, to warn you that rebels took us by surprise.' He looked down at his feet. 'The army is routed with many dead and injured.'

'How many rebels were there?'

'Many thousands, my lord, too many to count.'

'Irish mercenaries?'

The soldier looked back up at Jasper. 'They seem to be poorly equipped, my lord.'

'Yet they are well led, for they took you by surprise?'

'They came at night without any warning.' The soldier frowned at the memory. 'They must have captured or killed our sentries. The first we knew of it they were amongst us.' He studied his boots.

'What of Lord Clifford?' Jasper sounded more conciliatory.

'Retreated to defend the city of York, my lord. He sent me to warn you and ask for reinforcements.'

'Can you make it back to York?'

'I can, my lord.'

'Then tell Lord Clifford the king's orders are to hold the city at all costs. The king has raised an army to defeat these rebels, whatever their numbers.'

The man accepted the gold coin Jasper slipped into his hand, then left on his mission.

Henry rubbed his eyes, feeling the weight of responsibility on his shoulders. 'Oxford will intercept them?'

Jasper looked thoughtful. 'In good time. We're still waiting to hear from Rhys ap Thomas and your stepbrother about how many men they can bring. Lovell must have learnt from last time and seems to have raised an army.'

'What do you suggest?'

'I've placed Edward Woodville in command of our cavalry. I'd like to send the best of them north to get the measure of the rebels—and keep them at bay until our army can reach them on foot.'

'You think we can rely on him?'

'Of course.' Jasper raised an eyebrow at the question.

'Forgive me but I'm trying to be cautious about who we trust...'

'Edward Woodville has been loyal to you since France and fought with great courage at Bosworth.'

Henry stared at his uncle and back at the parchment map for a moment before replying. 'It seems we are to fight Bosworth all over again.'

They'd been riding at the marching pace of Henry's army since dawn when he spotted a single rider approaching in the bright yellow and red of Oxford. The messenger galloped to warn Jasper.

'The rebels are close by, my lord.' His deep voice carried well. 'They occupy a hilltop near the village of Stoke.'

'In what numbers?'

'Many thousands, sir, although there are no reports of cannon or cavalry in any numbers.'

Jasper glanced across at Henry. 'The vanguard is ready to engage them?'

The messenger nodded. 'Our archers have them in range, sir.'

'Good. Kindly tell the Earl of Oxford to draw them into the field. We are ready with reinforcements and will hold back until needed—as agreed.'

'Yes, sir!' The messenger grinned and bowed his head to Henry then turned and galloped back the way he'd come.

Henry's spirits rose at the news, for whatever the outcome he wished it over. Jasper reported superstitious rumours of strange lights sighted in the sky. Some thought it a good omen but others argued it must be a portent of ill-fortune.

After another sleepless night he'd risen early and thanked God as he knelt at his prayers. Reinforcements had arrived the previous day with the Stanleys and the Earl of Devon, then the Welsh army of Rhys ap Thomas marched into camp.

The sight of so many well-armed soldiers proved a boost to the morale of the men. Lovell and Lincoln might have thousands of mercenaries but Henry's army were more than a match for them.

Early morning sunshine further lifted Henry's mood as they marched five miles to the Earl of Oxford's position near East Stoke. He noted the men's faces were tense. Word of the rebel routing of Lord Clifford's army meant few expected an easy victory.

Jasper found them a vantage-point from where the enemy standards were visible on the opposite side of an open, shallow valley. Henry waited with Jasper at his side. They'd agreed to hold back the main force until they had the measure of the rebels and would rely on Oxford to goad them into advancing.

Oxford's archers strained as they hauled back their yew longbows and watched for his order, then let loose and darkened the sky with a storm of deadly arrows.

Despite having the better ground, the rebels were unprepared for the onslaught. Men cried out in pain as sharp bodkin arrowheads pierced flimsy armour.

Henry watched as the leading rebel mercenaries fled for their lives. The fast-flowing River Trent cut off their escape to the west, so they found themselves heading back through their own ranks. Then the rebel commanders urged their men to charge forward. Jasper's plan had worked.

He flinched at the roar of the cannons they'd dragged all the way from the royal armoury. Iron shot cut through the ranks of advancing mercenaries like a scythe through dry stalks of corn. From his vantage-point Henry guessed more than a hundred men had already fallen, yet the rebels continued undeterred, pressing forward and hacking at Oxford's men in savage fury.

The sharp sound of a distant trumpet broke through the noise of battle and a new wave of men appeared from behind the enemy hilltop. Carrying banners Henry couldn't identify, they looked better armed and equipped than the Irishmen, including many with crossbows and several carrying heavy handguns.

Jasper cursed. 'Germans!' He drew his sword. 'These are experienced fighting men—and they've used the Irish to force our hand!'

They watched as more Germans poured over the hill like a swarm of angry bees, yelling so loud Henry could hear them across the battlefield. Oxford's archers bore the brunt of the savage attack, which pressed through without slowing down. The rebels began heading towards Henry's position and not for the first time he feared for his life.

The sun glinted on Jasper's sword as he raised it high,

the signal for Rhys ap Thomas to take his Welshmen to reinforce Oxford's vanguard. He pointed as the long flowing banner of the black raven rose above the battlefield. 'I pity the Germans when they meet our Welshmen!'

Henry heard the pride in his uncle's voice. Holding up a hand as if to shade his eyes from the sun for a better view he wiped a tear from his eye. He knew the rebels brought this on themselves yet he felt overwhelmed with deep sorrow. This might be God's will but each death added to those already on his conscience.

The grey smoke of gunpowder drifted in the air as their cannons boomed again and again. 'Just as at Bosworth,' He muttered. 'yet now I've brought the Welsh to war against the Irish...'

'We have no choice, Henry.' Jasper sheathed his sword, which he'd held ready, and stared into the carnage. 'I'm still holding Devon's men in reserve, and Edward Woodville's cavalry, but I pray we won't need to commit them...'

'Amen to that,' agreed Henry. He turned away from the sight of men murdering each other and hung his head to pray for salvation and forgiveness.

The sun rose high overhead before the last of the rebels threw down their weapons in surrender. Against Henry's wishes the battle-bloodied Welshmen pursued their fleeing enemy and slaughtered those trying to escape.

A weary John de Vere joined Henry and Jasper to report on the search for the leaders. Apart from a purple bruise on his cheek where his missing helmet must have taken a blow he looked in good spirits.

'Another great victory for Lancaster, Your Grace!'

Henry forced a welcoming smile. 'Well done, John. We owe you a debt we can never repay.'

'The men fought well, I'll grant you—and so did those German mercenaries!'

Jasper stepped forward. 'Have you captured Lovell or Lincoln?'

'Lincoln's dead.' John de Vere glanced back across the battlefield, where bodies were already being stripped of weapons and armour. 'Lovell's vanished yet again. My men are questioning the wounded and prisoners to identify more leaders,' he gestured to his waiting guards, 'but I have captured one of the ringleaders.'

Henry felt sympathy for the nervous young boy, who looked about ten years old. He wore an ill-fitting velvet robe with a gilded York livery collar around his neck contrived to suggest a noble appearance. A long moment passed before Henry spoke. He'd been remembering the hardships of his own life at the same age as the prisoner of the surly Welshman Sir William Herbert.

'What's your real name?'

The boy stared ahead, unblinking, perhaps in shock at the change in his fortune. When he spoke, his high-pitched voice showed his youth yet he had a cultured accent. 'Simnel, Your Grace.' He looked wary of Oxford's guardsmen and Henry wondered if they'd treated him roughly.

'Who told you to pretend to be the Earl of Warwick?'

The boy stared at his feet. Henry guessed he still had loyalty towards those who'd made him their figurehead. He understood. He'd only been twelve years old when they executed William Herbert after the Battle of Edgecote. For all his rough ways, Henry had grieved that the man who'd been like a father to him met such a savage fate.

'Answer the king, boy!' Oxford's voice sounded stern.

Henry held up a hand. 'We know you've been used by those who should know better than to mislead the people.' He stared at the boy for a moment. 'You are pardoned in the king's name—and shall work in my kitchens, where we can keep an eye on you.'

Jasper smiled at the suggestion. 'What do you say, young Simnel?'

Simnel bowed his head. 'Thank you, Your Grace.'

Henry turned to John de Vere. 'I also grant an amnesty to the common men and mercenaries, who are to return to Ireland, Germany—or wherever they came from. Please see that they do?'

'Yes, Your Grace.' John de Vere glanced back across at Henry's standard, now flying high on the hilltop where the rebels had camped. 'The leader of the German mercenaries is dead but the Irish noblemen surrendered. What do you wish us to do with them?'

Henry hesitated. Some might see pardoning rebel leaders as a sign of weakness. Worse still, they could regroup and return to fight another day.

'The price of their freedom is an oath of allegiance, then they are free to go and tell the people of Ireland we wish for peace. The Irish are to be our allies—not our enemy.'

♔

Crisp autumn leaves swirled in golden brown drifts in the courtyard of the Tower of London as Elizabeth prepared for her coronation. Londoners were in celebratory mood and ready for the York princess to finally become crowned queen. Dressed in a kirtle of purple velvet under a mantle of ermine, a circlet of gold shining with rare pearls and precious stones, adorned her long hair.

Elizabeth made her procession through cleaned streets decked with flowers and lined with liveried soldiers. As she passed the crowds cheered, shouting 'God save the Queen,' and 'Long live the Queen!'

A noisy fanfare of trumpeters greeted her arrival in Westminster, although by tradition Henry sat out of view. Concealed in a private pew, he watched with only his mother for company.

Lady Margaret strained to see her daughter-in-law entering the great entrance to the abbey. 'This must be costing a fair penny, Henry?'

'That's what I wish the people to think.' Henry gave her a knowing look. 'I've levied heavy fines and forfeiture of estates for those who failed the test of their loyalty. The money raised has more than covered the costs of my army in the North, as well as this coronation.'

'You will have to grant Elizabeth her own income now, as queen.'

Henry ignored the edge to his mother's voice. 'Richard Foxe has taken care of that. Her mother's estates will be transferred to her, together with their income.'

'She has little enough use for them now she has retired to Bermondsey Abbey.'

Henry stared at her as a thought occurred to him. 'At your suggestion?'

'Contented poverty is an honourable estate, Henry.' Before he could reply she pointed as the precession entered the nave. 'Your Uncle Jasper looks splendid in his new livery.'

'I've appointed him Great Steward of England.'

'You've rewarded loyalty well, Henry. I heard John de Vere is your new Lord Chancellor—a good choice.'

Henry agreed. 'If not for him...' He decided not to mar the day with black thoughts. 'The Earl of Derby is also made Constable of England.'

Archbishop John Morton appeared, dressed as finely as any king in cloth of gold. Loyal to the Tudor cause since Brittany, he'd been made Archbishop of Canterbury, securing Henry's grip over church and state. A choir of children, all dressed as angels, sang tunefully as Elizabeth wore the golden crown for the first time as Queen of England.

Henry gave thanks to God. He'd defended his throne with honour, surrounded himself with trusted men, and chosen the most beautiful woman in England as his queen.

Chapter Four

March 1488

Elizabeth took Henry's arm in hers as she led him on a tour of Sheen Palace. Once part of her mother's estate, it fronted the River Thames some nine miles upstream of the Palace of Westminster and twenty by royal barge from the palace at Greenwich.

The hammer-beamed great hall, empty of furniture, echoed when they spoke. Faded tapestries hinted at former glory and Henry shivered as the cold air made him mindful of ghosts of the past. Elizabeth wore a gold brocade cape with a fur hood over her gown, and her eyes shone with the excitement as they explored dusty rooms and the maze of narrow passageways.

'King Henry the Fifth chose Sheen as his palace,' she pointed to the Plantagenet crest above the stone fireplace, 'but he died during a winter siege in France before it could be finished.'

Henry laughed at her serious tone. 'Not the best of omens, if I am to be persuaded to make this our family home?'

Her eyes sparkled. 'I've happy memories of this place. My father told me Sheen once meant the basest form of shelter.'

'And then he gifted it to your mother.'

'She wished for a place of her own, when...' A shadow of sadness passed over her face at the memory, then she brightened. 'Let me show you my ideas for the gardens.'

Henry pulled his heavy fur-trimmed woollen cloak around his shoulders as she led him through a narrow doorway into the outer courtyard. The last signs of the morning's frost glistened like diamonds on the cobble-stones and their breath froze in the air. He wished he could be inside, in front of a good log fire.

At the same time, he felt happy to indulge his wife and pleased to see her recovering, to be the girl he first met. She rarely mentioned her mother, although he knew Elizabeth visited her whenever she could. If the stories of King Edward's many mistresses were true, they would explain why his wife lived away from his salacious court.

A tangle of thorny briars looked as if it could once be a rose garden. Early stinging nettles were reclaiming the borders, like an invading green army. Elizabeth led him through an overgrown orchard of stunted apple trees to a stone bench overlooking the river. She brushed away dead leaves and sat, gesturing for him to do the same.

Henry watched morning sunlight sparkling on the Thames. A pair of swans floated past, the only sound the gentle rippling of water. He'd become used to the bustling city downriver, with boatmen clamoring for fares. Now he found the riverside scene tranquil and calming.

His predecessors chose this place with good reason. The deep, wide moat made it easy to defend and the old stone jetty provided good access to Westminster. The buildings needed work and the grounds had become a wilderness, yet he could see the potential.

'I like it here.' He reached across and took her white-gloved hand in his. 'We shall make Sheen into a palace fit for a royal family.'

Elizabeth squeezed his hand in agreement. 'I would like that.' She gave him a conspiratorial look. 'This is my most secret place. A sanctuary.'

Henry stared into her bright amber eyes. 'You spent many months in sanctuary... yet you've never spoken of it?'

'At first I didn't understand the danger we were in.' She stared, wide-eyed into the far distance as she remembered. 'My mother made a game of it, said it would be a great adventure. Years later she told me my father abandoned us and she thought our enemies might murder us all.'

'That's why she took you to the sanctuary of Westminster Abbey.'

'With my sisters—and she gave birth there to my brother Edward.'

Henry held the silence, intrigued to learn more of her past. Elizabeth's mother showed great courage in adversity but the experience left its mark on her. He began to understand why she seemed so distrusting of his mother's motives, or his own, for that matter.

'The abbey monks protected us.' Elizabeth looked into his eyes. 'We should reward them for their kindness.'

'And the others who helped you.'

'In truth we saw little of anyone. A few loyal friends brought us food. My mother taught us to read from her book of hours. I later learnt we were there for almost six months but it felt like more like six years.'

'And when you could leave the sanctuary of the abbey your father promised you to the Dauphin of France?'

'Not right away. I must have been seven or eight by then.'

'Old enough to understand...' Henry felt an irrational surge of jealousy at the idea.

'They began preparing me to become Queen of France. My father did his best to coach me, although I wonder if he had any idea.'

'I heard you were his favourite?'

Elizabeth shook her head. 'Edward had always been his favourite. His heir...' She flashed him a strange look and Henry wondered if he might be about to learn what she believed happened to her brothers. 'Those were... difficult times when my father died.'

'Your mother took you back to the abbey?'

'For our own safety.' Her eyes misted at the memory.

'She didn't trust your uncle, King Richard?'

She remained silent for a moment, watching a busy robin foraging in the grass, then looked at him. 'He declared her marriage invalid—and all us children illegitimate.'

Henry heard the edge to her voice. He recalled rumours he'd heard in France that she'd been in love with King Richard and dismissed them. It seemed impossible after the way he'd treated her family. He found it easier to believe Richard desired her for his new queen to replace Anne Neville, although he'd also heard he had planned to marry her off to the King of Portugal.

He watched her face. 'How did he persuade your mother to come out of sanctuary?' He sounded indifferent to her answer, although he held his breath.

'First he tried threats and placed armed guards on every entrance to prevent our escape. Then he made a promise to ensure our safety.'

'Your mother believed him, after all that had happened?' Henry resisted the temptation to refer to the fate of her brothers.

'He swore an oath on the Gospels before the Great Council. We had no choice other than to trust him.'

Their conversation echoed in Henry's thoughts many times after he returned to Westminster, where the towering spire of the old abbey dominated the skyline. As agreed with Elizabeth, he'd privately granted a generous sum to Abbot John Esteney, who'd given her sanctuary, to pray for lasting peace.

Now Richard Foxe spread out the master builder's new plans for Sheen Palace and its grounds. As well as new tennis courts, the drawings included a tiltyard for jousting tournaments, complete with a fine grandstand for spectators. He'd learnt the value of outward display from the French. As well as becoming their family home, Sheen would serve as a place to entertain and impress foreign nobles.

'Elizabeth wishes to retain as much of the interior as possible,' Henry studied a list of proposed improvements to the great hall, 'which should reduce the cost.'

Foxe produced an itemised list of the builder's estimate. 'I took the liberty of anticipating this, Your Grace. It seems only proper these expenses are met from income from the queen's estates, transferred from her lady mother.'

Henry tutted as he checked the totals, although he approved Richard Foxe's advice. The costs far exceeded his expectations, yet Elizabeth would enjoy the distraction of overseeing the work herself. Taking his quill, he dipped it in the silver inkpot and inscribed his initials. He'd seen how men would take advantage of his generosity and ordered the Treasury only to make payments he had authorised.

Foxe gathered up the plans and tied them with a scarlet ribbon. 'There is another matter, Your Grace. I refer to the... predicament of your benefactor, Duke Francis of Brittany.'

Henry sighed at the reminder. 'His ambassador still waits for our reply?'

'He does, Your Grace, and I understand his instruction is not to return to Brittany until he has secured it.'

'We are well aware of the ambitions of Madame la Grande.' Henry recalled his first meeting with Anne, Regent of France until her brother Charles would come of age. He'd always suspected her support for his cause and now guessed she might be in league with Margaret of Burgundy.

He looked out of the leaded-glass window at the bustling city below. 'The French will no doubt invade Brittany whatever we choose to do.' He knew Richard Foxe deserved an answer yet he worried about the downfall of Brittany, a land with so many memories.

'I owe my life to good Duke Francis.' Henry made a decision. 'I am meeting my Uncle Jasper in Southampton to view the Venetian galleys—he will know what to do.'

'There is also the letter from King James of Scotland, Your Grace.'

'I've not forgotten—but we cannot afford the expense of sending an army all the way to Scotland. He must learn to control his rebellious lords.'

'My understanding, Your Grace, is that King James is currently raising his own army.'

'You are suggesting we do nothing?'

'The rebels support the kings' young heir, James,

Duke of Rothsay. I have drafted a letter for your consideration, supporting the efforts of the Archbishop of St Andrews, who hopes to reconcile the king with his son.'

'Keep me informed. I for my part shall pray we can avoid war with these troublesome Scots, whatever the outcome.'

'We have reliable informers in both camps, Your Grace.'

Henry returned to the window and studied the narrow streets below. 'Tell me, Foxe, what is your opinion of Rodrigo de Puebla?'

'He seems an honest enough man, for a diplomat... although King Ferdinand of Aragon will have chosen him with good reason.'

Henry turned sharply. 'Can he be trusted—or is he a spy, sent to worm his way into our confidence and learn our weakness?'

Foxe returned Henry's stare with his usual unblinking coolness. 'He confided he'd been sent to report to his master on the suitability of your son, Your Grace.'

Henry began to pace the room as he thought. He stopped and turned to Foxe. 'Do you know what he has reported?'

'I understand he offered a most positive account, although... I also learnt he has yet to receive any payment from Spain since his arrival last year. We provide his accommodation, yet how he survives if this is true is something of a mystery.' Foxe raised an eyebrow. 'As for whether he can be trusted, Your Grace, that remains to be seen.'

'So you are suggesting his co-operation, if not his trust, might be bought?'

'Without question, Your Grace. May I ask what you

have in mind?'

'We need an alliance with Spain. It's time to begin negotiations with King Ferdinand.' Henry smiled. 'You are to secure the services of ambassador de Puebla to ensure the betrothal of King Ferdinand's daughter, Catalina, with a dowry of.... shall we say two hundred thousand gold crowns?'

Cheering crowds called out 'God save the King!' and 'God save the Queen!' and threw flowers as the grand procession made its way to the Chapel of St George in Windsor. Henry decreed a special feast in honour of St George's Day. Blessed by warm spring sunshine, it proved the perfect time to display his court in all its finery.

Henry rode in the lead on his favourite white charger, caparisoned with cloth of gold, preceded by heralds and followed by standard-bearers carrying his royal standards alongside the flag of St George.

Knights of the Garter in their colourful livery followed, including Sir Jasper Tudor and Henry's stepfather, Sir Thomas Stanley. Behind them rode the queen and Henry's mother in a gilded carriage drawn by six white horses. Henry provided them both with matching gowns of the Order of the Garter trimmed with brocade of gold and had never been more proud of them.

His concern that Elizabeth might resent his mother's constant presence in their household seemed unfounded. They now chose to spend much time in each other's company and his mother often stayed overnight in her own suite of rooms at Sheen Palace as well as at Windsor Castle.

In place of marching guardsmen, who now lined

their entire route, twenty-one of Elizabeth's ladies-in-waiting in gowns of crimson velvet rode on white palfreys, decorated with bright ribbons and bells. The musical tinkling of bells competed with fanfares of trumpets and the clatter of hooves on the paved road, creating a celebratory atmosphere.

A thanksgiving banquet in the great hall of Windsor Castle followed the service, where Elizabeth's uncle, Sir Edward Woodville and Henry's uncle, Viscount John Welles, were both rewarded for their loyal service by being made Knights of the Garter.

Henry sat between his mother and Elizabeth as they were entertained by tumblers, who formed a human tower the height of four men. Minstrels playing lutes accompanied a choir of young girls dressed in colourful gowns and singing songs composed for the occasion.

Servants carried platters of venison and the centrepiece of a golden hind, surrounded by lifelike wildfowl. Wine and ale flowed and Henry applauded the performance of a fire-eater, who sent great plumes of flame high into the air.

Henry's mother caught his attention. 'You should say a few words, make a speech of thanks?'

Feeling in good spirits, Henry had the hall called to order and rose to propose a toast. 'My lords and ladies...' he paused to survey their familiar faces. 'It warms my heart to see so many good loyal people here today. I give thanks to God we now enjoy peace and prosperity in this land.' He raised his silver goblet in the air and proposed a toast. 'To our patron saint, St George!'

A hundred deep voices echoed his words and his mother nodded in approval. Word of this would spread far and wide. The people wanted a strong and chivalrous king, as well as a devout one, and he would not disappoint them.

Henry tasted the salt in the bracing sea air as he inspected the bustling dockside at Southampton with Jasper. Men shouted orders in several languages as ships were loaded with cargo. Others climbed high in the rigging to prepare sails, oblivious to their royal observers. As they watched, a basket of silvery fish spilled its contents over the quayside to a roar of curses from the foreman.

Jasper pointed out a high-masted ship being loaded with bales of wool. 'A Genoese galley. Designed for use in calmer waters, the lateen sails make the most of light winds. They carry great loads yet are light enough to be rowed when becalmed.'

Henry shaded his eyes from the spring sunshine and realised the row of holes above the waterline were for fifty long oars. The design reminded him of his gilded royal barge and a thought occurred to him.

'We need new ships to control the Channel. We should learn from the Venetians.'

Jasper studied the lines of the Venetian ship. 'If we built them well, galleys could be used for trade all the way to the Mediterranean yet carry an army if needed.'

He led Henry further down the dockside to where a handsome caravel waited for favourable winds. Henry studied the lines and could see she'd been recently built, with fresh paint and bronze swivel guns mounted fore and aft. He looked up at the top of the mast and recognised the flag of Portugal.

'Even the Portuguese have better ships than our tired old cogs.' He turned to Jasper. 'I shall commission new ships to be built without delay.'

Jasper grinned. 'You remember your first crossing to France?'

Henry laughed at the memory. 'I feared we'd be wrecked on the rocks and drowned. We have come a long way since then.' He looked back at the caravel. 'My new ship will be the greatest ever to sail from Southampton and I'll spare no expense in her equipping.'

'You must call her *Regent* —and your mother shall have the honour of launching her.'

'I like it.' He looked out towards the horizon. 'Command of the seas will set us apart—and if there is to be war in France, we must be prepared.'

Jasper's smiling face became serious. 'You plan to support Duke Francis?'

'I planned to seek your advice Uncle. We might not be here now if not for the good duke, yet I've no desire to risk war.' He lowered his voice so only Jasper could hear. 'In truth we cannot afford to raise such an army, even if we had the ships.'

'I knew as much. And you would have to forbid anyone such as Edward Woodville taking his cavalry to protect Duke Francis?'

Henry looked into his uncle's dark eyes. 'Of course. I would have to forbid it.'

Richard Foxe's lined face looked graver than ever as he arrived to bring Henry bad news. 'I regret to inform you King James of Scotland has died in battle, Your Grace.'

'You are certain he hasn't escaped?'

'I understand the rebels made sure of it and already proclaim his son king.'

Henry shook his head. His foray to the south coast

had improved his mood and allowed him to forget the trouble in the North. By all accounts King James had been a good, devout man, trying to do his best against impossible odds—not unlike himself.

'He reached out to us for help. We failed him.'

'We had no choice, Your Grace.'

'We must learn from this, Richard. There but for the grace of God...'

'Even if we had wished to support King James, the Treasury could not fund an army in time.' Foxe hesitated. 'Perhaps it is time to talk to Parliament about raising taxes?'

Henry groaned at the thought. 'At the risk of destroying my fragile support in the North?'

'The world must not learn of our vulnerability, Your Grace. If you wish to ask Parliament to raise new taxes, make no secret of the reason.'

Once again, Richard Foxe surprised him. Henry thought for a moment. 'You are right. Instead of one ship, I will commission an entire fleet. Instead of wasting money on mercenaries, I'll order every fit and able man to learn to use a bow, shoot straight and true.' He liked the idea. 'England has the means to pay for a new army and it shall do so.'

Henry prayed alone at dawn in the Chapel of St George at Windsor Castle. He prayed for forgiveness and for the good, loyal friends he had lost. A single, battle-weary survivor managed to return to England with his story of Edward Woodville's doomed venture to Brittany.

Henry recalled Edward's unswerving support for him during those long years in exile and his courage at

Bosworth. His leadership and cavalry had carried the balance at the Battle of Stoke. The notion that Edward Woodville could be killed never entered Henry's mind. He'd seemed invincible, a true chivalric knight.

Whether brave or foolhardy, Edward Woodville took on the might of the French army with a few hundred bowmen and paid the price. The only man to escape told of Edward's small army being massacred by the French without mercy. The news spread like wildfire through England, hardening the resolve of Parliament to raise taxes for an invasion of France.

He lit a votive candle in memory of Elizabeth's loyal uncle, who could have been king, the last of his kind. While his taper still flickered in the still air of the chapel Henry lit a second candle for his old friend Duke Francis of Brittany. A tear ran down his face as he remembered the duke's great kindness.

As a boy, he'd looked up in awe at the powerful ruler of Brittany. He learnt much from observing good Duke Francis. The duke always honoured his word, despite many opportunities to profit from their protective custody. He provided five ships at his own expense to support their invasion of England, including his own flagship, and asked nothing in return. Henry would always regret how poorly he'd returned the favour.

The short and bloody battle for Brittany forced the ailing duke to concede the hand of his only daughter, Anna, now eleven, to Charles of France. He'd lived only long enough to know the humiliation of his beloved Brittany before succumbing to his long illness, a defeated man.

Chapter Five

April 1489

Reaching out with slender fingers, the latest gift from the King of Spain munched at the succulent grape as if it were an apple. Less than a foot high, with a long, thick tail, the monkey had brown fur except for a cap of black. It fixed Henry with a pleading stare and held out a hand for more.

He offered another grape, which it took and began to suck at the sweet juice. 'Do you think it has too-knowing eyes?' Henry smiled. 'I feel it can read our thoughts.'

Elizabeth spoke in a hushed tone, as if frightened of alarming it. 'Does it have a name?'

'I thought to call him Rodrigo,' Henry laughed at her surprised expression, 'after our esteemed ambassador. I wonder if this little monkey has also been sent to spy on us?'

'Will the ambassador not be... offended?'

'He should take it as a compliment that I consider his name worthy for my new pet.' Henry gave her a grin. 'Others have given us presents of lions, yet I received a monkey as a gift from his master.'

'You plan to keep it in our private apartments?' Elizabeth frowned with concern as she watched Henry feed the creature another ripe grape.

'It amuses me.' He grinned at her discomfort.

Elizabeth studied the thin gold chain which ran from

a leather collar around the monkey's tiny neck to prevent it escaping. 'It has sharp little teeth...'

'I think Rodrigo is clever enough not to bite the hand that feeds him.'

'The ambassador...' Elizabeth lowered her voice so the ever-present servants could not overhear. 'Has he made progress with his negotiations?'

Henry nodded. 'It seems we've found a suitable princess for our son. I expect a considerable dowry—and if de Puebla's word is to be relied on, Princess Catalina is a pretty girl and bright for her age.'

'It must be difficult to be certain.' Elizabeth looked doubtful. 'I understand the princess is only four years old...'

'Arthur is only two years old, yet you agree he's as handsome as his father—and as quick-witted as his mother?'

Elizabeth smiled at the thought. 'Of course, but then as you often remind me, he is a Tudor.'

'Half Tudor, half prince of the House of York.'

'And soon there might be another...'

Henry embraced her. 'Elizabeth!' He stared into her amber eyes. 'You are with child again?'

'God willing.' She failed to prevent a giggle at his enthusiasm for the news.

'I prayed for God's blessing upon us yet it seemed to be tempting fate to ask for another child.' His voice became serious. 'I haven't forgotten the toll Arthur's birth took on you.'

'It is a small enough price to pay.' A fleeting shadow drifted over her face, the fear of all parents, then the moment passed.

'I will pray for your good health and that this time it goes easier for you. Now we must celebrate our growing family!'

John de Vere took a deep drink of ale. He'd arrived at Sheen late in the evening at the end of a long journey all the way from York. Elizabeth and most of the servants had retired for the night and they sat in the private, oak-panelled room Henry chose as his study.

A luminous crescent moon glimmered through unshuttered windows, glazed at Elizabeth's expense. The cavernous stone grate, usually filled with blazing logs, stood empty due to the warm evenings. Tall candles cast their flickering light over the ageing earl's weather-beaten face, revealing fine grey stubble on his chin.

Before continuing his report, he lifted the heavy silver jug and refilled both their cups, unconcerned at spilling a little on the polished oak table. Henry took a sip. The ale tasted good, with a bitter aftertaste. More appropriate to their mood than the sweet Rhenish wine he'd become used to.

John de Vere half-emptied his cup in one go and wiped his mouth on his sleeve as he looked across the table at Henry. 'Do you recall the time I escaped from Hammes Castle, Your Grace?'

Surprised at the question, Henry had to cast his memory back to the day they first met. John de Vere arrived at their exiled camp in France looking like a beggar, with an unkempt beard and no cap or helmet to cover his straggling hair. If not for Jasper, he would never have recognised this vagrant as the Earl of Oxford.

'I remember you were helped in your escape by Sir James Blount, Captain of Hammes.' Henry took another sup of the strong ale, feeling it start to improve his spirits. 'It comes back to me now. You returned to the castle to rescue his good lady wife—at great personal risk, I've no doubt.' He studied his old friend's face as he recalled those troubled times. 'We were glad to have loyal men of your experience join our mercenary army.'

John de Vere leaned forward in his chair and fixed Henry with a serious look. 'My escape plan had a near-fatal flaw. I found myself high on the battlements with no way back. I had no choice other than to risk jumping into the moat.' He took another drink of ale before continuing. 'The drop proved much further than expected—and the water stank to holy hell.'

'Well I for one am relieved you survived to fight with us at Bosworth.'

'The reason I refer to it is we put Henry Percy in a similarly impossible position. The poor fellow knew he would be dammed if he did—and dammed if he didn't.'

Henry noted his critical tone and lack of formality but decided to allow it on this occasion. The ageing earl had been drinking and had travelled far with his news. 'They were his people, so who better than Henry Percy to collect the taxes due?'

'You are right, Your Grace, although we always knew there'd be trouble when we announced the new taxes.' He cursed. 'Who knows how many Yorkists rebels lurk there, waiting their chance?'

'Henry Percy visited to warn me in person and put the case for the people.' He frowned. 'He wanted me to agree concessions but the timing made it impossible. The Grand Council had committed six thousand men to support Anne of Brittany.'

John de Vere raised an eyebrow. 'I understood the cost has been repaid in full by Brittany?'

'Only after it had been incurred.' Henry drained his cup and placed it on the table with an irritated thump. 'How could we allow one part of the country to pay less than the taxes due?'

'Henry Percy handled the task badly, by all accounts. He failed to win over the dissenters and called them knaves. I liked him, though. You know he had command of King Richard's reserves at Bosworth?'

'And refused to engage them against us.'

'He deserved better than to be lynched by a mob, but foolish to leave himself unguarded at such a time.'

'I heard rioters attacked him in their thousands?'

'An exaggeration, Your Grace. All we found were a few hundred men, armed with pitchforks and sticks. It proved easy enough to capture the ringleader and after that they ran for their lives.'

'You executed the leaders?' Henry already guessed the answer—more deaths to add to those already on his conscience.

'Only one, a yeoman, hanged in York when he admitted his treason. The main Yorkist troublemaker, Sir John Egremont, has either gone to ground or fled the country. He's no doubt become Margaret of Burgundy's new lapdog—a fitting reward for his disloyalty!' De Vere's deep chuckle echoed in the stillness of Henry's study.

'And now your advice is we should progress to York to restore order?' Henry struggled to see the humour in the situation, particularly if his own life would be put at risk once more.

'We've done it before and can do it again, Your Grace. We need to serve the northerners a reminder— while there is still time.'

Henry appointed former Yorkist Sir Thomas Howard, Earl of Surrey, Lord Lieutenant of the region once governed by Henry Percy and ordered him to ride ahead with a vanguard. Howard carried the sword of state at King Richard's coronation and had been taken prisoner after the Yorkists were routed at Bosworth. Henry decided to release him from the Tower after three years, relying on his instinct rather than his advisors.

The ride of over two hundred miles north from Sheen Palace meant a stop at Leicester, where they took the opportunity to recruit more men before pressing on to Nottingham Castle. Successive kings created the finest deer parks in the country at Nottingham but Henry felt in no mood for hunting.

After a restless night, rising early for his prayers, he prayed for Elizabeth. He missed her but judged it too great a risk for her to travel with him. He also missed his Uncle Jasper, who'd always been at his side on visits to York but was now too old for such long journeys. At the same time, he knew it would be good for the people of York to see him as his own man, not in the shadow of his uncle—or of his wife.

Heralds and sergeants-at-arms cleared their way through the narrow streets of York yet Henry glanced from side to side, looking for shadows in doorways. He'd not forgotten the savage anger of the man who attacked him with a dagger three years earlier and might have killed him if not for his uncle's swift action.

He also noted less enthusiastic cheering from the crowds, who seemed more curious to see their king. His badge of the Tudor rose still decorated doorways, although he spotted some of the more defiant wore the white rose of York. He consoled himself with the thought it remained the queen's chosen emblem.

'Welcome to York, Your Grace!'

He turned to see a smiling Thomas Howard, who'd been waiting to greet their arrival. 'Earl Surrey, we trust you've had no further trouble with rebels?'

Surrey looked pleased with himself. 'I've charged six more with treason and ordered them to be hanged in the morning.'

Henry froze. It wasn't the answer he'd expected. 'Let it be known these six will be the last, Sir Thomas. I've come to York in peace.'

'What is to be done with the other rioters we've captured, Your Grace?'

'Tell them the king offers them pardons in return for swearing fealty.'

♚

The archbishop's voice echoed in Westminster Palace as he read aloud the orders to create young Prince Arthur a Knight of the Bath. Arthur fidgeted in his long blue robe, oblivious to the meaning of the ceremony.

'You shall honour God above all things, be steadfast in the faith of Christ. You shall love the King your Sovereign Lord, and his right defend to your power.'

The archbishop paused as he heard someone ordering the men guarding the door to stand aside but, at a sign from Henry, continued with the formal ceremony.

'You shall defend maidens, widows, and orphans in their rights, and shall suffer no extortion, as far as you may prevent it, and of as great honour be this order unto you, as ever it was to any of your progenitors or others.'

The doors burst open to admit the queens' chamberlain, elderly Sir Thomas Butler, Earl of Ormond, responsible for reporting to Henry on progress with her confinement. He didn't need to speak, the look he exchanged with Henry was enough. Their new child, next in the growing line of Tudors, was about to make its dangerous way into the world.

Henry nodded to dismiss Sir Thomas. 'Pray continue, Archbishop.' He glanced at the long line of those waiting their turn. 'We have seventeen more knights to be created this evening and I wish to attend to them all.'

He tried to focus on the formal words, recited so often it could be difficult to note their meaning. Little Arthur looked up at him, as if sensing something had changed in his father. Henry allowed himself a brief smile to reassure his son. Something had changed, as it does for any parent, new responsibilities, new possibilities and new worries.

Elizabeth seemed in good spirits as he visited her chamber for the last time before her confinement. As usual, she'd distracted his questions about her health with a request. He understood why she wished her mother to be brought out of her retirement to support and represent her. Happy to do anything in his power to help her, he agreed.

His own mother attended to the minutest detail of the birthing, leaving little for Elizabeth's mother to do other then hold her hand and pray. As for representing the queen, the steady flow of foreign ambassadors requesting an audience made it easy to find some of little consequence for Elizabeth Woodville to meet. All the same, he ensured his mother would also be in attendance.

As the final new Knight of the Bath was created,

Henry announced his news. He asked them all to adjourn to the king's chapel to pray for the good health of the queen and his new child. Something at the back of his mind prevented him from saying they were to pray for his son. In a moment of insight, he realised Elizabeth never mentioned it might be another boy. He recalled her once telling him a mother knew, so there could be good reason for her silence.

He glanced down at Arthur and took his little hand, leading him through the candlelit passageways that would take them to Elizabeth. He was proud of his son, now a knight of the realm and soon to become the Prince of Wales. A daughter created new possibilities and he'd long ago resolved there could only be one choice of name.

The faces of those waiting outside Elizabeth's chamber told him everything he needed to know. He handed Arthur to her ladies-in-waiting and, gesturing for her guards to open the doors, passed through the outer rooms to her privy chamber.

It took a moment for his eyes to become accustomed to the poor light of her inner sanctum. The delicate scent of lavender mixed with exotic incense. A fire burned in the hearth and the warmth of the room contrasted with the chill stones of the corridors.

In place of precious tapestries, all the walls and even the ceiling was hung with cloths of deep blue arras, ornamented with golden fleur-de-lis. Elizabeth's bed had a high canopy of cloth of gold and a velvet counterpane embroidered with beautiful roses of Lancaster, his mother's personal contribution.

Surrounded on both sides by her silent ladies, Elizabeth sat upright in her grand bed. After Arthur's birth she'd been bathed in sweat, yet now she wore a new silken robe, with her long golden hair combed over her shoulders. Her eyes sparkled with joy and Henry realised he'd been holding his breath.

'We have a daughter, a perfect, beautiful daughter.'

Henry reached out to take her pale hand in his, noting red marks where her gold rings had been pulled from her fingers. 'Thanks to God.'

The midwife, Alice Massey, who earned Henry's respect at Arthur's birth, brought the baby forward. Wrapped in pure white linen, their new daughter gazed at him with large round eyes. Henry stared back into her pink little face in wonder. 'Her eyes are the most delicate blue...'

The midwife glanced at Elizabeth for her permission to speak. 'Babies are often born with blue eyes, Your Grace.' She spoke softly yet with authority. 'The true colour might show after a few months although I've known it to take over a year.'

Henry laughed at his own lack of knowledge. 'Perhaps, good Mistress Massey, our daughter will prove to have the dark eyes of the Tudors!'

For the first time Henry recognised the woman standing to his wife's side as her mother, Elizabeth Woodville. When he'd last seen her the former queen had been a great beauty. He'd even asked Richard Foxe to see if she could be married off to King James of Scotland.

Her once golden hair was under a coif and gable hood, although even in the low light he could see it had turned grey. Her pale face looked lined, her eyes a little sunken, yet they fixed on him with the look of one who is more than equal. When she spoke, her voice sounded husky, older than her years.

'My daughter is strong, thank the merciful Lord, as is

my new granddaughter, Your Grace.' She cast her eyes down, as if realising what her outspoken display of confidence might cost her.

Henry gave her the briefest nod of acknowledgement and looked across at his mother, standing on the opposite side of Elizabeth's bed. The glint of Beaufort steel flashed in her eyes, although her face was impassive. He guessed old rivalries must have resurfaced. Richard Foxe had been right to suggest Elizabeth's mother deserved a peaceful retirement. He resolved to ensure she returned to it for good, for the sake of the peace between his mother and his wife.

'I thank God I have lived to see such a wondrous day—and wish to thank you all for the support you have given my wife and new daughter.' He paused as he glanced again at his mother, still standing in the shadows. 'I've always known the name of my first daughter... she is to be called Margaret, in honour of my lady the king's mother.'

Shining pearls of water dripped back into the Thames as ten rowers of the gilded royal barge raised their oars as one. Yeomen in royal livery at the bow and stern threw mooring ropes to those waiting at King's Bridge pier, while the king's heralds blasted a raucous fanfare of welcome. Prince Arthur was unperturbed by the pageantry. It was all he'd known since birth.

With him in the royal barge were four bishops and seven earls. His mother's own minstrels, dressed in York livery, played her favourite tunes on lutes and flageolets, although neither she or his father were present. This was his moment and neither wished to divert attention from their son.

A wintry breeze tugged at the long pennants and

standards on the barges of the Mayor of London, the trades and guilds following behind. All wore their finery and added to the air of celebration with happy cheers and shouts of 'God save Prince Arthur!'

Few would guess that Arthur celebrated his third birthday two months before. He dressed like a miniature king, with cloth of gold and a bright ruby gleaming in his new cap. Henry prepared him well for what was about to come, taking the time at Sheen Palace to explain each step of the ceremony.

'Your great-grandfather, Owen Tudor, came from a long line of Welsh princes, Arthur.' He studied his son's face searching for a sign of understanding. 'He would be so proud to see you become the new Prince of Wales.'

He gritted his teeth with impatience that his son was still too young to even make sense of his words, let alone the significance of this day. Henry reconciled himself with the knowledge that day would come. The innocent child in front of him would be King of England and Prince of Wales.

He'd been king long enough to know he'd taken the crown poorly prepared. Despite the best advice and guidance of Jasper and his mother, he'd had no option other than to employ those who'd served two Yorkist kings. He already planned how he would school Arthur in the skills of kingship. He would teach him to keep his enemies close, to be a merciful king and how to win the love of his people.

He would also teach his son to take pride in his Tudor roots. For a moment Henry recalled the stories his Uncle Jasper entertained him with during their long sojourn in Brittany. Looking back, he wondered if some were too fanciful to be true yet, however unlikely it seemed, a Welsh servant had somehow married the beautiful, widowed queen of a warrior king.

He took Arthur's hand in his and placed on it a gold ring, so small it fitted perfectly. 'This belonged to your great-grandmother, Queen Catherine of Valois.' He looked deep into Arthur's dark eyes to stress his point. 'It is precious beyond price... all we have to remember her by.'

Arthur examined the gold ring. 'Je vous... remercie, mon Père.'

Henry smiled in surprise at the confidence in his young son's angelic voice. 'Master John Rede tutors you well, Arthur, yet now you must use English.'

Arthur looked up at him in bewilderment. 'Yes, Father.' Arthur twisted the ring on his finger. 'I shall care for it.'

'Take care *of* it,' Henry corrected, 'for one day, you will pass it on to your own son.' He took comfort in the thought, which seemed to put all the hardships and danger he'd endured into perspective.

Chapter Six

August 1490

Elizabeth sat close to the leaded-glass window for the light as she worked on her embroidery, two of her favourite greyhounds at her feet. She employed a French embroiderer and all her ladies were expert with a needle, yet she chose to embroider Henry's new Garter robe herself. Using gold Venetian thread, she'd spent a month on the Latin motto alone. Now she stuck the needle into her pincushion.

'What do you think, Henry?' She held her work up for his opinion.

Henry scratched a cryptic note in the margin of the ledger. He wished he'd taken his mother's advice to hire ships when needed. He'd underestimated the running costs of his new fleet and would have to ask Parliament to vote for more money. He laid down his quill and turned away from the chamber accounts he'd been checking for the past hours, to study her handiwork.

'Honi soit qui mal y pense.' He raised an eyebrow.

Elizabeth looked down at the golden lettering for a moment. 'Shame on him who suspects the worst of other's motives.'

'Then I must be shamed. Five years have passed since Bosworth—yet still no one is quicker than I to wonder at people's true intent!'

'Like my mother?' Her voice sounded matter-of-fact

yet he heard the note of bitterness.

'Your mother played a full part in our daughter Margaret's christening...'

'You returned her to the abbey before Christmas.' She studied him for a moment. 'If I didn't know better I could think you were punishing her for something.'

'Don't be foolish, Elizabeth.' Henry ignored a twinge of conscience. 'Your mother is the only godmother to our son—and you forget I increased your mother's pension to four hundred pounds, although I wonder what she finds to spend it on.'

'I grant you agreed to my request.' Her voice was softer now. 'You know my mother spends little enough on herself. She pays for prayers to be said for her sons...'

Henry cursed inwardly as her mention of her brothers reminded him of yet another new conspiracy he must deal with. 'You are free to visit your mother whenever you wish, although as far as I know, you've not done so for some time?'

Elizabeth didn't reply and busied herself tidying away her needlework. He wondered if she knew how her silence infuriated him. He would speak to his own mother about this. She always knew what to do. It would be good for Elizabeth to take the children to stay with her at Woking Manor.

Henry put away the ledgers and accounts and placed the stopper back on his engraved silver ink pot to prevent it drying out. He once told his confessor he'd committed the sin of wishing Elizabeth's mother dead. He regretted that now and returned to his original point.

'When I referred to people's motives, I was thinking of the motive of men like King Ferdinand. First he gives me a present of a troublesome monkey—and now he writes to you?'

Elizabeth finished packing away her needlework and prepared to leave. Her greyhounds stood waiting. 'I'm sure King Ferdinand means nothing by it...'

'So I am mistaken if I see it as a slight,' He interrupted her explanation, 'that my future daughter-in-law's father tells you of his victories over the Moors in Granada?'

'You know the rest of his letter was of little consequence, as was my reply.'

'He plays games with us, Elizabeth. These people...' he struggled to think of something to justify his annoyance, 'they have no respect for the proper order of things.'

Yet again, Elizabeth refused to be drawn. Henry realised he should have complimented her on her work, rather than raise such matters. Her deft fingers crafted plain velvet into a magnificent robe fit for a king.

He wondered if she had any idea he sometimes envied her skills. Not only her needlework, for he'd watched as she turned battle-weary knights and the most astute ambassadors into her lap-dogs.

In a break with tradition, he often sent for Elizabeth to keep him company while he worked. Alone, apart from the guards outside the door and occasional servants and messengers, they could speak without being overheard. His mother once told him such candour was good for the soul.

Greenwich Palace lacked the warren of private apartments of Sheen, separated by a moat from the court. Henry valued the privacy of his study. Built by the wealthy Duke Humphrey, brother of King Henry V, the palace had been remodeled by Queen Margaret of

Anjou. The glazed tile floor at Henry's feet was still decorated with her fleur-de-lis and marguerite emblems.

As well as being convenient by river for Westminster, Henry enjoyed riding and hunting in the two-hundred-acre deer park. He crossed to the window, which had views out over the Thames. A tall-masted merchant ship floated past, men hanging from the rigging ready to change the sails as they proceeded upriver to dock.

A Thames ferryman strained his oars against the tide, making poor progress despite his best efforts. His passengers seemed to be remonstrating with him, rather than offering any encouragement. It reminded Henry of his long struggle to win over the Yorkist faction. Whenever he thought it safe to relax, any progress he made was soon lost.

He turned to Elizabeth. 'Do you believe there is any chance either of your brothers could still be alive?'

She was standing, about to leave but stopped and stared at him with questioning eyes. 'I do not. Although...'

'You've heard the rumours?'

She hesitated. 'There are always rumours. I sometimes wonder if people enjoy nothing better than to gossip. I once ordered my ladies not to repeat anything they knew to be rumour. I never heard them so silent.'

'I'll wager they forgot your instruction soon enough. I met with my Uncle Jasper last night. He told me there might be yet another pretender, this time disguising as your poor brother Richard.'

'Where did he hear this?' Elizabeth sounded disinterested yet Henry doubted it.

'A Flemish merchant adventurer, returned from Calais.' Henry scowled. 'If it's true, I would suspect the hand of Margaret of Burgundy. Our agents report how your aunt collects Yorkist waifs and strays and continues to plot against us.'

'You reminded me five years have passed since Bosworth. Is it not time to end this bitterness?'

'Reward her treachery? Margaret of Burgundy justifies her actions because her brother died opposing us.' He realised he was raising his voice and calmed himself. 'In truth she schemes because I've not allowed her to profit from trading agreements granted by your father.'

Elizabeth crossed the room to join him at the window, her long gown swishing on the tiled floor. She took his hand in hers, something she'd not done for a long time. 'It can't be good for you to dwell on such things. We have much to thank the good Lord for.'

Henry wanted to embrace her, feel the warmth of her body through the silk of her gown, yet he did not. Instead he gave her soft hand a gentle squeeze. 'That's why I need you here while I work on my accounts. Seeing how the costs are rising could make any man turn to gloomy thoughts.'

'Even the richest man in the land?'

'Particularly the richest man in the land—if he wishes to remain so.'

'You need a rest from matters of state, Henry. You've surrounded yourself with good men to take care of it for you, yet you still initial every expense.' There was a note of admonishment in her voice.

'You don't understand, Elizabeth. I have no choice. However, you are right, we should make the most of this fine weather. I have a gift for Arthur, a new crossbow made by Swiss craftsmen.'

A look of anguish crossed her face. 'He's far too

young for such things...'

He grinned. 'I think our son will surprise you—come with me and watch!'

Prince Arthur looked delighted at the sight of the little crossbow. With a carved ash stock, its polished and engraved silver fittings gleamed in the warm sunshine. No toy, it fired sharp bolts with great force yet fitted well into his little hands.

Elizabeth looked at the crossbow. 'Be most careful with it, Arthur. This weapon could kill a man.'

Arthur seemed not to understand and looked up at Henry. 'Father?'

'Let me show you, Arthur.'

He pulled back the arming lever and placed the first bolt in the groove. Taking aim at the painted wooden target he pulled the trigger and heard the bolt find its mark with a satisfying *thunk*.

Arthur clapped his hands and looked up at Henry in admiration. 'Me now, Father?'

Henry grinned at his son's enthusiasm. Elizabeth had been right. They needed to spend more time like this, as a family. He reset the crossbow before handing it to him. 'You need a steady hand, Arthur. Brace your arm against your side, like this.'

He demonstrated and was pleased to see Arthur copy his stance. Placing a second little bolt in the groove he showed Arthur how to take aim, sighting on the target. His son misunderstood and pulled the trigger, sending the bolt flying high into the air.

Elizabeth called out in alarm and stepped forward to intervene. She turned to Henry. 'We should wait until Arthur is a little older.'

'No!' He immediately regretted the note of

annoyance in his voice. Their moments together as a family were rare enough and Elizabeth was right to show concern. He took the miniature crossbow from Arthur and reset the cocking lever.

'I learnt to use a proper bow at little more than his age.'

Arthur, no longer smiling, looked close to tears.

Elizabeth stepped forward. She picked Arthur up to comfort him, seeming to struggle to control her anger as she turned to Henry. 'He's tired. I shall take him back to the nursery.'

Henry still held the little crossbow and cursed to himself as he watched them leave. He understood Elizabeth's concern for their son but she didn't understand why this was important. These skills took years of practice. He was already thinking of having a yew longbow specially made.

Arthur would learn more than chivalry and diplomacy. His son would learn skill with the bow and sword and ride at the joust as soon as he could hold a lance. Arthur would not need to rely on men like John de Vere to fight his battles for him. He would make his son into a warrior king.

The setting sun glowed like a ripe peach in a pastel October sky by the time their entourage rode into the cobbled courtyard of Ewelme Manor. Deep in the Oxfordshire countryside, it was once the property of the treacherous Earl of Lincoln until Henry forfeited Lincoln's estate under an Act of Attainder.

He'd also claimed the well-appointed old manor house, which he now let to the late earl's younger brother, Edmund de la Pole. Despite his professed fealty, being the last remaining York heir made Edmund a possible focus for malcontents.

Henry would have slept better in his bed at nights if Edmund de la Pole was held under guard in the Tower. Instead, all he could do was have his agents keep close watch on Edmund, yet he'd allowed him to resume the title of Earl of Suffolk in recompense.

They'd travelled to the country at the suggestion of his Italian physician, who advised that the foul air of London caused Henry's toothache to worsen. He'd begun to suffer with his teeth since May and several had begun to turn black, despite his perseverance with odious herbal remedies and his daily prayers for relief.

Henry also welcomed a respite from the constant demands of court and state. Ambassadors from countries he'd never heard of arrived with every ship, wishing to discuss trade and alliances. Parliament required his attendance whenever new statutes were passed, involving long and often tedious meetings. Worse still, the noble families of England had finally woken up to the way he'd whittled at their power.

From early morning prayers until midnight mass there seemed to be constant meetings and decisions to be made, leaving him little time to spend with his family. Elizabeth chose to take no part and showed little interest in affairs of state, other than the charities, religious and educational foundations she supported with his mother.

Prince Arthur now spent more time with his tutors. Although Henry looked forward to his weekly visits, there was rarely time to spend more than an hour with his son. He feared Arthur would become a stranger to him. He could hardly recall when he'd last spent time with his daughter Margaret. Still in the care of her nursemaids at Sheen Palace, as had her mother before her, he'd forgotten his baby daughter.

The dull ache from his tooth did little for his patience with dim-witted servants. One was recently dismissed for talking too loudly in the antechamber and another for dropping a plate he was serving. Henry even raised his voice when Richard Foxe suggested he should rest for a week. Now he was glad he'd taken his loyal secretary's advice.

The limited accommodation at the manor house meant only essential servants accompanied them. After much debate, they brought Henry's elderly priest to conduct the mass, his physician and the green and white Tudor liveried yeomen of the King's Guard.

Henry left the Lord Chancellor, Bishop John Morton, together with Richard Foxe, to oversee matters at Westminster during his absence. Although seventy years old, Henry relied on the bishop's experience and trusted him implicitly. At Henry's side since his exile in France, the bishop proved skilled at overcoming objections to the new taxation.

Even the most vocal objectors struggled to argue with the bishop. He maintained that those with the money to save should invest in the future of the state, while those with money to spend could afford the king's taxes.

Now Henry could clear his mind of the concerns of kingship for the first time since leaving Brittany all those years ago. After a sound night's sleep, he rose early for mass in the simple chapel, little more than a small-windowed room furnished with a wooden altar. An old tapestry of the figure of Christ on the cross hung above the altar. Fresh rushes made it tolerable to kneel on the cold stone floor.

Already less distracted by his aching tooth, he prayed for the health of his mother, his wife, son and daughter. He raised his eyes to the faded tapestry and asked only that his people could be allowed to live in peace. To Henry's great relief there had been no further talk of impostors or bands of Yorkist rebels.

He'd sent Richard Foxe to Scotland to renew his treaty negotiations with the fifteen-year-old King James IV. Others were in Ireland, doing what they could to prevent it becoming a haven for Henry's enemies. He thanked God for the good men who risked their lives to keep the peace.

Now only events across the Channel continued to worry him. King Charles was due to come of age and at twenty-one would rule in his own right. He feared the worst news each time he read the reports of his agents in France. Henry prayed that his taxes would never be needed to finance war with the French.

After a platter of roast beef, served with a trencher of bread still warm from the oven, Henry decided to take a walk in the manor gardens with Elizabeth. She looked happier than he remembered for ages, with a fur-edged cape over her satin gown. Pearls and diamonds flashed in the sun from the edging of the fashionable cowl covering her plaited hair.

She took his arm in hers, a habit he found comforting. 'I've missed having you to myself, Henry.' She smiled, 'I know you work hard to keep the country at peace, yet I worry at how it takes its toll on you.'

'You are right. I find it too easy to become immured in matters of state.'

'Well, now we shall see if the country is able to cope without your endorsement of every decision.' Her eyes twinkled with mischief. 'Instead your duty can be to attend to your own desires for once.'

Henry stopped walking and embraced her. The yeomen guards following them at a distance looked away as he kissed her. He recalled the memory of a cold Christmas Day in the great cathedral of Rennes. That was when he'd first pledged to marry Elizabeth, King Edward of York's eldest daughter, a girl he'd never set eyes upon.

Arranged by his mother it was no love-match but a calculated plan to win over those loyal to the House of York. Henry had worried the people would whisper behind his back that he owed his throne to Elizabeth. When he thought he would lose her to her uncle, King Richard, he began to consider alternative brides.

Now he knew for certain it had always been his destiny to marry Elizabeth. He marveled as she returned his kiss. They'd had their disagreements yet their union had somehow become a love-match after all. His love and respect for her grew even stronger after coming so close to losing her after the birth of their son. He thanked God each day for the miracle of her recovery.

They walked in silence down the grassy path through the well-tended orchard heavy with apples. Henry picked a ripe one and inspected it before offering it to her as a gift. 'The forbidden fruit.'

Elizabeth tasted the flesh and smiled in approval. 'Now I have knowledge,' she laughed as she played along, 'you must also.' She handed the apple back to him.

Henry took a bite. The sharp sweetness took him by surprise and he laughed. 'This might not be the Garden of Eden, yet I name you my Eve, my lady.'

'And you are my Adam, no longer the innocent!' She

shared another bite of the apple as they continued to explore the gardens, their armed escort following at a discreet distance.

That night they watched the sun touch the western horizon and drank a flagon of rich red wine between them before retiring to bed. The ancient, creaking staircase providing access to their room was so narrow their guards had to remain on the ground floor.

Elizabeth slid across the heavy iron bolt securing their door, and gave Henry a knowing look, leaving him in no doubt of her intentions. She pulled off her velvet slippers then removed her stiffened gold headband and coif cap, shaking her long hair free of its silver pins and plaits.

He watched as she combed it with her long fingers, like golden threads of pure silk in the moonlight. She reached for the fastenings at the front of her long-sleeved, damask silk over gown, without taking her eyes from his face. Then she let the rich fabric fall to the floor at her feet, followed by her scarlet petticoat and fine wool stockings. Unable to resist any longer, he crossed the room and took her in his arms, holding her close.

He whispered in her ear, as if they might be overheard. 'I love you, Elizabeth of York.'

She embraced him and looked into his eyes. 'I love you, Henry Tudor.' She kissed him on the cheek, her eyes twinkling. 'You know I am unable to remove this kirtle without assistance?' She turned and waited for him to unfasten the back.

Henry studied the neat spiral of lacing for a moment. In all the years they'd been together she'd always left such matters to her ladies. He pulled at the thin silk ribbon that tied it at the neck, then started to unfasten the back.

As it came loose she cast the restraining kirtle aside then slipped out of her fine white linen shift to stand naked before him. Her favourite pearl and ruby pendant, on a fine gold chain around her neck, served only to emphasise her beauty.

Henry marveled at the smooth paleness of her skin and the perfect curves of her body. Even after bearing two children, to him she was still the most beautiful women in England, fluent in four languages, daughter of one king, wife of another and mother of the next.

She reached out and pulled him close. He kissed her again, with more passion this time, feeling her respond to his touch, no longer a king and queen but lovers without a care in the world.

Chapter Seven

June 1491

Henry ran across the courtyard from the stables, his riding boots splashing in puddles, feeling exhilarated by the heavy downpour. Once in the shelter of the hallway he stood dripping on the polished floor while a young servant pulled off the heavy boots and unfastened his wet cape.

'Good hunting, Your Grace?'

Henry turned to see his old friend John de Vere waiting to greet him.

'Good for the stags!' Henry had to recover his breath after running and grinned at his own joke. 'They know how to outwit us, by running where the bracken grows too thick for our horses. We would still have pursued them but for this rain.'

'They say this wet June is a threat to the harvest, Your Grace. What is not good for farmers is not good for the country.'

'You are right, Sir John. We must pray for the proper season to return.'

Henry gestured for de Vere to follow him to his study and called for a servant to bring them warmed mead. A fire crackled in the grate and Henry warmed his damp tunic in front of the flames.

'How is the queen, Your Grace?'

'Elizabeth is in her confinement.' Henry grinned with pride. 'Good Mistress Alice Massey is back to her duties.' He gave de Vere a conspiratorial look. 'I can confide in you she thinks we are to expect another son.'

Henry's serving-girl arrived and set out silver cups, then poured them each a measure of the sweet mead. Henry tasted a sip and gestured for the girl to leave the jug on the table.

De Vere raised his cup. 'May it be God's will, Your Grace. To the health of the queen.'

Henry raised his cup in reply. 'The queen's health.' The smooth, fermented honey warmed his throat. 'Am I right to presume you haven't journeyed here on a wet day without good reason?'

'Indeed, Your Grace. I need to discuss the future of our alliance with Anne of Brittany.'

Henry nodded, 'We've yet to reply to the letter from Maximilian, after King Charles took Nantes two months ago...'

'Well, we understand King Charles has now laid siege to Duchess Ann in Rennes—and refuses to recognise her marriage.'

Henry stood and started pacing his study as he thought through the implications of John de Vere's news. He stopped and turned to de Vere. 'Her marriage to Maximilian... it is valid in the eyes of God?'

De Vere shrugged. 'Her marriage was a betrothal by proxy,' he gave Henry a knowing look, 'and as far as we know was never consummated.'

'So, Charles of France intends to claim Brittany by conquest and win young Anne for himself?'

'He has the men to do it—and the Breton army has never recovered from their defeat at Nantes.'

Henry cursed. 'We should have been better prepared for this. The signs were there for anyone to see.'

'We've prepared as well as we could, Your Grace.

This could be the chance we've been waiting for...'

'What?' Henry's question echoed in the stillness of the room. He turned on de Vere. 'I owe a great debt to the late Duke Francis and pledged to support his only daughter, yet I can't believe it is God's will for me to make war with France.'

'Forgive me, Your Grace, for taking a soldier's view. Will you permit me to explain?'

Henry sat back in his chair and refilled his cup with the rich golden mead. 'You have a plan?'

'King Charles has dug in for a long siege. The last thing he'll expect is an attack from the rear!' John de Vere chuckled at his joke and took a sip of his drink and savoured the taste before continuing.

Henry raised an eyebrow. 'How do you propose we could surprise them?'

De Vere placed his empty cup on the table. 'Your fleet is now the finest this country has ever seen. We must move swiftly, reinforce our garrison at Morlaix and march on Rennes before the French realise what's happening.'

'Rennes is over a hundred miles west of Morlaix.'

'Our men could march across country at night, avoiding the main roads in the small hours to make the most of the element of surprise.'

Henry had misgivings about de Vere's plan. With typical arrogance he underestimated the resourcefulness of the Bretons. The seemingly unpopulated countryside was home to a close-knit community. The notion that an army of Englishmen could march to Rennes without being seen was laughable. All the same, he'd sworn to do what he could to protect Anne and had no wish to see her birthright stolen by the French.

He glanced across and realised John de Vere waited

for his reply. 'I shall have to think on this.'

John shook his head. 'Your Grace—there is no time to lose.'

'Then make good the preparations—but not one ship is to sail until I give the order.'

John de Vere prepared to leave. 'Understood. I shall start right away.'

Henry sat alone while he finished his drink. He threw a fresh log on the fire. As he watched it blaze he recalled his time in exile and the young Breton girl he'd left behind. She'd talked with such pride of her city of Rennes. It seemed strange to think she would be over thirty, no longer the dark-haired elfin beauty of his memory but more likely a thick-waisted matron, old before her time with the hardships of childbearing.

For a moment he imagined her grateful thanks for his heroic return with his army to liberate her city from the French, then dismissed the idea. He crossed to his desk and wrote two brief, identical notes. After reading them both through, he lit a taper from the fire and melted a little of his dark red sealing wax, then sealed them with his signet ring.

He called for a servant. 'Have these delivered to my lady the king's mother—and also Sir Jasper Tudor. Tell the messenger to explain the king requires their presence regarding a matter of some urgency.'

Lady Margaret arrived early, soon after Henry emerged from the chapel where he'd been praying for guidance. She was accompanied by her priest and confessor, Christopher Urswick, Archdeacon of Richmond. Henry hadn't seen Urswick since Arthur's christening and greeted them both warmly.

'I trust, by God's grace, you are able to remain here

until after the child is born, lady Mother?'

'Of course. There is much for me to do—and I pray your lady wife is in good health?'

'She is, and will be comforted to know you have agreed to help her.'

In his heart Henry doubted it, yet the lie was a modest sin to keep the peace between them. Elizabeth made a good pretence of her affection for his mother, yet he knew her too well. He showed them both into his study and offered them a seat before turning to Christopher Urswick.

'We are indebted to you for your services while we were in exile, Archdeacon. It is good fortune to have you with us. Now we must make an important judgement on matters in Brittany.'

Christopher Urswick gave a slight bow. 'Thank you for your kind words, Your Grace. I've followed the news of recent events and appreciate the dilemma they present.'

Henry's mother was more forthright. 'You cannot allow that scoundrel Charles of France to take advantage of the poor girl Anne.' She stared at Henry, her eyes wide. 'She is fourteen years old, little more than I was when you were born. Furthermore, I understand Charles is already betrothed to the daughter of Maximilian?'

'It seems King Charles feels he may do as he pleases now he is of age.' Henry shook his head. 'Are you saying I should agree the Earl of Oxford's proposal to go to war with France?'

His mother cast her eyes down. 'It is a dilemma, Henry. I would not wish you to go to France unless we are certain of your safety.'

'I agree, lady Mother,' Henry exchanged a look with

the archbishop, 'which is why I wait for my Uncle Jasper's advice.'

Jasper arrived late in the evening after Lady Margaret retired to her rooms. Instead of riding on horseback he travelled in a high-sided wagon. Henry noted it was also laden with his uncle's luggage, a sign he'd conceded to Henry's request to keep him company until the child was born.

Henry embraced him. 'It has been too long, Uncle. I'm glad to see you.'

'By God I'm glad to see you too, Henry!' His deep voice echoed. 'I'm also relieved to be out of that old wagon. I know every bump and rut in the road! Curse this back of mine.' Jasper loosened his jerkin and stretched. His visits had become fewer now he was less able to manage long rides.

'You must be hungry after your journey?'

Henry sent for venison, Jasper's favourite, and led him to the great hall where places were set for them both at the long oak table. Jasper admired the new tapestries of hunting scenes. Richly embroidered horsemen galloped through green forests in pursuit of their quarry.

'A gift from King Ferdinand.' Henry explained.

Jasper took a closer look. 'They put me in mind of hunting wild boar in Suscinio.'

Henry remembered. 'Those years at the duke's château in Suscinio seem so long ago and far away... although I might return to Brittany yet, if John de Vere is let off his leash.'

'You make him sound like one of the queen's greyhounds!' Jasper laughed. 'De Vere has already told me of his plans.'

'I trust you told him he doesn't have a chance of surprising King Charles at Rennes?'

Jasper grinned at the thought. 'I admire John de Vere's ambition, Henry, if not always his battle plans.'

Henry agreed. 'I sent him to prepare the fleet. Perhaps the sight of our new ships will make King Charles reconsider?'

'Send your ships, Henry—but be clear they are not to make landfall without your order.' Jasper grinned. 'We'll put on a show for the French.'

'You seem to forget, Uncle—you are half French yourself—and I am one-quarter Valois.'

'You're right, Henry—and you are half English and one-quarter Welsh. We Tudors are turning into a mongrel breed.'

A cheerful northern woman, who had served Henry since Bosworth, brought thick slices of steaming hot roast venison on a silver tray, with a loaf of bread and an earthenware jug of strong Breton cider.

Henry watched as she filled two tankards and Jasper grinned in approval after tasting the cider. 'By the heavens, that brings back memories, Henry!'

'I've been keeping it for you, Uncle.'

Jasper cut a trencher of bread with his knife and filled it with steaming slices of venison. 'You've already eaten?'

'I'll join you with a cup of cider—we have to drink the rest of the barrel now we've opened it.'

Jasper pointed to the tapestries with his knife. 'Can your good ally King Ferdinand not come to the aid of our Breton friends?'

'He has yet to agree the dowry for his daughter's marriage to our son Arthur, although your suggestion is a good one, and a useful test of our future alliance.'

Jasper agreed and filled Henry's tankard with the golden cider. 'A toast is in order, Henry. You've been so concerned with King Charles; you seem to have forgotten we expect the next in our line of Tudors!'

Henry raised his tankard. 'To our son, wishing him a safe and healthy welcome to this troubled world!'

Jasper refilled his own tankard and held it high. 'To the Tudors, may God keep watch over us all.'

Heavy rain continued to drum on the roof of Greenwich Palace as Henry paced in the corridor. His mother promised to keep him advised of Elizabeth's progress, yet several hours had passed since her last appearance.

Jasper snored in a comfortable chair nearby, having been given the privilege of free rein in Henry's wine cellar. A messenger had been send with an urgent letter to the Earl of Oxford in Dover, with orders to patrol the coastline but not to land or engage the fleet without the command of the king.

King Ferdinand's ambassador, Rodrigo de Puebla, was summoned from Westminster to help word a letter to his master. Without any knowledge of their language, Henry had no option other than to place his trust in the ambassador.

For his part, de Puebla seemed grateful and promised to deliver Henry's request to King Ferdinand in person. It was the best Henry could offer to Brittany in the circumstances, and now all he could do was wait for news of the outcome.

Henry recognised the sound of his mother's voice as her hand shook his arm to wake him. Unwilling to retire to bed he'd followed his uncle's example and fallen asleep in a chair.

'The good Lord has blessed you with another son.' His mother looked tired yet happy to bring him the news.

'Elizabeth?'

His mother gave him a rare smile. 'She is well.'

Henry embraced his mother and her thin body tensed at his unexpected show of emotion. 'We thank the good Lord our prayers are answered.' A thought occurred to him. 'I wish to see the baby—and Elizabeth.'

His mother glanced back towards the queen's rooms. 'Her physician advised her to rest—but I know Elizabeth will be pleased to show you your new son.'

She led him into the inner sanctum where Elizabeth lay, her eyes closed as if she was sleeping. Henry held up a hand to show the midwife he'd no wish to disturb her. He peered into the gilded cot where his new son lay sleeping and turned to his mother, waiting behind him. 'His reddish hair might owe more to his Plantagenet grandfather than the Tudor line.' He kept his voice low, to not wake the sleeping mother and child, and smiled. 'We shall name him Henry.'

Two hundred yeomen lined the route from Greenwich Palace to the house of the Observant Friars. On a command from Jasper, they lit blazing torches to light the way on the moonless night. The scent of pitch blended with pine resin carried in the still air. The bright orange flames dazzled Henry as he led the procession of bishops, barons and earls for the christening of his second son.

Fresh rushes were strewn over the ground for every

step, as prescribed by Lady Margaret's ordinances, which set out every detail of the christening. Elizabeth rode on a canopied gilded litter, supported by velvet cushions, their new baby, wrapped in a mantle of cloth of gold trimmed with ermine, cradled in her arms.

Nobles from all over England and Wales cheered and applauded at the sight. The River Thames glittered with the lights of a thousand lanterns as the people of London took to boats to catch a glimpse of the great spectacle. The mayor and aldermen had been rowed to Greenwich on barges, and were dressed in all their finery as they formed a line to greet the new prince.

In the church the light of a hundred candles glinted from the silver font, brought from the cathedral at Canterbury. Surrounded by Elizabeth's ladies-in-waiting, a canopy of crimson satin fringed with gold hung over them.

The honour of conducting the service was granted to Richard Foxe, now Bishop of Exeter. Lady Margaret Beaufort looked pleased as she watched her newest grandson named Henry. Foxe made the sign of the cross on the sturdy child's head. Little Henry would be prepared for a life of religious devotion. One day he would become an archbishop and a cardinal of Rome, caring for the spiritual life of his elder brother Arthur, when he became King of England.

Henry squinted as he reread the troubling letter from Rodrigo de Puebla, as if there might be some clue he'd missed the first time. He stayed at Sheen Palace as often as matters of state allowed, and it suited him that Elizabeth accepted his mother's visits with good grace.

He placed the letter to one side as Elizabeth entered. Still recovering from the delivery of their robust son, she claimed to be in good health yet he worried that she spent so long sleeping. She glanced at the unfolded parchment then back at his face.

'What is it, Henry?'

He gestured towards the letter. 'You remember the impostor who claimed to be your brother? He's landed in Ireland and they've proclaimed him Richard of York.' Henry passed her the letter to read and watched her face as she studied it. She looked pale and tired, yet when she finally spoke her voice sounded determined.

'King Ferdinand wishes to delay payment of Catalina's dowry because of this... impostor? My brother is dead—I am certain of it.' She studied his face with sadness in her eyes. 'My mother would have told me if she thought, for a single moment, that he still lived.'

'If there were only some way we could convince the people of that, yet I'm at a loss to know what to do. If I send ships to Cork to make his arrest...'

Elizabeth reached out and took Henry's hand in hers. 'The letter says he bears a likeness. If he were my brother I should know it.'

Henry gave her gold-ringed fingers a gentle squeeze. 'These things are sent to try us, Elizabeth. It's a cruel trick these Yorkists play, yet they threaten the lives of our children. I must act against them—while there's still time.'

Chapter Eight

May 1492

With Elizabeth expecting her next child, Henry welcomed the distraction of the May tournament at Sheen Palace. Planned to last for the entire month, the event attracted competitors and spectators from noble families as far as Germany and Spain, all flying colourful banners and standards.

Hundreds of canvas tents and a sprawling May fair filled every space in the palace grounds and gardens. The tang of wood smoke from cooking fires and lively music from bands of minstrels added an atmosphere of boisterous celebration. Shouting vendors touted their wares and the once peaceful river bustled with boats and barges.

The grand tournament provided Henry with a much-needed opportunity to display the new wealth and prosperity of the country. With his court plagued by rumour and treasonable talk, he'd cursed Margaret of Burgundy for welcoming the impostor and claiming to recognise him as Richard, Duke of York. To Henry's further anger, King Charles had taken Brittany and forced Duchess Anne to become Queen of France at an illegal and secret dawn ceremony.

Henry's relationship with his trusted commander John de Vere suffered when the earl claimed he could have prevented it, given the chance to do so. Then he'd reported that King Charles' army marched towards their border with Italy, where he planned to seize the wealthy city of Naples. If true, there might be no better time to take an army to Calais.

Henry pulled his favourite longbow to full extent and focused on the distant target. A crowd of spectators watched as he loosed the arrow. He kept the problem of his failing sight a secret from all but Elizabeth and his mother. He shaded his face with his hand as he squinted to see his arrow sticking from the outer ring.

'A good enough shot... for a king!'

He bowed at the ripple of polite applause. He'd been right to take part in the competition. His mother said he must be seen by his people if he wished them to love him, and he was determined not to disappoint her. At the same time, he knew what they were saying behind his back. If they were to invade France, even Jasper said he would have to sail with John de Vere.

Henry joined his uncle under the royal canopy of cloth of gold, high on the grandstand overlooking the tiltyard. On his sign, a fanfare of trumpets announced that the day's tournament was about to begin. Hundreds of spectators thronged the arena as knights in full armour prepared to joust on great warhorses.

Velvet cushions protected Jasper's back from the hard wood of their seat. Henry noted how his uncle grimaced in pain when he moved and how the shadows under his eyes seemed darker. The powerful figure he'd always looked up to was starting to look like an old man.

'I must have my physician take a look at you, Uncle. His herbal potions might ease your discomfort?'

Jasper shook his head. 'The ravages of age, although I couldn't stop your grandfather riding into battle with us when he was sixty!'

Henry recalled the stories Jasper had told and retold during the long years of their exile. His grandfather, Owen Tudor, was executed on the orders of Elizabeth's father after their defeat at Mortimer's Cross.

'Not only did he take on York at the age of sixty—he fathered a child with his serving-girl when he was little younger than you!'

Jasper laughed at the memory. 'A Tudor, A Tudor!' He bent double with a fit of coughing.

Henry called for a cup of wine for his uncle and made a mental note to speak to his physician. He remembered Elizabeth's concern at news that her mother, now frail at fifty-five years old, had made her will and was not expected to last the month.

He wondered if he should ask his mother, staying at Sheen to oversee Elizabeth's confinement, to visit her at Bermondsey Abbey, then thought better of it. Her husband had shown no mercy to his grandfather. Jasper had been made to live with the burden of guilt for his part in that day ever since.

The wine improved Jasper's spirits. They both cheered and applauded as a Flemish knight raised both hands in the air in mock surrender, calling out for the king's mercy. It was not the show of great chivalry Henry hoped for, yet the crowd seemed to enjoy the spectacle.

'Next in the list is a Welshmen from our exile in Brittany.' Jasper had to raise his voice to be heard over the cheering. 'Sir Hugh Vaughan of Kidwelly.'

Henry remembered him. 'A good man—and loyal. He has a dispute over a coat of arms with Sir James Parker.'

'Could you not settle it, Henry, for old times' sake?'

'He requested a judicial joust.' Henry surveyed the

cheering spectators. 'The spectacle has drawn the biggest crowd of the day.' He grinned at his uncle. 'I'm hoping Sir Hugh will show the folly of challenging the king's man!'

'And a Welshman!' Jasper pointed at Vaughan's banner.

The spectators fell silent as the two knights readied their lances, then charged. Sir Vaughan's lance shattered as it smashed into his challenger's face with such violence he was flung from the saddle and crashed to the ground. Some in the crowd groaned, yet many more continued to cheer the victorious Welshman as yeomen carried his challenger's limp body to a nearby tent.

Jasper stood for a better view, a look of concern on his rugged face. 'I fear this dispute has been settled, although not as Sir James might have wished.'

Troubled by the incident, Henry visited Elizabeth before she retired to her chamber. He made a judgement not to mention the death of Sir James at the joust that day or of the spectator struck by a stray arrow. Instead, he contrived to appear cheerful, knowing it could be a month before he would see his wife again.

Elizabeth smoothed the silk gown covering her bulging middle and looked up as Henry entered the room, where she sat surrounded by her ladies.

She dismissed them and waited until they closed the doors, then took his hand and placed it over the child.

'Can you feel her moving?'

'You think it's another girl?'

She looked tearful. 'I have a great favour, if you will?'

'If it's a girl, might we name her Elizabeth?'

'After your mother...'

'Pray for us, Henry.'

'You have cause for concern?'

'Only that... this child seems eager to enter the world. I was not fully recovered from little Henry...'

'We will pray for you, our two Elizabeths!' He turned to leave, then looked back. 'I love you, Elizabeth of York.'

'I love you, Henry Tudor.' She raised a hand and smiled, although her eyes misted with sadness.

He wiped a tear from his cheek and struggled to compose himself as he made his way back through the maze of corridors. Henry fixed the memory of her smile in his mind and fought to dismiss the thought he might never see Elizabeth alive again.

St George's chapel in Windsor echoed to the solemn words of the priest. He ran through the absolution of the dead with professional detachment, a man doing what was required of him. A bouquet of white roses on the simple wooden coffin seemed a fitting tribute to the former Queen of England, although there were few enough guests to see them.

Her daughter Elizabeth remained at Sheen Palace in her confinement, together with her sister Lady Cecily. Elizabeth's remaining son, the Marquis of Dorset knelt with his hands clasped in prayer, with her other daughters, Lady Anne, Lady Catherine and the youngest, twelve-year-old Lady Bridget, who travelled to Windsor by river barge, with several of their ladies.

Henry remembered Lady Elizabeth Woodville in his prayers that Whit Sunday. It troubled his conscience that the full cost of her funeral had to be met by Thomas Woodville. Her only son paid for her to be laid to rest alongside the man she had loved, the enemy of the Tudors, Edward IV.

Henry rubbed his eyes as he lost another hand of cards. Four pounds could keep a family fed for a year yet he'd let it slip through his fingers in less than an hour. His mind was on Elizabeth and he closed his eyes for a moment in silent prayer.

He'd made the mistake of taking her love for granted. Lost time they could have spent together filled instead with discussions about revenue or what to do about the York impostor. Now he could lose her he realised he'd seen more of his mother than his wife since the birth of little Harry.

Bishop Foxe caught his eye yet his face had its usual impassive expression. He excused himself from his gambling party and followed Foxe into the relative privacy of the anteroom.

'You have a daughter, Your Grace.' Richard Foxe gave him the briefest smile. 'May I be the first to offer my congratulations?'

Henry sensed a great weight lifting from his shoulders as he followed Foxe through dimly lit corridors. He pledged to himself he would be a better husband to Elizabeth, a better father to his children— once he returned from the war in France.

The midwife Alice Massey seemed to be holding something back as she confirmed the news of his daughter. Having been through the tension of Elizabeth's confinement three times before, Henry knew the buxom woman well and was concerned by her subdued manner.

'All is well with the queen, Your Grace.' She avoided his eyes, choosing instead to look at Henry's shoes.

'The baby—is there some problem?'

Alice Massey hesitated long enough for Henry to fear the worst. 'Your daughter is small, Your Grace, yet has a good pair of lungs.'

Henry allowed himself to breathe again. He passed her the purse of gold coins he carried. Ten pounds seemed a small price to pay for her service to his family. 'Please tell the queen I wish her well—and pray for our two Elizabeths!'

♛

Henry stared up at the sails of his flagship *Regent* billowing in a fresh autumnal breeze. His standard, the red dragon of Cadwallader and the cross of St George, flew proud and high on the topmast. He said a silent prayer for his army, readying weapons as the fleet neared the coast of Calais. After months of preparation they were finally going to war.

Much to his disappointment, the people of England welcomed his difficult decision. It seemed they longed for him to be a warrior king, not a peacemaker. The men of Kent lined the streets of Sandwich to see the fleet off, throwing coins to the sailors and shouting for them to give Charles of France a bloody nose.

Jasper's shout broke through his reverie. 'A fair wind, Henry, a good omen!'

He'd urged Jasper to remain at home, yet his uncle insisted he was still Henry's guardian, pledged to protect him.

'The wind brings the colour back to your face, Uncle.'

'It's good to be at sea. I wondered if I'd ever set foot in France again.' Jasper studied the fleet, which followed behind them into the far distance. 'We sailed from France with a handful of borrowed ships, yet we return with too many for me to count.'

'There are more than five hundred in the fleet,' Henry heard the pride in his voice, 'enough, I pray.'

'John de Vere was right, Henry.'

'Right or not, we've rolled the dice.'

Jasper grinned. 'Well, I pray you have better luck with dice than you do with cards!'

Sir John de Vere led the first wave of ships into Calais, where over fifteen thousand men prepared to disembark. In no time the quayside became a mass of soldiers, unloading horses, siege weapons and supplies for a long campaign. Henry's ships soon filled the harbour to the entrance, the greatest invasion of France in a generation.

Sir Edward Poynings, a veteran of Henry's exile and one of his oldest commanders, waited to greet him in the great hall of the old castle. Now over seventy, Sir Edward needed a stick to walk yet brandished it in the air like a weapon.

'Welcome to Calais, Your Grace.' He recognised his old friend Jasper, 'and to you, my lord!'

'It's good to see you, Sir Edward, and we thank you for clearing our way of the French.'

'All we met were a few Flemish pirates!' He shook his head. 'They ran before we could even fire a shot.'

Henry took his seat at the head of the table and the others joined him. 'My lords...' Henry glanced around the table at the members of his war council. Many had been loyal to him before Bosworth. 'You will not be surprised to learn that I hope for peace with France—not war. My problem is that since we took the throne, our efforts to maintain that peace have cost more than half the revenue of our country.' He paused and glanced at Sir John de Vere. 'The French must repay that cost in full—and swear to never support our enemies.'

Sir Edward Poynings was the first to reply. 'If they refuse, Your Grace?'

'If they refuse, Sir Edward, then we shall assert our sovereignty by force.'

The room fell silent for a moment. For the first time, Henry realised they looked at him with new respect. He'd forgotten the thrill of taking such great risks. Jasper was right. He'd lost more often than won at his games of cards. Now he played for the highest stakes, and gambled with his life, and the lives of all who sailed with him to France.

At a signal from Henry, John de Vere spread out a parchment map. 'We have but a toe-hold here in Calais.' He pointed to the coastline south of them. 'Sir John Savage will lead a siege of Boulogne, whilst our ships blockade the port. The plan is to divert the French as my men push north and eastwards and establish our front around Calais.' De Vere glanced around the table. 'If the French decide to attack us here in Calais, they will find us ready.'

'Thank you, Sir John. All our resources are at your disposal as our commander in the field.' Henry glanced at his uncle. 'Sir Jasper will lead our diplomatic mission. We can allow him only one month, and then this council must declare war on France.'

Gulls screeched overhead as Henry waited at the rail of his flagship in the staple port of Étaples, at the mouth of the River Canche. Only two weeks had passed since they'd set a deadline at that meeting in Calais, yet to Henry it seemed much longer.

Unable to do anything other than wait for news, he'd spent long hours at prayer. Then Sir John's forlorn men returned to Calais carrying his body, wrapped in a canvas shroud. Their ships continued to prevent access to the old walled port, but the siege ended when the French launched an ambush under the cover of darkness.

Jasper seemed to read Henry's mind. 'Sir John Savage was one of the first Yorkist commanders to support us. You recall his men wore white hoods at Bosworth?'

'I do. He fought for York at the Battle of Tewkesbury and captured Queen Margaret of Anjou—but told me he never trusted King Richard.'

Jasper frowned. 'Don't take it to heart, Henry. If Sir John and a handful of men are the only casualties of this... adventure, we should count ourselves fortunate.'

'We must see his family are cared for.' Henry pointed to approaching riders carrying a white flag of truce. 'It seems the moment of truth approaches, Uncle.'

They watched as the men dismounted and approached the guards on the quayside. Henry counted them—six men wearing the royal livery of the House of Valois, the once familiar blue-and-white surcoats with golden fleur-de-lis. He would have wished to meet King Charles in person, but on Jasper's advice agreed to negotiate with his ambassadors.

'You are certain they will agree to our demands?'

Jasper grinned. 'We shall find out soon enough—but winter is coming, Henry. Our cousin Charles prepares his army to invade Italy, so I believe he has little choice.'

'I pray you are right, Uncle. Many lives depend upon it.'

The negotiations proved a formality, as the king's

ambassadors carried a treaty that only required Henry's signature. As well as reparation in full for all expenses incurred over the past six years, King Charles committed to never support the Enemies of England, including pretenders or claimants to the English throne.

After the French left Henry embraced his uncle and called for strong drink to celebrate.

Jasper looked pleased. 'I think this is known as a king's ransom. Three-quarters of a million crowns is more than I could have hoped for.'

'We've won, Uncle. Yet in my heart I know the people of England will not understand.'

'Then you must see to it that they do, Henry. It's time to consider what matters most—that's the true measure of a king.'

Henry watched as their mooring ropes were cast off and sailors scrambled to catch the wind. His uncle was right. He bit his lip to focus his mind. He was doing God's will. He'd defied the odds yet again to prove himself worthy of the crown of England. He'd defeated his enemies, overcome his secret doubts and knew he would make his mother proud.

Chapter Nine

January 1493

Christmas at Westminster Palace was marked by a nativity feast of fat geese, painted with saffron butter to give them a golden glow. A private family occasion, a choir sang to the accompaniment of musicians with lutes and dulcimers, as well as Henry's precious new clavichord, paid for from his own purse.

To Henry's left sat his son Arthur, then his mother, Lady Margaret and her white-bearded husband, Sir Thomas Stanley. Beside him sat Sir Jasper, with his beautiful young wife Catherine Woodville. At the side of the queen sat her sisters, Lady Anne and Lady Catherine, both yet to be found suitable husbands.

The great yule boar, carried by four men to a fanfare of trumpets, seemed to snarl at them with gilded tusks and glittering diamonds for eyes. Henry's kitchens excelled themselves with a nativity scene of sculpted sugar, complete with shepherds, wise men of the East and angels suspended overhead on fine silk thread.

Sir Jasper, as the elder of the Tudors, stood to propose the toast to peace and prosperity. He spoke of Christmases past, when Henry had been a child young Harry's age, then in Brittany, where the late Duke Francis had shown them great kindness. He finally raised his goblet and dedicated the feast to the honour of her grace Lady Margaret, the king's mother.

Later, at a midnight mass in the Royal Chapel of St

Stephen, Henry knelt at the side of his mother and gave thanks to the Lord for his many blessings. He liked to make a new pledge before God with the dawn of each new year, and chose to honour the promise he'd made to himself to become a better father. His fears of losing his youngest daughter reminded him he'd become too preoccupied with matters of state.

His children were becoming strangers to him. It didn't help that his family were dispersed over several palaces. Prince Arthur, now in his seventh year, had been hidden away with his tutors at Farnham in Hampshire. A thin-faced, serious boy, he'd hardly spoken to Henry since returning to London.

Their daughter Margaret, turned three the previous November, looked like a miniature version of Elizabeth, with a reddish tint to her golden hair and large, amber eyes, and seemed in awe of him. With little Harry, she'd been brought to Westminster from Eltham Palace. Once a hunting retreat and a favourite palace of King Henry IV, Eltham now served as the royal nursery.

Harry had the red hair of the Plantagenets and the build of his grandfather, Edward of York. Able to walk unaided much earlier than Arthur, he'd already learnt to run at every opportunity, a trial to his nursemaids. Henry was relieved that Arthur owed more to his Tudor heritage. He wondered how much work it might take to prepare his high-spirited second son for a life of devout contemplation in the church.

Elizabeth hardly ventured away from Sheen as she recuperated from the birth of their newest daughter. Little Elizabeth's size and frailty had been a great worry to them both, yet at last she seemed to be thriving, thanks to the care and attention of her devoted wet-nurse, the likeable Lady Cecily Burbage, daughter of a neighbouring nobleman.

'We shall mark the Twelfth Night as a family,' Henry announced, 'with music and singing, magic and disguisings!'

He placed his hand on Arthur's shoulder. 'I have a present for you, a fine new bow crafted from Spanish Yew. We'll try it out at the butts tomorrow?'

'Yes, Your Grace.'

'Father.' He corrected his shy son. 'You must call me father.' Henry studied his son's thin, pale face and glimpsed an echo of himself at the same age. 'You are growing into a fine scholar, Arthur,' he grinned, 'but we must make time for merrymaking. We shall spend more time together. I will teach you how to lose your money at cards!'

'I should like that, Father.' Arthur smiled, the first time Henry had seen him do so since he'd returned to Westminster.

Elizabeth picked up little Harry, already escaping on sturdy legs. 'And you, sir, shall have sugar fancies.'

Harry's bright eyes shone with affection for his mother, although he seemed not to even recognise his father. Henry produced a silver bell on a red silk ribbon from the pocket of his doublet. The shining bell tinkled musically as he dangled it in front of his youngest son.

'A present for you, Harry!'

Strong little fingers grabbed the ribbon and Harry started swinging the silver bell so violently Elizabeth had to take it from him. He bawled in loud protest and she called to her ladies-in-waiting.

'Fetch the minstrels to play, if you will.' She smiled at Henry. 'Music seems to calm him.'

'As it does his father. Let there be music—and fools

to cheer my son!'

Servants carried steaming cups of mulled wine for Henry and Elizabeth, as well as sweet treats for the children, who were brought low chairs and velvet cushions to sit on. A colourful satin curtain pulled back as if by magic, to reveal a candlelit wooden stage, with a canopy of state supported by long wooden poles, painted in spirals of Tudor green and white.

A musician beat his drum and the king's trumpeters blasted a discordant note as Patch the fool appeared on the stage. Dressed as a knight, with a coat of knitted woollen mail and a cooking pot on his head, he began the entertainments as master of ceremonies, mimicking the arrogant tone of Sir John de Vere, Earl of Oxford, as he read from an over-large scroll.

He drew an enormous wooden sword, which he waved at the children while bellowing a humorous song of his great bravery. In a flash of smoke, another of Henry's fools appeared. A stocky dwarf dressed as a bright red dragon, he did his best to avoid the oversized sword, roaring and dancing around Patch as Elizabeth's minstrels played a lively jig. Little Harry clapped his hands in delight as the unconvincing dragon fell over his own tail and tripped from the stage.

Next came another of Henry's fools, carrying a shepherd's crook and wearing an absurdly high, gold-painted bishop's mitre. Disguised as the Bishop of Misrule, he proceeded to wag his finger in the air and lecture the king and his family in a stentorian voice, yet none of his words made any sense.

'He mocks Bishop Foxe!' Elizabeth laughed.

'A poor resemblance,' Henry grinned, 'yet his manner is unmistakable.'

A troupe of Flemish jugglers amazed them with their

skill, throwing heavy wooden clubs to each other and spinning them high in the air. As the last of the jugglers vaulted from the stage, Patch the fool returned and bowed to Henry and Elizabeth with exaggerated reverence to announce the finale.

The choir of Westminster Cathedral entered, all dressed in white and wearing silver wings of angels. Their caroling echoed through the palace as they sang Henry's favourite songs, accompanied by musicians with drums and flutes.

After the children retired for the night Henry gestured to his waiting servant to bring him a box tied with a ribbon of silk. He handed it to Elizabeth.

'I have a gift for you.'

She unfastened the ribbon and took the richly decorated volume from its box. 'A book of hours.' She opened it at a page showing the hours of the Virgin. The colours dazzled and the gold lettering glowed in the candlelight, as if with some magical inner fire. 'It is a thing of great beauty. Thank you Henry, I shall treasure it.'

'I also give my pledge to be more attentive to you, Elizabeth.' He took her hand in his. 'I love you... with all my heart.'

She leant forward and kissed him, regardless of the servants. 'I love you, Henry.'

He squeezed her pale fingers, their secret sign of the bond between them. Despite threats from impostors and another difficult birth, the past year had been a good one. He was proud of his family, the new generation of Tudors, and resolved they should spend more time together.

Bishop Foxe waited with a friar who wore the long cowl and brown robes of the Augustinian order. The friar turned his tonsured head at the sound of Henry's approaching footsteps. Henry called out to his old friend, the renowned scholar and poet, Bernard André, whom he'd not seen since the coronation.

'You've done well, Master Bernard, I hear?'

'Thanks in no small part to your generous patronage, Your Grace. I have taught at the universities of Oxford and Cambridge.'

'Bishop Foxe tells me you are also qualified as a doctor of law?'

'Indeed. It has taken me a good many years, yet I have secured mastership in both civil law and canon law.'

Henry placed a firm hand on the friar's arm. 'Well done, Master Bernard, you are an inspiration to us all. Come in and I shall explain why I've asked you to travel all the way from Oxford.'

He guided the friar into his privy chamber and led him to an empty chair, indicating to Richard Foxe to join them.

'We have a proposal for you, Master Bernard.' Henry turned to Foxe. 'Kindly explain, Bishop?'

'The king wishes to appoint you as his poet laureate, Master Bernard, and also to seek your assistance in helping to prepare his son, Prince Arthur, for kingship. You are to become his tutor once he reaches the age of ten years.'

'It is a great honour you do me, Your Grace. I understand Prince Arthur is a studious boy?'

Henry agreed. 'He has been tutored well, yet I need to consider his future education. You have an excellent knowledge of the Roman and Greek classics, Master

Bernard, as well as an enquiring mind. I wish my son to understand how the classics contain the lessons one needs to lead a moral and effective life.'

'It warms my heart to hear you say such enlightened words, Your Grace.'

'A lesson I'm determined to pass on to my son is that a king must speak and write with eloquence and clarity.'

'The Humanist moral philosophy, Your Grace. A modern king must engage in civic life and persuade others to be virtuous.'

'I take it you accept my proposition, Master Bernard?'

'Gladly, Your Grace.'

Richard Foxe saw Henry's nod for him to continue. 'There is another matter we wish to discuss. His Grace also wishes to commission you to write a book—a history of the life of Henry Tudor.'

Foxe glanced across at Henry. 'There are conditions. The king requires this work to be kept secret, and for you to prepare your account without... embellishment. The book is to be a gift for Prince Arthur, when he comes of age.'

Friar Bernard remained silent for a moment as he considered the implications. 'I am most grateful to accept this commission, Your Grace, although I profess not to know much of the events of your life before Bishop Foxe first introduced me to you in Brittany.'

'My uncle, Sir Jasper, will be happy to tell you about his father, my grandfather, and the circumstances of my birth. My lady the king's mother can also be taken into our confidence about this work.' Henry spoke to himself. 'Even I do not know the extent of her involvement in events leading up to our victory at Bosworth.'

Friar Bernard clasped his hands across his broad chest, then turned sightless eyes to Henry. 'I trust, Your Grace, there is no particular... urgency for this commission?'

Henry looked across at them both and fought back emotion. He bit his lip to focus his mind. 'Last year, the queen's lady mother passed away. She was aged fifty-five—and before that in good enough health.' He took a deep breath. 'My own mother is now fifty years old, Master Bernard.'

'I understand, Your Grace.'

'You are no doubt aware there are also those who plot against us. I shall keep this fragile peace, with the grace of God—but write your story, Master Bernard, for who can know how it will end?'

♔

Henry was uncertain about what to make of Sir Robert Clifford. A handsome but impoverished knight, he'd been with a group of men arrested for plotting against the crown and now imprisoned in the Tower. Tired of continued rumour and speculation about the pretender to his throne, Henry decided he must question Clifford in person.

Sir Robert had been overheard claiming to have actually met the troublesome impostor in Burgundy. In all the time since Henry first became aware of the rumours, this was the closest he'd come to his elusive adversary. To his annoyance, Clifford remained tight-lipped and seemed prepared to take his secrets to the grave.

Henry chose not to tell Sir Robert he'd spent most of June and July back at Kenilworth Castle, preparing for a rumoured invasion from the pretender's supporters.

The attack never came but caused him sleepless nights and the expense of maintaining his army ready to move at one day's notice to ensure his safety.

He ordered the removal of the iron manacles on Clifford's wrists and shackles chaining his ankles. He knew there were ways of extracting the information but he needed more than a confession. Henry wanted a way to capture the pretender and put an end to his damaging escapades.

'For a man so keen on talking, you have little enough to say to your king?' He leant forward in his chair. 'Tell me how and where you met the impostor.'

Clifford hesitated, glanced once at Henry, then cast his eyes back to the tiled floor as he spoke at last. 'It was at the court of Margaret of Burgundy, Your Grace.' His voice sounded well-educated yet dispirited, as if he'd lost all hope.

Henry raised an eyebrow. He'd recently imposed a total ban on trade with Burgundy in the hope that Margaret would hand over the pretender. It came as little surprise that men such as Sir Robert Clifford seemed happy enough to ignore his commands.

'What took you there?' Henry tried to control his annoyance. He needed Clifford to continue talking.

'I travel to all the foreign courts...'

'My agents think you were in Burgundy to plot with the impostor against us.'

'I was not, Your Grace.'

'And the Duchess of Burgundy introduced you to the impostor?'

'I understood he was nephew to the duchess...' He studied Henry as if making a judgement. 'Only later I realised he was...' Clifford stopped as he chose his words. 'The one calling himself the Duke of York.'

'What did you make of him?'

'I...' Clifford stared down at his shoes. 'He may be an impostor, yet he is convincing, Your Grace.'

Henry studied the man. It was not the first time he'd heard the pretender described as convincing and probably not the last. Bishop Foxe had a theory that Margaret of Burgundy could be schooling the boy in details of the York family and their court. If true, this made him a greater threat than young Lambert Simnel, now slaving in Henry's kitchens, ever was.

'You were overheard saying you believe him to be Richard, Duke of York. What do you say to that?'

Clifford hesitated. Henry wished to make an example of such men, a warning of the perils of disloyalty to the crown, yet there was something about Sir Robert Clifford that set him apart.

'I confess that I'd been drinking, Your Grace, and the wine loosened my tongue. In truth, I regret the day I ever set eyes on the... impostor.'

'You were knighted for your bravery at the Battle of Stoke Field, risking your life to defend us against Yorkist rebels.' Henry stared at Clifford. 'Now you face charges of conspiracy and await the gallows for your treason, yet you don't seem afraid of the fate that awaits you.'

Clifford looked forlorn. 'I beg the King's gracious mercy to forgive a moment of foolishness.'

Henry sat back in his chair. 'Foolishness? You are right. This foolish business has cost a great deal—to learn this troublesome lad is the son of a Flemish boatman. His true name is thought to be Perkin Warbeck.'

He fixed his eyes on Clifford's to see his reaction to the news. 'We believe his deception came about by accident. A Breton wool merchant named Pierre Jean Meno took him to Cork. Warbeck dressed as a nobleman and the Irish mistook him for the Earl of Warwick, escaped from the Tower.'

Clifford looked surprised. 'I thought...'

Henry shook his head. 'We'd have released young Warwick from the Tower by now if the Yorkists were not so keen to replace me with him.' He stared at Clifford. 'You must understand that Margaret of Burgundy has good reason to recognise this impostor as Richard of York. She hopes to profit from it at our expense, as it seems the lad has promised much not in his gift. You told my men you make a living as a merchant adventurer?'

Clifford nodded, 'I've had to make my own way in the world, Your Grace, as a third son I have no inheritance.'

'Well, I have need of someone with your knowledge, Sir Robert, although your life might depend on your ability to show discretion.'

Clifford regained his composure a little. 'You may rely on my loyalty, Your Grace.'

'I pray that's true, Sir Robert. We suspect that someone paid you to travel to Burgundy to make contact with Perkin Warbeck. We wish to know the name of that person.'

Clifford seemed to make a decision. 'It was... Sir William Stanley.'

Henry sat back in shock, his mind reeling. 'My kinsman, the Lord Chamberlain?'

'You will have him arrested?'

'Not yet, Sir Robert. First, you will gather evidence of his disloyalty. I must be certain of my facts before arresting the brother of my stepfather.'

'I understand, Your Grace.'

'You must return to Burgundy and learn what you can about Warbeck's intentions.' Henry studied his face. 'Do you think you could win his confidence?'

'I do, Your Grace.' Clifford brightened and stood straighter.

'We will meet your expenses—and if you are able to assist with his capture, you'll be well rewarded.'

Clifford bowed to Henry. 'I thank you, Your Grace.'

'I understand one of those arrested with you is your wife's father.' Henry saw Clifford's despairing nod. 'I shall show mercy to your co-conspirators, including your father-in-law, and free them from the Tower with the same warning that we give to you. If you ever conspire against us again, you will be taken to Tyburn and hanged.'

Chapter Ten

July 1494

Henry ran a calming hand over the smooth withers of the fine Welsh mountain pony, a birthday gift for Harry. 'There now, my beauty.'

Elizabeth glanced at the young groom holding the bridle, although she looked at Henry as she spoke. 'You've checked the girth is tight enough?'

Henry gave the fine new saddle a tug. 'I have—and I've adjusted the stirrups long, as it's his first ride.'

She turned to Harry, waiting with his sister Margaret. 'Take care now Harry, be sure to listen to your Father?'

'Yes, Mother.' He didn't take his eyes off the pony.

Henry lifted his son onto the saddle. 'Now place your feet in the stirrups, like this... and try to keep your heels in line with your ears.' He grinned as he passed Harry the rein. 'You sit with a good straight back, Harry. That's good—but try not to lean forward.'

He took his son's hand. 'Now, you hold the rein like this, with your little finger under and the other fingers over it.' He demonstrated, helping Harry to find the proper grip. 'Turn your hand so your thumb's on top. Don't pull too hard.'

Harry glanced around for his mother and beamed. 'My own horse, Mother! I'm riding my own horse.'

Henry grinned. 'She's a Welsh pony, like I learnt to ride on when I was little older than you, Harry. Treat her well and she'll soon come to know you.'

Harry sat tall in the saddle. 'Can I ride now, Father?'

Henry laughed and led the pony to walk in a slow circle around Elizabeth and Margaret.

'Look at him—a natural horseman!' Henry beamed with pride in his young son, yet his happiness was tinged with regret. He'd been far too busy when Arthur learnt to ride and would never have that time over again. At least he'd honoured his pledge to spend more time with his family.

Elizabeth called out. 'Keep a firm hand on that bridle—he'll be off at a gallop if you give him the chance!'

Henry laughed at the thought. 'He looks as if he'll turn into the image of your father.' He patted Harry on the back. 'You're strong enough for a boy twice your age.'

Elizabeth smiled at Henry. 'My father loved riding in the parks here at Eltham. You know there are over a thousand acres? He would have been so pleased to see his grandson ride here.'

'Even though he's a Tudor?' Henry doubted it. He thought King Edward would more likely turn in his grave if he knew the House of York had been so thoroughly defeated by his old enemy.

There had been numerous arrests since Robert Clifford became his spy amongst the Yorkist exiles in Burgundy. Henry's commissioners had been tasked with investigating numerous treasons and several of the pretender's supporters now languished in the Tower.

Most of the men arrested had been quick enough to swear fealty and pay Henry's fines in return for their freedom. Those who did not would have to await their fate at the king's pleasure. His advisors told him he must have them hanged if he wished to put an end to treason, but for now he preferred to let them stew.

A thought occurred to Henry as he noted how well his son sat in his saddle. 'We shall mark this day by making our son the new Duke of York.' He was pleased to see Elizabeth brighten at his suggestion. 'We cannot allow this... Perkin Warbeck,' Henry scowled as he said the name, 'to claim the title any longer—and we will hold a royal tournament in his honour to make certain everyone knows.'

The leaves faded to a crisp golden brown on the trees before Harry's first public appearance in London, escorted by six of the king's trumpeters and a grand procession of the mayor and aldermen, followed by the men of the trades in their colourful liveries.

The knights of the Order of the Bath, dressed in mantles of crimson silk, with bright gold chains and tassels, led Harry on his first rite of passage. He would be the youngest ever admitted to the order, although Henry doubted that he understood.

Harry rode the powerful black courser as if he'd been born to it. Chosen for its good temperament, the warhorse would prove daunting for any other three-year-old. Harry beamed at the crowds thronged along the entire route to Westminster. He waved a hand as they cheered, 'Long live Prince Henry!'

Elizabeth watched with Henry from under a painted wooden podium, erected for the occasion, as the procession reached Westminster Palace. 'He is a credit to your coaching, Henry.'

Henry smiled at her compliment. 'I can't take all the credit. He rides well for his age, I must say. Sometimes... I wish Arthur showed a little more of

Harry's spirit.'

'Suum cuique pulchrum est.'

Henry agreed. 'Yes, to each his own.'

'Arthur is becoming a scholar, far beyond his years.'

He heard the defensive note in her voice. 'Arthur loves his books, I'll grant you, yet when he becomes king he'll need to lead by example.'

'He's young and will learn.' She smiled back at him. 'Arthur has achieved great skill with his bow.'

'Thanks to my patience, Elizabeth, yet he shows little appetite for hunting or tennis. I believe he prefers his own company. The other night, when he was supposed to be sleeping, I found him reading by candlelight.'

'Exactly like his father!'

'Well, Harry follows you, Elizabeth. He's already able to manage some Latin and French, yet he has a mischievous sense of humour. He even plays his tricks on my good lady mother!'

'Yet Lady Margaret calls him your fair sweet son and shows him favour over her other grandchildren. I would never have thought it. She brings him special gifts—and always asks after him.'

'My mother suggested we should consider appointments for Harry. I'm minded to make him Earl Marshal of England, Lord Lieutenant of Ireland and Constable of Dover. He needs an income now he is Duke of York.'

'You don't think so many titles will be a heavy burden of responsibility for our youngest son?'

Henry gave her a conspiratorial look. 'In truth it means the actual holders of the posts have only temporary tenure. It helps to keep them on their toes, as they know they can be replaced at any time.'

Wearing their crowns and robes of cloth of gold, Henry and Elizabeth presided over the first day of the tournament. With them sat their sons Arthur, Prince of Wales, Harry, the new Duke of York and their daughter Princess Margaret. The royal grandstand had a canopy of cloths of estate of blue arras, embellished with gold fleur-de-lis.

Next to them sat Sir Jasper, Duke of Bedford, his wife the duchess and Lady Margaret, with her husband Sir Thomas Stanley, Earl of Derby, with many earls, barons and knights.

Henry was pleased to see so many spectators attending, despite the earlier rain showers which threatened to turn the roads to mud. A light breeze now tugged at the pennants and standards of all the great houses of England as the first day began with a fanfare of trumpets.

Four young ladies wearing white satin gowns with crimson sleeves rode fine white horses. They led the knights on horseback into the lists by ropes woven from white and blue silk. The knights rode horses caparisoned with black velvet edged with gold brocade.

They wore the king's livery of green and white with the queen's crest of murrey and blue on their helmets. After saluting the royal family, the first two lined up with lances, either side of the tilt to compete for the king's prize.

The Master of the Joust shouted his command and heavy hooves thudded on hard packed earth. The jousters closed with a smash of wood on metal, taking turns until one was judged a winner.

The champion of the joust, Sir Edward de la Pole, Earl of Suffolk and younger brother of the Earl of Lincoln, was presented with a diamond studded gold ring by five-year-old Princess Margaret. Dressed like her mother, she looked like a miniature queen.

The finale of the first day was a violent mock battle between all the participants, who'd been formed into two opposing sides with sashes of red and blue. They fought on foot and made a great spectacle as swords clashed and men yelled out, pretending to fall with mortal wounds.

Prince Harry wore the same robes of cloth of gold trimmed with ermine as Henry, the only difference the colourful and precious feather of a popinjay in his cap. He stood and called out in his powerful young voice, waving his arms to encourage his chosen side, the reds, to victory.

Arthur seemed not to mind his young brother becoming Duke of York and being the centre of attention. 'Look, father!' He pointed a gloved finger as a towering knight rode into the thick of the melee. He was followed by a mounted standard-bearer carrying Henry's standard, the red dragon of Cadwallader and cross of St George. The tall knight drew his sword, raising it high in the air.

For a moment Henry was reminded of the carnage at Bosworth. As he watched, the knight raised his visor and called in a deep, bellowing voice for the blue-sashed army to lay down their weapons in surrender. Only then did Henry understand the mock fighting was a re-enactment of the battle at Bosworth. The mounted knight represented himself, portrayed as the hero of the day.

He turned to Arthur. 'I pray you will never witness a real battle.' They watched as those pretending to be dead were commanded to arise and staggered to their feet. 'These play-actors might count themselves fortunate. The wounds of a real fight are more fearsome than a man could imagine.'

'I've no wish to become a soldier, Father.' Arthur's face had the same look of concern as his mother.

'Nor I, Arthur.' He tried to reassure his son. 'I plan to hand you a kingdom at peace, on good terms with its neighbours.' His eyes narrowed. 'The sad truth is, Arthur, you will find that men like to fight each other.'

'Why is that, Father?'

Henry had to think for a moment. 'There are many reasons. Some seek glory, others fight to become rich.' He studied his son's attentive face. 'Many fight for what they see as their duty to the will of God and loyalty to a noble cause.'

'You fought for such a cause?'

He studied his son's face as if seeing him for the first time. 'You will learn that sometimes your destiny leaves you with no other choice.'

Henry suspected he'd read too much into the question from a boy not yet eight years old. With a jolt, he realised although his son was half Tudor, he was also a son of York.

Henry cursed as he missed yet another ball from his courtier and tennis partner, Lord Robert Curzon. He'd yet to show real skill at the game but it proved a good diversion from matters of state. He enjoyed learning the tactics. Lord Curzon sliced at the ball with a cutting stroke, which gave it an unpredictable spin.

Unfortunately for Henry, his weakness for gambling had already got the better of him and tennis was proving an expensive pastime. As well as the cost of building the courts, Henry chose to retain the full time services of a Spanish tennis master. He'd yet to win a single game.

Lord Curzon called out, his voice echoing in the high-walled court. 'Do you wish to take a rest, Your Grace?'

'I do not—although I regret accusing you of going easy on me.' He grinned and took a firmer grip on the handle of his racket. 'Your service, again, Lord Curzon.'

Henry feared the real cause of his problem was not the fault of the Spaniard's poor coaching so much as his own weakened vision. Still keen to keep such an unkingly defect from the world, he was aware it had become something of an open secret amongst his closest courtiers.

This time he reached for the ball and managed to return it, much to the surprise of his partner, who seemed to be caught off guard. Henry wiped the sweat from his eyes and watched for the next service. He might never become a competent tennis player but it would not be through lack of trying.

♛

'Is there to be no end to this... treachery?'

Foxe regarded Henry with a grim expression. 'I regret, Your Grace, that I had no cause to suspect the dean, or else...'

'I've known Master William Worsley, Dean of St Paul's, for more than twenty years,' Henry shook his head, 'and now he plots against me—to support Perkin Warbeck!'

Bishop Foxe nodded. 'He's one of the wealthiest clergymen in England, Your Grace. I considered him a friend until I heard of his arrest.'

'You would have reported him to me yourself, if you had known?'

Foxe seemed unperturbed by Henry's tone. 'Of course, Your Grace, without hesitation.'

'Well, I thank the Lord my commissioners have exposed his disloyal servant's treason. The man must think us fools that he can mock us with impunity?'

'It seems Dean Worsley remained loyal to York and waited his opportunity all these years.'

The continued dull ache from Henry's tooth had worsened and he felt in no mood for clemency. He paced the floor as he tried to think, a habit he'd tried to rid himself of. 'There are those who'd have him hanged, as an example to others.'

'Might I ask Your Grace to consider the many years of service the dean has given to his church and country?'

Henry stopped pacing and turned to face Foxe. 'Does it not make his crime so much worse that he was in a position of our trust?'

Bishop Foxe remained silent, as if he knew better than to press his point until Henry had calmed a little.

Henry knew Foxe well and understood his silence. 'I meant no criticism of your good self—I just wish an end to this treachery.'

'May I make a suggestion, Your Grace?'

'Please do. I am at a loss to know how to deal with these...' Henry stopped himself from cursing. 'These traitors who plot against us!'

Foxe looked at Henry in silence for a moment. 'Dean Worsley comes from a well-connected family and inherited a great deal of land from his late uncle, Archbishop Booth. I understand, Your Grace, the bequest included estates in Hackney and Tottenham, as well as an income of some two hundred pounds a year in rent.'

'You seem particularly well informed, Bishop.' Henry realised it sounded like an accusation. 'I recall hearing he owns a fine house, more of a mansion, in Hackney. I thought at the time this was unusual for a dean, even of a great cathedral like St Paul's.'

'My suggestion, Your Grace, is a suitable punishment would be to impose a fine in return for your gracious pardon. You could also demand the income from his estates.'

'If he hangs, his estates will be seized by the crown...' Henry's aching tooth made it hard to think.

'Yet instead you could have him pay to you, say, two hundred pounds a year, for the rest of his life?'

'You are right, Bishop Foxe. This business has cost me, both in sleepless nights and the cost of my commissioners. It's about time we had some financial return.'

Henry lay awake before dawn, listening to the strange, nocturnal noises of the old Palace of Westminster. Shutters rattled in a gust of wind, eerie echoes haunted empty, dark corridors. A dog barked outside, then yelped as its noise was cut short.

He'd doubled the guards outside his door. Good loyal men, yet now he strained to hear their whispered conversation. Only a few words reached him. The conspirators would celebrate if they knew how well their efforts disturbed him. Troubled by his conversation with Bishop Foxe, he'd been unable to sleep.

The conspiracies made him suspect everyone. Richard Foxe did whatever he asked, even risking his life in his Scottish negotiations, yet he'd been ready to question his loyalty. He recalled the bishop's wounded expression. Such loyalty was hard won yet could be so easily lost.

He recalled how King James of Scotland was murdered by his own subjects who replaced him with his own son. Henry worried his tax raising and limiting the power of the barons could be fuelling dissent. He struggled to imagine Arthur having any part in such a rebellion, yet the new King James claimed he'd not known his father would be killed.

He closed his eyes and tried reciting prayers, yet the whispering somewhere in the back of his mind continued. He imagined he heard what his guards were saying. Warbeck was Richard, the true Duke of York, and they would not oppose him when he returned to claim his right to the throne.

Henry sat up in bed and shouted for a servant to light a candle. For the first time, he contemplated the implications of Margaret of Burgundy being right. His commissioners told him the man was an impostor yet could have been saying what he wanted to hear.

If the man he knew as Perkin Warbeck was the missing Duke of York, his beloved wife could side with her brother, as could his treasured sons. Even members of his own mother's family had been implicated in supporting Warbeck's scheming.

The only person he could trust without question was his Uncle Jasper. He knew what his uncle would say. Urged on by the good intentions of advisors like Bishop Foxe, he'd shown too much leniency. Even those he'd pardoned could be laughing behind his back. It was time to act like a king. His life depended on it.

Chapter Eleven

February 1495

Henry decided to visit his mother in person with his grim news, rather than send a letter or imposing the indignity of summoning her to his presence. He'd rehearsed his words many times as he rode the twenty miles south from Sheen Palace with his Yeomen of the Guard.

Now his mother's grand manor house in Woking came in sight his courage slipped away. He'd had to act fast, as the news would reach her within a day. He could think of no way to soften the blow and cursed the man who'd caused him to upset her.

His mother was at her prayers when he arrived. An elderly servant in his mother's livery bowed and showed him into the great hall. He declined the offer of wine and looked around the hall as he waited, struck by its lack of decoration.

The stone walls, once hung with fine tapestries, were bare except for the carved and gilded Beaufort portcullis over the fireplace. The polished oak table stood empty, as if rarely used. Henry guessed it had been some time since his stepfather, Sir Thomas Stanley, last stayed there.

The door opened and his mother entered, dressed, as she often now chose to, in the black robes of a nun, with a tight, starched white linen coif and pale grey hood concealing her hair. She carried a small prayer-book bound in black leather.

'I bid you welcome, my most dear son.' Her eyes, as sharp as a hawk, studied his face. 'I was not expecting your visit. I trust all is well?'

Henry hesitated to answer. 'These are... difficult times, lady Mother. With sadness in my heart I bring news of a traitor within our family.' Henry glanced at the door. 'We need privacy, while I explain.'

He watched as she crossed to the door and dismissed her servant waiting outside before closing it and inviting him to be seated. She took a firm hold on her prayer-book in her thin fingers, as if preparing herself.

'I wish you to tell me, Henry. Who is this traitor... and what crime have they been accused of?'

He sensed the note of sadness in her voice but knew he could not keep it from her. 'Sir William Stanley,' Henry avoided her eyes, 'is to be executed for treason.'

'Our own dear Will?' She seemed to age a little before Henry's eyes. 'There must be some mistake?'

Henry shook his head. 'I find it difficult to understand those who plot against us, yet this is so much worse to comprehend.'

'Will has been like a brother to me. He fought for you at Bosworth. He has served you...' Her words tailed off.

He took a deep breath. 'He's made a confession— that he supports the pretender, known to us as Perkin Warbeck.'

They sat together in the silent room for a moment while she considered the implications of Henry's words. He longed to take her frail hand in his and offer some words of comfort, yet he'd never been more conscious of a distance between them.

'Has my husband...' She studied his face as if

dreading to hear the answer, 'Has Thomas been implicated in any way?'

'I pray he has not, Mother.' He rubbed his eyes.

'I know my good husband, Henry. You will not find a man more loyal—whatever his brother has done.'

Henry flinched at the sharpness of her tone. His mother always spoke to him with great affection. He could not recall hearing a cross word from her, yet he knew she'd defend her husband. For the briefest moment he suspected she might be hiding something, then dismissed the thought.

'You know how people like to make mischief and must prepare yourself for gossip.'

She studied him with weary eyes. 'Have you come all this way to test me, Henry?'

'Both your husband and his brother have served us well but were once loyal to York. I have come here to explain why I can't show Sir William leniency.'

'Not for my husband's sake? This could do great harm to his reputation.'

'I cannot, even for your own sake, Mother, although it grieves me to say these words.'

'Sir William is a wealthy man. I understand you have fined others, attainted their lands?'

'I must tell you a great secret, Mother, which you must promise never to repeat, even to your husband.'

She gripped her prayer-book. 'You have my word.'

'I have an agent at the court of Margaret of Burgundy. His information has resulted in many arrests, including our steward, Lord Fitzwater. Sir William has been in contact with our agent for over a year to keep in touch with the pretender to our throne.'

She nodded in silent understanding.

'I shall meet the expenses of his funeral and ensure

he does not suffer unduly.'

Henry made the long journey back to London with a heavy heart. He'd prayed with his mother for the soul of William Stanley, once a trusted friend, now his enemy. He'd also prayed to the Holy Virgin that his mother and her husband would understand he'd had no choice.

Sir John de Vere looked tired from his ride. Concerned at reports that Perkin Warbeck landed at Deal in Kent, Henry had sent him with five hundred men to investigate.

'He never came ashore, Your Grace.' De Vere scowled. 'Word is he's sailed on to Ireland. They counted fourteen ships, some flying the flag of Burgundy.'

'Yet you are certain it was Warbeck?' Henry studied his old friend's battle-scarred face. 'Or was it all rumour, put about by our enemies?'

'He was there. We found some of his men.' De Vere shook his head. 'Seems he abandoned the men he'd already put ashore—to save himself.'

'As we had to in Dorset,' Henry made a quick calculation, 'nearly twelve years ago.'

'I'd forgotten—we almost lost Jasper in the confusion!'

'Warbeck's men, were they foreign mercenaries?'

'At least a hundred and fifty died but those we found alive were quick enough to talk.' De Vere shook his head. 'Some were English and confessed they'd planned to gather enough supporters to march on London.'

'Yet the men we had watching the coast of Kent saw them off?'

'They served you with loyalty, Your Grace.' He

grinned. 'Warbeck's men didn't have a chance.'

'We must note this as a warning, Sir John. We learnt from our near disaster in Dorset.' He raised an eyebrow at the memory. 'I'm encouraged to know our defences proved sound, yet what if he'd landed in the North?'

'Then... we might have a problem, Your Grace.'

Henry turned to him in surprise. 'We have men to watch the coast, and our agents in Ireland can try to learn what he plans to do next?'

'I pray you are right, although you know there have been riots after Sir William Stanley's execution. The Stanley family always had great affinity in the North. They considered Sir William as one of their own...'

'Now they use his death as an excuse to rebel against the taxes. It would have gone easier if I'd spared Sir William—although I could never again count him as loyal.'

'You sent a clear message, Your Grace, that no one is beyond the reach of the law.'

'And it has cost me. Now, Sir John, we must be sure to catch this troublesome impostor.'

There never seemed to be a good time to make a progress to the North, but Henry judged it necessary to win back the support of the great families there. In a public show of support, his mother and stepfather hosted their visit to their grand manor house at Lathom in Lancashire.

Henry accepted Sir Thomas' offer to see the view from the roof parapet. From his high vantage-point, Henry could see the unfinished house was surrounded by a six-foot wall and a wide green moat with a high drawbridge defended by a tower.

'You've built a castle here, Sir Thomas.' Henry meant

it as a joke yet felt a little envious.

'Stone is cheap enough in the North, Your Grace, as is the labour of masons. I pay them half what it would cost in London.'

Henry appreciated his stepfather's efforts to be civil, yet there was an edge of bitterness to his words since the death of his younger brother.

'There will be eighteen towers,' Sir Thomas continued, 'and I've named the tall one in the middle the eagle tower.' He saw Henry's raised eyebrow. 'Yes, we do have eagles here. When it's finished you'll be able to see for ten miles at least.'

Henry heard a muttering behind him and turned to see the earl's fool, a grinning imbecile wearing a cap adorned with pheasant's tail feathers. The fool spoke with such a thick Lancashire accent he couldn't make out his words. Sir Thomas seemed to understand and cuffed the fool around the head, sending him scuttling back the way he'd come.

Only on the ride back to Sheen Palace did Henry realise what the fool had said. 'Remember Will.' Although a fool, he was strong enough. Henry realised the fool could have pushed him over the low parapet to his certain death. He must take more care from now on.

Elizabeth stared out of the window and smoothed the front of her gown, already expanding with her latest pregnancy. 'I remember when she was born. So tiny, like a little mouse.' She turned to Henry. 'I prepared to lose her then, you know. The midwife, Alice Massey, told me...'

Henry placed a comforting hand on her shoulder. 'Good Alice Massey might have delivered more babies than she can count—but our baby was a fighter.'

Elizabeth studied him with sad amber eyes. 'She was, Henry.'

'Half Tudor, you see...'

'And half York.'

Henry bit his lip. He had to be strong for her. He fought the dreadful feeling of regret. He should have learnt from Arthur's lost youth. In three years, he never tried to know his little daughter Elizabeth. He'd been more interested in securing her a husband, the hand of the one-year-old Francis, to be the future French king.

He listened to his wife's sobbing as she cried herself to sleep. He prayed for her and remembered the story of Atropos, the Greek goddess of fate and destiny, who chose the mechanism of death and ended the life of mortals by cutting their thread.

Little Elizabeth's coffin, brought on a chariot drawn by six black horses, seemed so small. One hundred poor men, all dressed in black, sat like silent crows in every spare seat, paid to pray for a princess taken before her time.

Henry commissioned a skilled engraver to write an inscription on a gilded plate so her name would never be forgotten: *Here, after death, lies in this tomb a descendant of royalty, the young and noble Elizabeth, an illustrious princess. Atropos, most merciless messenger of death, snatched her away. May she inherit eternal life in Heaven!*

Kneeling at Elizabeth's new, grey marble tomb in the peace of Westminster Abbey, Henry forced himself to focus on his prayers. He'd always believed in his destiny, yet struggled to accept the loss of his little child was the will of a merciful God.

Duchess Catherine welcomed Henry to Jasper's manor house at Thornbury in Gloucestershire. Still a beautiful woman, in a shimmering gown of scarlet satin and long, gold brocade sleeves. A large ruby flashed in the light on a thick gold chain around her neck as she greeted him with a graceful bow.

'You do us a great honour, Your Grace, to travel here so close to Christmas.' Her brief smile was not matched by the concern in her eyes.

Henry knew the reason. He asked the question that had urged him on for the past three days, despite biting winter winds and icy roads. 'How is my uncle?'

She avoided his gaze. 'His physicians fear...' She seemed to struggle to say the words. 'They tell me he won't last the week. I sent the charlatans away, their daily bleedings and foul potions made my husband worse.'

'I left as soon as I received your letter.' He waited while Jasper's servant took his damp cloak and gloves. 'I am grateful to you, Lady Catherine.'

He warmed himself at the stone hearth, where a log fire crackled and spat glowing embers. His fingers tingled as the feeling returned. He'd feared the worst. There was only one reason his uncle's wife would write. The journey west was long and cold, yet he'd not hesitated to come.

A buxom servant brought mulled ale hot from the kitchens. Henry took a grateful sip and glanced across at Catherine. Only a year younger than himself, Lady Catherine looked more like Jasper's daughter than his wife. Her waist had grown thicker under her gown, the legacy of four children by her first husband, the ill-fated Duke of Buckingham. The darkness under her eyes spoke of the strain she must now be under.

'I imagine my uncle complains at being kept in bed?'

'I've done what I can for him, Your Grace.'

Henry heard the coolness in her voice and remembered her marriage was not a love-match. Elizabeth was right. He'd offered her to Jasper like a trophy of war. He knew his uncle would always treat her with kindness, yet could not expect her to thank him for it.

'May I see him now?'

'Of course, Your Grace. He knows you are here and will be glad to see you.'

Henry sensed a resignation to her voice and realised his uncle's poor health must be difficult for her. He finished his cup of mulled ale then followed Catherine into a dark hallway and up a flight of creaking wooden stairs.

He recalled Jasper telling him he wished he could live by the sea in Tenby and walk down to the harbour in the evenings. The journey to London from the far west of Wales was too long for him, so he'd settled in Gloucestershire, half way between London and his beloved castle at Pembroke.

Jasper sat up in his bed, propped up on velvet cushions. He grinned as he recognised Henry in the doorway. 'You made it here despite the snow!' he coughed, a dry, rasping sound, then reached out a hand in welcome.

Henry shook his hand. 'Good to see you, Uncle. It would take more than a little snow to keep me away!' Last time they met he'd joked at how his uncle's once iron-hard muscles were turning to fat, yet now his hand felt thin and frail.

'I was sorry to hear about your daughter...'

Henry sat in a chair at the side of Jasper's bed and

realised he'd not seen him since before little Elizabeth's death. He would have liked to visit Thornbury more often but there had been too much to do, and Jasper was no longer fit enough to travel to London.

'Thank you, it has been a... difficult time for us all.' Henry fought the emotions welling up inside. 'You know we are expecting another child? Elizabeth thinks it might be another girl.'

'Well done, Henry.' Jasper's voice sounded weak but his eyes twinkled with mischief. 'Your father would have been proud.'

'My father was ambitious.'

Jasper nodded. 'I remember how happy Edmund was the day he married your mother, one of the wealthiest heiresses in England.' He stopped to gather his breath. 'You know her grandfather was the eldest son of John of Gaunt and gained the confiscated estates of Owain Glyndŵr?'

Henry forced a smile. He'd heard the stories many times, yet Jasper never tired of reminding him. His mother rarely spoke of his father, so the picture of him in Henry's mind had been formed from his uncle's memories.

'He wanted to make his mark on the world, and has—through you.' Jasper sounded wistful, 'Edmund would have been pleased to know his son has become so great a king.'

'I wish I could have known him, Uncle, yet you've been more than a father to me.' Henry looked into Jasper's dark eyes. 'I could not have done it without you.'

'Who can know?' Jasper smiled. 'You do well enough without my help.'

Henry shook his head. 'I've missed your good advice,

Uncle. It is hard, being king—harder than I ever imagined when we were in Brittany.'

'Sometimes we must be guided by our destiny, Henry.' He coughed again, his face showing the pain as his chest heaved. He sat in silence for a moment, recovering his breath. 'Queen Charlotte of France once told me... whatever happens to you has been waiting to happen since the beginning of time.'

'I wish to tell you a great secret, Henry, while there is time....'

Henry placed his hand on his uncle's shoulder and spoke softly. 'I can't believe there is anything you need to confess to me, Uncle. I've never known a better man than you.'

Jasper peered up at him. 'I killed a man once, Henry.' He drew a deep breath. 'His name was Roger Vaughan, a fellow Welshman. I captured him at Chepstow castle. When he asked for mercy I said I'd offer him the same courtesy he allowed my father. I took my sword and cut off his head.'

The great effort of saying the words seemed to take the spirit from him. Henry knew the Vaughan family bore a grudge against Jasper yet never understood why, until now.

'We were at war, Uncle. I carry the burden of many deaths on my conscience.'

Jasper recovered his breath. 'I took his life out of vengeance, Henry. He executed your grandfather. William Herbert might have given the order but it was Roger Vaughan of Tretower who carried it out.'

'I forgive you, Uncle. We shall pay to have prayers said for Roger Vaughan.'

'Thank you, Henry, it would mean a lot to me.'

'You've always known my great secret, that I never

wished to become king.'

'You told me as much back in France before we even had an army.' His voice sounded weaker now, as each breath became a greater effort.

'You told me a king doesn't have to fight in wars, that if I were king, I could end wars, bring peace to this country...'

'I could not be more proud of you, Henry.' His voice became a whisper. 'Pray for me.'

Henry's eyes filled with tears.

Chapter Twelve

March 1496

The deep sense of loss of his loyal uncle hung over Henry like an ominous cloud, darkening his mood. The long, freezing winter finally gave way to spring, yet the cold still lingered in his bones. He suffered with his bad teeth and could not recall when he'd last had a good night's sleep.

He worried about his dwindling finances and needed to raise more taxes to maintain his hard pressed army. The new dockyard in Portsmouth was ready yet he had no money to build new ships. He'd taken to gambling to pass the time and take his mind off Perkin Warbeck, but lost a small fortune at cards and dice.

Henry missed his Uncle Jasper. He missed his wife, shut away in her rooms to give birth to their fifth child. It should be a time of great anticipation, yet he feared the worst. Elizabeth grieved for the loss of their daughter and looked like a pale ghost when he saw her for the last time.

One consequence of his uncle's death was that his mother forgot their differences over the execution of William Stanley. She moved to Sheen Palace with an entourage of servants. His mother had come to care for Elizabeth and promised to remain until after the baby was born.

She liked to keep him company while he checked through his chamber accounts, although unlike

Elizabeth, she preferred her books to needlework. She also liked to discuss matters of state and would distract him from his work with her questions.

'I understand your Uncle Jasper's will allows only that his wife will have such dues as shall be thought to appertain by law and conscience.' There was a note of satisfaction in her voice.

Henry glanced up from checking the lists of expenses. Although he'd spoken once of having fathered two daughters in Wales, his Uncle Jasper left no legitimate heir. He'd shown great generosity in providing for his household servants with a year's wages, yet he hadn't made his wife an executor of his will or left her anything specific.

'You've never approved of the Woodville family, Mother, but Lady Catherine cared for my uncle as well as anyone could.' He laid down his quill and turned to face her. 'As for his will, he divided his fortune between us and benevolences to the church.'

'Your uncle was right to limit her inheritance. Has she not already remarried a young courtier?'

Henry raised an eyebrow. 'I am sure you know, Mother, this courtier comes from a good Lancastrian family—and is a man with excellent prospects.' He frowned, 'It was done in haste, I grant you, and without our consent.'

'I am surprised at your tolerance. Lady Catherine should be in mourning.' She spoke as if to herself.

Henry turned back to his work. He doubted Jasper would have wished his wife to mourn him for too long. He imagined his uncle would have laughed to know she married a man younger than herself so promptly. He wished her well and would have given the marriage his blessing.

His mother still wore her mourning dress for Jasper. He knew she prayed for a week after his funeral at Keynsham Abbey, long into the night. He'd sometimes wondered how close the two of them had been at the time of his birth in Pembroke Castle. He asked Jasper once. He'd deflected the question, like a swordsman parrying a blow, as if there might be something he wished to hide.

Henry glanced at his mother, who had returned to studying her book. He could ask her now but decided it was too late for her answer to be of any consequence. Some things are best left unspoken.

He returned to the letter from Bishop Foxe, who was in Scotland to negotiate a betrothal between Henry's daughter Margaret and King James. Henry read the letter aloud to his mother for her opinion, something he'd rarely done with Elizabeth.

His mother listened until he finished and then shook her head. 'I confess I never was in favour of this scheme, Henry. How old is your young daughter now?'

'Princess Margaret was six years old last September. I appreciate your reservations, Mother, but these things take time.'

'Well, now King James supports the impostor, will you order Bishop Foxe to return?'

'We have all the more reason for him to persist with his discussions. If there is any chance of persuading King James to hand over Warbeck, we must take it.'

Henry found he was thinking aloud. An alliance with James of Scotland could solve all his problems. In the meantime, Richard Foxe was taking the opportunity to learn what he could of the intentions of the Scots.

'Bishop Foxe advises you that Warbeck is married now—to a Scottish lady, a cousin of King James.' She looked thoughtful. 'That suggests he either thinks the impostor tells the truth or could be turned to his advantage.'

'The good bishop has known King James of Scotland since he was a boy. What do we have to lose by trying?'

'A daughter.'

'She would become the Queen of Scots and begin to work for peace.' Henry doubted the words even as he said them, yet he found these debates with his mother helped focus his thoughts. 'We have a truce with France, Sir Edward Poynings has brought the Irish lords into line, and Bishop Foxe has a deal with Philip of Burgundy. Only the Scots now threaten our peace.'

He pointed with his quill to the chamber accounts, piled up on his desk. 'In truth, Mother, we cannot afford a war if the Scots choose to invade with Warbeck. Even with all the fines we've been imposing, we'd have to raise new taxes—and risk more dissent in the North.'

His mother returned to the study of her book. Henry understood. She had offered her opinion and considered their discussion to be ended.

Henry studied parchment maps of the Atlantic Ocean spread out by the bearded Viennese adventurer, John Cabot and his sons. Intrigued by tales of fortunes in trade to be made in distant lands, he'd agreed to give them an audience. He'd also asked his trusted chancellor, Sir Thomas Lovell to the meeting.

Sir Thomas stroked his beard as he considered the possibilities. 'You have a suitable ship in Bristol?'

John Cabot produced another parchment. 'We do, sir, a fast and able ship, the *Matthew*, of fifty tons, with a crew of eighteen men.' He glanced at his sons. 'I am a master mariner—and my sons have spent their lives at sea.' He spoke in a deep voice in a curious West Country accent, although his first language was Italian. 'This is our list of supplies, enough to last our crew twelve months.'

'What do you seek from us?' Henry was cautious not to reveal the poor state of his finances.

'We ask for royal patronage, Your Grace. Bristol merchants will invest if we have the king's warrant.'

'And what do you expect to discover?' Sir Thomas still sounded unsure.

'Little is known of these lands, sir.' He pointed to the western Atlantic on the parchment map. 'I was in the spice trade, following the ancient routes, and heard stories of fabulous wealth in Asia.'

Henry smiled, 'I have also heard of mysterious people across the sea. You could secure us trading rights?'

'We would hope to, Your Grace. I believe the route to Asia could be shorter from the north than along the trade winds, although the adventure is through discovery.'

'You will bear the whole costs and pay the king one-fifth of any profits?' Sir Thomas had a duty as chancellor to protect Henry's interests.

Cabot grinned. 'We will, sir—and claim new lands for the King of England.'

Henry saw Sir Thomas' nod of approval. It seemed there was little enough to lose in the venture. 'We shall grant you letters patent, Master Cabot. You and your sons will sail under the English flag to seek out and discover lands unknown to Christians.'

After they had gone, Sir Thomas turned to Henry. 'An interesting fellow, I wish him well.'

Henry agreed. 'He was recommended to me by an Augustinian friar. His real name is Giovanni Caboto and what he says is true. The Italian merchants of London will finance his voyage.'

'So we have nothing to lose, Your Grace?'

'And everything to gain, Sir Thomas. There is a whole world beyond these shores. Who knows what he might find?'

Henry held his newest child in his arms. A daughter, she had entered the world without fuss or cause for concern. Her swaddling robes were loosened, freeing her arms. He laughed as a tiny hand reached for his nose.

The tragic death of their daughter Elizabeth meant he'd prepared himself for the loss of another. Only now did he realise they'd not even discussed names or planned the christening. He breathed a great sigh of relief and thanked God to see both the baby and Elizabeth in good health.

'What shall we name her?'

Elizabeth looked up from her bed. 'I was thinking— we could name her Mary, after my beloved younger sister, who died when she was only fourteen.'

'Mary Tudor... a good name,' Henry smiled in approval, 'and she is a good size.'

'I thank the Lord for his grace. There has been enough sadness in our household.' She smiled as she watched the two of them together. 'Our little Mary shall mark the start of spring. A new season is beginning for our growing family.'

Henry handed the baby to her young nursemaid, Mistress Annie Skearn, telling her he needed a private moment with his wife. He sat on the edge of

Elizabeth's bed. Taking her pale hand in his, he gave her thin fingers a gentle squeeze.

'Our physician says you are to remain in bed for a few weeks until you regain your strength.' He looked into her eyes. 'Each of our children seems to take something from you.'

'I'm tired, Henry, although...' She hesitated.

'What is it, Elizabeth?'

'I need to rest before we have another child.' She watched for his reaction. 'You know what I'm saying?'

Henry understood and kissed her hand. 'I agree to abstinence until you feel well enough.' He saw she still had a look of concern. 'What troubles you?'

'I was thinking of my mother. You know how many children she had?'

Henry shrugged. 'Too many to count?'

Elizabeth laughed for the first time since her daughter's death. 'My mother had twelve children. She was forty-three when my youngest sister Bridget was born.' She squeezed his hand. 'My mother warned me, when I was expecting Arthur, of the consequences of not meeting your needs.'

Henry recalled the stories of her father's many mistresses. The rumours even reached him in Brittany, such was the late king's indiscretion. He understood. 'You need have no concern, Elizabeth.'

'It would only be until I feel strong again.'

He smiled at her. 'A small price to pay to see your health restored.'

Henry pretended dismay as Elizabeth took his black knight, left undefended. He'd arranged for the chess board to be placed on a special table that she could use while remaining in her bed. As well as helping the time pass more easily for her, he was determined to spend more time in Elizabeth's company.

The tuneful song of a blackbird drifted in the fresh spring air through the unshuttered window as Henry moved his bishop to take one of Elizabeth's pawns. A small victory, and he laughed at her frown of annoyance. A skilled player, she usually won their games.

'I have some good news about our son's betrothal.'

Elizabeth moved her queen to protect it. 'I was beginning to wonder if we shall ever see Arthur's Spanish Princess.'

'Well, Rodrigo de Puebla believes we will, and soon. It seems they've tired of using the pretender as an excuse for delay.' Henry moved his remaining knight, threatening Elizabeth's bishop. 'King Ferdinand needs this alliance more than we do.'

She pondered for a moment, then moved her queen. 'Checkmate, I believe.'

Henry studied the board, looking for a way out. 'A king, beaten by a queen.' He smiled, glad to see the colour restored to her face at last. 'I expect we'll soon hear King Ferdinand has agreed to pay the dowry.'

'Should we not be more concerned to see his daughter, if she is to be the future Queen of England?'

'Of course, although we must make sure there is enough money for her upkeep—until she is married.'

He watched as Elizabeth replaced the chess pieces in their correct squares, ready for another game. It was an encouraging sign of her recovery, as before she'd been too tired to manage more than one game of chess.

Henry hid a pawn in each hand and held them out for her to choose. 'I think you are well enough to join me on a summer progress to the West Country?'

'I should like that, Henry.' Elizabeth brightened as again she chose white, her lucky colour. 'We should take the older children.'

Leaving Sheen in bright May sunshine, they stopped at Eltham and Greenwich to collect Arthur, Harry and Margaret before setting out on the long ride to Chertsey in Surrey. One of the oldest market towns in England, it seemed the entire population turned out to welcome the royal cavalcade.

Garlands of flowers decorated the narrow streets and fresh rushes paved the way for the royal family. Arthur, who would become ten in September, led with Henry on their black chargers. Elizabeth, Harry and Princess Margaret followed in a carriage drawn by two pairs of white horses.

One hundred members of the Royal Guard rode with them, with as many servants, Elizabeth's ladies and several knights of the realm. Behind them followed wagons laden with beds and tapestries, clothing and the king's plate, all the essentials of the Tudor court in progress.

Henry peered up at the great stained-glass window of Chertsey Abbey. The crucifixion scene took on a surreal glow as it reflected the sunshine behind. It chilled him to know the body of King Henry VI had lain in state in the nave not far from where he sat, after his murder by Yorkist assassins.

He glanced to his side and could see young Arthur listening attentively to the sermon, yet he noticed his son Harry seemed bored. Not for the first time Henry doubted if his younger son should be prepared for a life in the church. He'd already shown a great interest in ships. Henry wondered if his son would one day command the royal fleet.

After the service, Henry lit a candle for his daughter Elizabeth and another for Jasper. As he watched the flames flicker in the coolness of the abbey he prayed to the Holy Virgin for their souls. He'd not had time to see much of either of them in their last year of life and vowed to not make the same mistake again.

The *Regent* strained at her mooring ropes at the dockside in Southampton, Henry's colourful standard flying in a warm summer breeze. Sailors shouted to each other from high on the yard-arms while others coaxed nervous horses up a narrow gangplank. Henry placed a hand on the shoulders of each of his sons as they watched.

'Your first sea voyage—mark this moment boys, as it will be the first of many.'

Henry stared out to sea. The wind blew in their favour, although he could see white foam cresting on the waves further out. He'd never been to the Isle of Wight before and thought it would be good for his sons to experience the short crossing on his flagship. Now he hoped it might not be too much of an adventure.

He remembered his first time, at the age of fourteen, braving rough seas and gales with his Uncle Jasper. They'd escaped York's men by sailing from Tenby at night. Their little ship was blown off course and in danger of being swamped by towering waves higher than the mast. He'd feared they would drown but their captain found shelter in the lee of the island of Jersey.

As they boarded to a fanfare of trumpets he raised a hand to the crowds who'd come to see them off. A voice shouted 'God save the King!' and the crowd gave a rousing cheer.

At last the heavy mooring ropes were cast off and the *Regent* headed out into the choppy waters of the Solent. The deck tilted as the mainsail filled, causing young Arthur to stumble.

'One hand for the ship, Arthur!' Henry shouted as his son made his way across the deck.

Arthur grabbed the rail at his side. 'I thought to take some air, Father.'

'Feeling seasick?' He studied his son's pale face under his wide-brimmed black hat. Tall for his age, his thin frame was hidden by a rich fur cape, despite the summer warmth. 'Keep your eyes on the horizon, that will help.' He grinned. 'It's a short crossing, ten miles, we'll soon be back on dry land.'

Henry glanced across the deck where Harry was being shown the guns by the captain and clearly enjoying the short voyage. Arthur was more interested to learn more about Sir Edward Woodville's brave but ill-fated foray to save Brittany.

'I ordered your uncle not to go but he was an adventurer, Arthur.' He pointed to the outline of the island dominating the horizon. 'I made him Lord of the Isle of Wight. It wasn't enough for him. He travelled to Spain to fight the Moors and was knocked unconscious in a fight. His front teeth were smashed, but he thought it a badge of honour. He wanted to make a name for himself, so he'd sailed to Brittany in secret with his army. They didn't stand a chance against the French.'

He looked down at his son. 'Learn from your uncle's mistakes, Arthur. He could have been waiting to welcome us now—and not buried in an unmarked grave, God rest him.'

The great hall of Carisbrooke Castle echoed to the sound of music and laughter at the banquet in Henry's honour. Seated at the top table with Elizabeth to one side and Arthur to the other, Henry applauded the choir of local women. He turned to Arthur.

'Are you not pleased you came with us?'

'Yes, Father. My first time at sea was an experience I'll remember.'

Henry picked at a plate of small birds. He'd hardly eaten any of the dozens of courses as his tooth ached, although he kept the dull pain a secret. As he watched a group of travelling mummers acting out their play he wondered what was going on in London.

'How can you be certain this was Warbeck?'

Ralph Neville, Earl of Westmorland, seemed sure. 'That's what they say, Your Grace. The villagers, whose cottages were burnt, said the attackers carried the banner of York. Their leader rode a fine horse and commanded well over a hundred armed men.'

'They could have been local raiders?'

'We're well used to the Scots, trying their luck over the border—this was different. They tried to persuade the local men to join them—and burnt their houses when they refused.'

'You can see how my instinct was to doubt it, Sir Ralph. It seemed unlikely Warbeck would bother looting a few cottages, yet now I see what happened.' He began to pace the room, his hands clasped behind his back as he thought. The boy who'd kept him awake at night had now become a man, with a Scottish army, paid for by King James.

Henry wished Warbeck had the nerve to ride into

York and proclaim himself king. Then, at least, they would have a fighting chance of capturing him. Instead, all they had were a few terrified villagers as witnesses to his crimes.

'How did you let him escape?' Henry heard the challenge in his voice.

'The border stretches for a hundred miles, Your Grace. We don't have enough men to cover it all.'

An idea occurred to Henry as he listened to Sir Ralph's excuses. He would call a meeting of Parliament and use this outrageous invasion to justify a new tax. Sir Giles Daubeney had been recalled from Calais to become the new Lord Chancellor in place of William Stanley.

The new taxes would pay for an army of twenty-five thousand men, and Baron Daubeney, who'd fought with distinction at Bosworth, would march them to the border. Next time Perkin Warbeck dared to cross, they would be ready for him.

Chapter Thirteen

June 1497

Elizabeth shouted to her ladies to hurry. Servants dashed from room to room, carrying clothes and boxes. More soldiers arrived to reinforce the guard, their weapons clattering as they marched. Sheen Palace was no longer safe and none of them knew if rebels could arrive at any moment.

The new taxes to pay for war with Scotland ignited embers of unrest. Not the smouldering remnants of York loyalty in the North but in the dry tinder of the poverty-stricken far west of Cornwall. Rumours spread of between ten and twenty thousand men marching on London, with more joining in every town and village.

Henry burst into Elizabeth's apartment wearing a sword at his belt with a silver breastplate strapped over his doublet. He carried his gleaming sallet helmet, bejewelled at Elizabeth's suggestion so his men would know him as their king. He surveyed the scene and turned to his wife.

'You must go, Elizabeth, now.'

She glanced around at the bustling servants, still folding and packing her satin gowns. 'How long do we have?'

'The rebels have already reached Farnham—there is no time to lose.'

'Arthur is at Farnham!'

He placed a calming hand on her arm. 'I sent men to

move him to the castle at Ludlow. I should have told you but it's all happened so fast. I have your escort waiting to take you and your ladies to Eltham. Take the children to my mother's house at Coldharbour. She's waiting there and you'll be safe within the city walls.' He placed his helmet on the table and gave her hand a gentle squeeze. 'Please stay there until you hear from me.'

'What are you planning to do?' Elizabeth's eyes narrowed with concern. 'Where are you going, Henry?'

'I wish I could stay with you—but I must do what I can to rouse men to guard London. I've sent for Baron Daubeney with his twenty-five thousand men—but until he arrives we must cover every entrance to the city.'

She kissed him. 'Take care. I shall pray for your safe return.'

He embraced her and returned her kiss, not caring about the servants. 'God speed, Elizabeth—and tell the children not to worry. We'll put an end to this soon enough.'

Sir John de Vere appeared in the doorway in his full battle armour. 'The men are ready to leave, Your Grace.'

Henry grabbed his helmet and gave her one last look before following the earl. As he stepped out into the bright June sunshine he wondered if he would ever see her again.

Henry rubbed his eyes and realised he hadn't slept for two days. Spurred on by stories of looting, the men of London turned out in force to help defend their property. He was beginning to believe the city would be safe from the rebels when John de Vere returned with worrying news.

'Our scouts report the rebels have reached Blackheath, armed and in great numbers. They are led by one of our own commanders, Baron Audley.'

'Why would Audley throw in his lot with the Cornishmen?'

De Vere shrugged. 'Word is they plan to storm the Tower of London.' He hesitated and lowered his gruff voice. 'It seems they believe they'll find you there, Your Grace.'

'Blackheath is less than two hour's march from here. We must prepare the men.'

De Vere agreed. 'We're as ready as we can be.' He peered into the evening sky. 'It will soon be dark. I doubt they'll come at night, so you should try to rest, Your Grace.'

Henry's instinct troubled him. The rebels had marched three hundred miles from Cornwall to Blackheath unopposed. It shocked him to know how vulnerable he'd become and knew he must deal with traitors such as Baron Audley.

'Is there any word yet of Baron Daubeney.'

'It's a long march down from the border, Your Grace. We can't depend on them arriving in time.'

Henry regretted his decision to send his army to the border with Scotland at such a critical time. He looked up at the men on the walls. Shopkeepers and landlords, they were armed with whatever they could find. They might hold off the Cornishmen for a while. He decided to take de Vere's advice and try to get some sleep while he could.

The queen's message was short. She'd decided to take the children to the Tower for safety and waited there with his mother. Henry cursed. At least Baron Daubeney had arrived. His men now guarded the walls and gates at Lambeth where the rebels were soon expected to arrive. He decided to join him there.

He arrived to find Baron Daubeney studying an old parchment map of Blackheath. The baron looked up at the sound of Henry's footsteps. 'Good day, Your Grace. I plan a raid to capture the rebel leaders,' he grinned, 'and cut off the head of the snake.'

'You've done well to bring your men to London in good time, Sir Giles. Now we can put an end to this.' He studied the ranks of well-trained soldiers. 'We need more than a raid. I want you to take as many men as you can spare. Oxford's men will surround the rebels while you... distract them.'

Over a thousand men died in the battle of Blackheath. The fighting became savage yet brief, the Cornishmen no match for Henry's trained soldiers. After their surrender the rest received the king's pardon and were sent home.

Henry watched as the dead were loaded like sides of beef onto wagons, for burial in mass graves. Mostly young men, they dressed in poor clothes and had been armed with tin mining picks and farming tools. He understood their resentment of a tax to pay for war with Scotland, yet they threatened the lives of his family.

He knew he must be strong and ordered the captured leaders to be taken to the Tower, to be hanged, then disembowelled and their bodies quartered. Their heads would be placed on pikes on London Bridge, a grim warning. Baron Audley would be shown the king's mercy and beheaded at Tower Hill.

Henry felt little joy as he led the victory march to Westminster, riding his black destrier and wearing his diamond studded sallet helmet with the visor raised. Elizabeth, their children and his mother joined him for a service of thanksgiving in St Paul's Cathedral.

The portly ambassador, Rodrigo de Puebla, presented his bad news with as much tact as he could. 'King Ferdinand is concerned that the man who calls himself Richard of York prepares for war in Scotland, Your Grace.'

Henry struggled to control his annoyance. 'How many times must we go through this... nonsense?'

De Puebla took a deep breath. 'I appreciate your situation, Your Grace...'

'Do you?' Henry interrupted. 'Is your master only going to be satisfied when I have Warbeck's head on a pike with the other traitors?'

The Spaniard looked at his shoes.

Henry calmed his voice. 'I have a message for your master. I wish the princess to come to England in two years when she reaches the age of fourteen.' He managed a smile. 'In the meantime I will deal with the impostor who has troubled this country for long enough. I shall also arrange for the formal betrothal of my son to Princess Catherine once I receive his positive reply.'

De Puebla bowed. 'I will convey this to King Ferdinand and Queen Isabella, Your Grace, and wish you good luck with this man Perkin Warbeck.'

Henry watched him leave. He'd decided not to tell the ambassador Warbeck had landed in Cornwall and was already marching on Exeter. There would be time enough to do that.

The report had come through a week before and this

time Henry was ready. With defeat still fresh in their memories, he'd expected the Cornishmen to turn their backs on Warbeck. Instead, they had declared him King Richard IV in return for promises to cut taxes, and some six hundred men marched with him to Exeter.

The sight of Henry's army was enough to send Warbeck running to the sanctuary of Beaulieu Abbey in Hampshire, where he was captured. Now he would come face to face with his adversary, Henry knew he must decide what to do with him.

The thought that troubled him most was that Elizabeth would recognise him as her younger brother. Such a thing could be a spark to the gunpowder of the Yorkist threat, enough to throw the volatile country into chaos.

Warbeck finally knelt before him, dressed in the fine clothes of a noble. His hands were tied behind his back with a length of cord and he'd lost his cap. His face showed dark bruises where he'd been dragged from his sanctuary on Henry's orders, yet it was the look in his eyes that surprised Henry most.

Over the years, Warbeck had become his nemesis. Henry expected defiance, perhaps even to see hatred on the face of his enemy. Instead, the pretender looked up at him with humility, no doubt knowing his life was in Henry's hands.

'I wish to confess, Your Grace, that I am an impostor.' He stared at Henry with wide eyes. 'I throw myself on your benevolent mercy.'

Henry shook his head. 'You are a traitor.'

'My name is Piers Osbeck, Your Grace.' He spoke with little trace of an accent. 'I was given the name Perkin Warbeck by the Bretons I sailed with.' He looked up at Henry. 'I was born in Tournai.'

'You will make a full confession—in writing?'

'I will, Your Grace.'

'Then you shall do so, and we will have a copy nailed to every church door in England and Wales.' Henry studied the man kneeling before him for a moment. 'Have you nothing else to say?'

'I ask a great favour of you, Your Grace. Not for myself. My wife is left in Cornwall in sanctuary at St Michael's Mount. I pray you can show her mercy, for she had no choice in coming here from Scotland. She is innocent and I am concerned for her safety now.'

'I understand your wife is a cousin of King James?'

Warbeck nodded. 'Her name is Lady Katheryn Gordon.'

With Elizabeth accompanying his mother on a pilgrimage to the shrine of Walsingham Priory in the North, Henry remained at lodgings in Exeter. He was glad of the diversion when he heard Lady Katheryn had arrived from Cornwall.

'Send her to me. I shall see what this Scottish woman has to say before I decide what to do with her.'

Bishop Foxe still hoped to negotiate a new peace treaty with King James. If the Scottish king cared for his cousin at all, it could do no harm to treat her as a victim of Warbeck's intrigues, although Henry was in no hurry to return her.

He looked up from his book as there was a knock at his door. His servant announced his visitor but Henry knew at once this must be Lady Katheryn. Slender and elegant, her sapphire blue eyes held his for a moment longer than they should.

She offered him a demure bow. 'I throw myself on

your good mercy, Your Grace.'

Her voice had a soft Scottish accent, which Henry found unexpectedly attractive. No one told him Lady Katheryn was a great beauty. He'd planned to ask if she had called herself Duchess of York. He'd thought to summon Warbeck and force him to repeat his full confession before her. Instead he found himself lost for words.

'You are in mourning?'

Lady Katheryn looked down at her plain black gown. 'I lost a child, my little son... may he find peace in Heaven.'

'I'm sorry... I didn't know.'

'Now I am to lose my errant husband.' She stated it as a fact yet Henry heard a note of hope in her voice.

'I've not decided your husband's fate. Although, I've learnt he is a foreigner, which means our laws of treason...'

He stopped talking as he noticed a tear run down her cheek. The last thing he had expected was to feel protective towards her, yet Lady Katheryn enchanted him with her youthful honesty. He wished he could offer her some comfort.

'You might show my husband mercy, Your Grace?'

Her pleading eyes touched some primitive emotion deep inside him. In an instant Henry understood why kings could ruin their reputation through infidelity. He fought to focus on his words, as he had when he first fell in love with the beautiful girl in Brittany so long ago.

'I shall consider my conscience, Lady Katheryn.' He offered her a smile, feeling a strange regret for the age difference between them, his thinning hair and poor teeth. 'Meanwhile you will become lady-in-waiting to my wife—the queen.'

His reward was a look of such gratitude and promise that he found himself unable to sleep that night. Before, it had been the threat of Warbeck, come to take his throne. Now it was his desire for Lady Katheryn, the wife of his enemy, who had come to steal his heart.

Henry struggled with the wording of a reply to a letter from King Ferdinand in his study. He dipped his pen and began to write when his thoughts were interrupted by raised voices, followed by a shout. Someone ran down the corridor outside his room then one of his guards banged open the door.

'Fire!' He shouted. 'Your Grace, the palace is on fire!'

'Where?'

The guard glanced behind into the outer room. 'I don't know. Your Grace, there's smoke—I thought to warn you...'

Henry knew the ancient timbers of the old palace would burn like dry kindling and prayed it wasn't already too late. Then the enormity of the danger they were in struck him. Their whole family were at Sheen for Christmas, including his mother and her household, as well as many lords and their ladies, members of his court.

'Come with me, we must rouse the queen!'

His guard was right. The distinctive smell of burning wood reached him as he stepped into the narrow corridor. The chapel bell began to ring, not the calm call to prayer but as a warning. He heard shouts and banging doors as more people were being warned.

His first thought was for Elizabeth. He dashed down the dark passageway that linked their private apartments and reached Elizabeth's room. She was still in her bed sleeping, despite the commotion.

'Wake up!' He shook her and pulled back the coverlet. 'There's a fire—we must save the children!'

Elizabeth looked confused as he led her to the door and coughed as she breathed the bitter tasting smoke. Holding the hem of her nightgown over her face, she followed Henry barefoot into the corridor, still looking dazed.

'You must get out, Elizabeth.' He glanced at the guards waiting to help them. 'Save yourself—I'll check the nursery, then make sure my mother is safe.'

'I must come with you—to save the children?' She was anxious now, looking down the smoky corridor.

'It's too dangerous, Elizabeth. Go and wait for me!'

He gestured to his guards, who led Elizabeth away, while another two followed him to the nursery. They entered to find the room deserted. Abandoned beds were already wreathed in smoke. His daughter Margaret's favourite doll lay on the floor as if dropped in haste. He hoped the children had been taken to safety by their nursemaids and tried to make their own escape.

'I pray to God they are safe...' Henry heard the desperation in his voice. 'We have to check my lady mother's room.'

One of the guards pointed to the far door leading to the back stairs. 'We must go, Your Grace, the flames are spreading fast. There's nothing we can do here!'

'No!' He shouted above the noise, which became a low roar, punctuated with bangs and sharp crashes as the fire took hold. 'I have to be certain my mother is safe.'

The guards followed him further down the narrow

smoke-filled corridors. Acrid fumes began filling his lungs and stinging his eyes. He could feel the heat prickling his skin. Their path ahead was blocked. Flames took hold of the old wooden panelling and there was no way past. If his mother remained in her room, they were too late to save her.

Henry's eyes filled with tears as he imagined his mother trapped in her burning room. A burly guard took his arm and guided him towards the stairway. He could hardly breathe and found it impossible to see where he was going. As he fumbled his way with his hands, the thick smoke made him cough and retch. The crash of a collapsing roof was followed by a distant scream.

'Who is there?' He yelled out at the top of his voice and stopped to listen for a reply. All he could hear was the crackle of the raging fire and crashes as more of the roof collapsed.

'Hurry, Your Grace!' There was a note of panic in the guardsman's voice.

Henry needed no urging now as he dashed between the flames and smelt his own hair singeing. One of his guards kicked with his heavy boot and the door burst open.

The shock of the freezing December air hit Henry as he fell to his knees, gasping for breath. He looked around for his family and recognised his steward approaching through the gloom. He gritted his teeth as he prepared himself for the worst news.

'The queen is safe, Your Grace, she is with your children.' His steward pointed. 'They've all been taken to the manor house.'

'Thank God... and my lady mother?'

'Your mother is also with the queen now. She was at

her prayers in the chapel, Your Grace.'

Henry flinched as he heard another thunderous crash. The main supporting beams must have burnt through. An enormous section of the roof collapsed into the flames with a shower of sparks. Burning embers drifted on the still air like evil, glowing snowflakes, threatening to cause more fires wherever they landed.

He shivered in the cold night air, despite the heat from the blazing palace, as he realised how close he'd come to being trapped inside. He accepted the offer of a heavy wool cape and pulled it around his shoulders. For the first time he realised he had blisters on both his hands and his skin was blackened with soot.

Henry wanted to be with his family, to see for himself they were all safe, yet couldn't take his eyes from the flames. Lords and ladies stood side by side with soldiers and serving-girls, many with soot smeared faces. The ground was littered with heaps of property salvaged in the flight from the fire. Precious gilt and silver plate glinted through a mound of priceless, smouldering tapestries.

'Are all the staff accounted for?'

The commander of his yeomen stepped forward. 'As far as we can tell, Your Grace, there are many with burns but no casualties.'

'I pray to God you are right, Commander.'

Henry watched as men carried water from the green moat in whatever they could find. A bucketful splashed with a sharp hiss on the nearest flames. It looked a hopeless task, yet they could not stand by and watch while the grand old building burnt to the ground.

He stared in disbelief at the ruins of his palace, until that night his family home. Dazzling orange flames now lit up the night sky. The fire reached the private chapel, where his mother had prayed an hour before. He knew there would be nothing left by morning.

He thought of his valuable papers, letters and reports—all taken by the flames. His study had shelves of rare books, collected over a lifetime. Elizabeth's precious jewels and treasured gowns were all now consumed by fire.

A movement in the darkness nearby caught Henry's eye. He was exhausted and emotional but there was no mistaking the distinctive square-jawed profile. Perkin Warbeck, under house arrest at Sheen Palace to be near his wife, gazed up at the inferno. The flames roared and lit up the young man's face. Henry thought he saw a look of triumph.

Chapter Fourteen

May 1498

Henry spread out the detailed plans of the new palace for his mother's approval. 'One Christmas I will always remember,' he gave her a rueful smile, 'and the most expensive, by a long measure.'

'I worried that the smoke had injured your health.'

'I'll confess to being a little short of breath, although the potion from my physician seems to be working.'

'I imagine the cost of the fire, including the crown jewels, was incalculable.' She continued to examine the drawings as she spoke. 'Let us thank the Lord not one person lost their life.'

Henry agreed. 'As you can see, I've resolved to rebuild. The new palace is to be our family home and main residence once more. I found inspiration from the scale of your fine manor house at Lathom.'

'I hardly saw your stepfather for a year while he built Lathom. He had little time for anything else, and now he only leaves Lancashire outside the hunting season.'

'My advisors think I spend too much time with the master mason Robert Virtue—but I insist on approving every detail of his plans.' He pointed to the drawing on the table before them.

'I plan to top these octagonal towers with gilded domes, decorated with brass weather vanes. You'll be able to see them for miles. There are to be three floors, with twelve rooms on each. Our family apartments surround a private internal courtyard with a grand water fountain in the centre—and panelled glass windows will flood the rooms with light.'

'It warms my heart to see how you've turned this disaster to good purpose, Henry.'

'In truth, Mother, the old palace of Sheen was full of York memories, particularly for Elizabeth.'

His mother agreed. 'I never felt at home there, for the same reason. I could feel the presence of ghosts of the past.'

Henry nodded. 'I've also learnt from the fire. Solid stone walls, with the roof lined with lead—and the risk of fire reduced with brick-lined chimneys to all the fireplaces.'

He studied his mother's face as he unrolled the final drawing. 'The finest decoration is planned for the new chapel.' He smiled at her nod of approval when she noted the prominent Beaufort portcullis motif. 'It will be built with white stone, with privy closets for private prayer and a plaster ceiling decorated with red and white roses.'

She laid a hand on his arm in a rare moment of tenderness. 'It broke my heart to see the old chapel in such a ruinous state, Henry. I would like to contribute to the cost of the new one.'

'Of course, lady Mother. I will dedicate it to you as our family chapel, a place of peace and contemplation. I have also decided to honour our heritage. We shall rename Sheen the new Palace of Richmond.'

Henry cursed at the news. 'It seems we manage to quell one rebellion only to see another breaking out in its place!'

He was visiting Sir Thomas Lovell, Chancellor of the

Exchequer, one of the few remaining friends who fought with him at Bosworth and Stoke field. A shrewd financier as well as soldier, Lovell was trusted with the most secret details of his accounts.

They sat at the refectory table in his great hall, where painted shields, trophies from long-forgotten battles, adorned the whitewashed walls. A procession of serving-girls brought choice platters of meat and fish, game birds and exotic delicacies.

Henry washed his hands in a bowl of rose-scented water and held them in the air while one of Sir Thomas' serving-girls dried them on a white linen towel. He watched as another servant filled two silver goblets with dark red wine.

Sir Thomas raised his goblet in the air. 'To your good health, Your Grace, and the success of Cabot's next expedition.'

Henry tasted the wine. Rich and sweet, he guessed it must be one Sir Thomas had saved for the occasion of his visit. 'John Cabot and his sons cannot be blamed for turning back because of bad weather. I am sure they'll prove as good as their word.'

Sir Thomas nodded. 'The London merchants have paid for them to depart again from Bristol, with five ships laden with English goods to trade for gold and spices from Asia.'

'I wish them well. The Treasury could use the income from this new trade.'

'We would not like to propose more taxes to Parliament, Your Grace, for a while at least.' Sir Thomas stabbed a finger in the air. 'Your late Uncle Jasper would have known how to deal with these Welshmen.'

Henry smiled at the mention of his uncle. 'He would

have talked them out of it, had them swear fealty and saved us another costly battle.'

Lovell considered this for a moment and sipped his wine before replying. 'The financial reparation after the Cornish revolt far exceeded the costs we incurred...'

Henry used his fingers to pull the meat from the bones of the small quails arranged on his plate. He'd become used to Thomas Lovell's subtle way of making his point. Few others knew the truth, but the fines demanded from those behind the last insurrection provided a much-needed boost to Henry's coffers.

'This is different, Sir Thomas, is it not?'

'If these Welsh rebels have taken the castle at Harlech, it seems the men of your garrison there were either incompetent or in collusion with them?'

They waited as servants carried a glazed suckling pig to the table. The pig seemed to stare at them with baleful eyes, until a servant removed the head with his knife and cut the meat into thick slices, over which he poured an orange sauce.

Henry tasted it and nodded in approval. 'You are right. I recall my Uncle Jasper telling me Harlech withstood a seven-year siege by being provisioned from the sea. It was the longest in our history.'

Lovell held up his empty goblet for his serving-girl to refill it. 'You could send Sir Giles, Baron Daubeney, with his army to root them out—but what if that takes another seven years?'

'It could make the rebels a focus for every dissenter in the land—but pardons in return for fines...'

Lovell took a deep sip of his wine and narrowed his eyes. 'It might offer them a way out of this alive and at no cost to the Treasury.' He looked pleased with himself. 'Keep your army at the Scottish border, Your

Grace, where it might focus the attention of King James?'

'I don't see what we have to lose, Sir Thomas, please arrange for my message to be delivered to Harlech Castle first thing in the morning.'

Henry returned to Westminster to discover that Perkin Warbeck was missing, despite a thorough search. The terms of his close arrest had been relaxed over the past months, although he was always followed by yeomen of Henry's guard. These stood before him now, unable to explain what happened.

'We pay you to watch over him, a simple enough task, yet he gave you the slip?'

The oldest of the guards spoke for them. 'We think he escaped through a window, disguised as a servant, Your Grace. When we found he wasn't in his rooms, we searched the palace and the grounds. There's been no sight of him.'

'I allowed him the use of a horse. Is it still in the stables?'

'It is, Your Grace, and we've accounted for all the other horses. We believe he can't have gone far on foot.'

'Don't underestimate Warbeck.' Henry scowled. 'He is a dangerous and resourceful man and must be found, do you understand? You are to find him and bring him here to me.'

A thought occurred to him. 'Warbeck's wife, Lady Katheryn, is with the queen at Eltham Palace. Two of you are to ride there and be ready if he tries to contact her—if he has not already done so thanks to your incompetence!'

He dismissed the guards. They had played their part

well enough. All he had to do now was wait. Even his lady wife would understand. Perkin Warbeck had broken the terms of his lenient confinement and deserved whatever he got.

He remembered his first meeting with the beautiful Lady Katheryn. He'd never been alone with her since, yet he'd allowed his adoration of her to cloud his judgement. Warbeck should be locked up in the Tower. He'd let him have too much freedom because of his desire to please her.

He knew he should have negotiated her return to Scotland. It would have shown good faith. The work of Bishop Foxe, to negotiate a new treaty with King James, as well as a betrothal, would have been made a little easier.

He liked to keep her at his court. Lady Katheryn seemed content as Elizabeth's lady-in-waiting. Elizabeth raised an eyebrow when she first heard his request, yet she'd said nothing, even when he paid for Lady Katheryn's fine gowns from his own privy purse. His priest confessor told him to remain mindful of the words of his Lord's Prayer; lead us not into temptation.

The elderly Prior of the Charterhouse of Sheen bowed his head. 'I came in person, Your Grace, to tell you the man named Perkin Warbeck has taken sanctuary with us.'

Henry studied the man. He recognised him as a regular visitor to the old chapel at Sheen Palace before the fire.

'We are grateful to you. Warbeck cannot be permitted sanctuary.' He looked at the prior. 'He must be taken into our custody.'

'You cannot violate sanctuary...'

'He is a traitor, a dangerous man, Prior.'

'Sacred places are protected from acts of violence, no matter how those acts are justified by law, Your Grace.' The prior's voice wavered a little as he spoke, betraying his nervousness at challenging the king.

Henry held up a calming hand. 'There is no need of any violence. He will be escorted to the Tower and well treated.'

The prior seemed doubtful. 'He'll not be executed?'

'He was detained within my own household on condition he respected the terms of his arrest.' Henry sat back in his chair. 'He will now be returned to the Tower until we are satisfied he has learnt his lesson.'

The prior seemed satisfied. 'In that case, Your Grace, I will decline his request for sanctuary.'

'A wise choice, Prior, for which we are grateful.'

After the old prior left Henry called for the captain of his guard.

'Take some men to the Charterhouse of Sheen and arrest Perkin Warbeck. He is to be pilloried in the public stocks in Westminster for one day, and for another at Cheapside, where he is to recite his confession to whoever will listen. Then you are to confine him in the Tower of London.'

'Yes, Your Grace.'

'And tell the Constable of the Tower to find a cell with no windows. We don't want him escaping again, do we?'

Elizabeth found Henry still at work in his study. She'd made the short journey from Eltham to Greenwich Palace as a surprise for him and seemed in good spirits. He turned at the sound of rustling satin as she entered.

'A new gown? It flatters you well, my lady.'

She gave him an elaborate curtsey, pleased with his compliment. 'My dressmaker follows the latest fashion from the Continent. One good consequence of that dreadful fire—an excuse to replace all my old dresses.' She leant down and kissed him. 'I've missed you, Henry.'

'I'm sorry, Elizabeth. I've been kept busy with the rebuilding, then dealing with the revolt in Wales and Warbeck...'

She placed a finger to his lips to silence him. 'I know how hard you've been working, Henry. I mean I've missed you,' she gave him a shy smile, 'in my bed.'

He studied her face for a moment. 'You are recovered?'

'With God's grace, as well as I'll ever be.' she blushed, more like a new bride than his wife of twelve years.

He took her hand. 'I'm glad to hear it,' he gave her hand a gentle squeeze, 'as I should like to have another son.'

Lying awake on his back in the darkness, unable to sleep, he felt her stir next to him. It had been well over a year since she shared his bed and he liked the feel of her warmth close to him. He caressed her curves with his hand, tracing the shape of her heavy breasts.

She turned to face him. 'You don't mind that I've put on a little weight?' Her voice sounded cautious, as if fearful of his answer.

'A little?' There wasn't enough light to see her face but he sensed her tense at his teasing. 'I love you as you are, Elizabeth, as God is my witness.'

He'd missed the physical side of their lives together.

She had lost her girlish looks over the past years yet now had a different, maternal beauty. He knew she was conscious of her double chin and thickening waistline yet it didn't bother him in the least.

'I am hardly the same man you married. I'm forty-one years old now, ready to be put out to pasture.'

She propped herself on a cushion and he thought her eyes sparkled with amusement in the poor light. 'Is there something you wish to confess, Henry Tudor?'

'Well, let me see. I confess I am now too short of breath to play tennis or exert myself at the hunt. I still suffer with my teeth, my hair is thinning and...'

'Enough!' She laughed. 'Although you forgot to mention your poor eyesight?'

'I thought that was my best kept secret?'

'I'm glad you don't see all my wrinkles. I know you too well for you to have secrets from me, Henry, and I love *you* just as you are.'

'Thank you, Elizabeth.' He reached out and let her long hair run through his fingers like golden silk as he had done when they first married. 'There is something else I must confess to you, Elizabeth, something I've told no one.'

Her body tensed again. He thought she might be holding her breath while she waited to hear what he had to say.

'My physician, the Italian Master Parron, is an astrologer. He professes to read the future in the stars.'

'Lady Margaret told me you have been seeing him. She does not approve. I imagine she considers fortune-telling the work of the Devil.'

'She might well be right. All the same, I asked him what he could see of your future.'

'I don't wish to know.' There was a serious note to

her voice now. 'I think I'd rather be ignorant of God's plan for me...'

'He says the stars forecast that you will live a long and happy life, Elizabeth. I thought you'd be pleased to know.'

'He tells you what you wish to hear, Henry—don't you know in your heart it is impossible to tell the future?'

'Master Parron publishes his predictions in an almanac so their accuracy can be verified. I must say he is convincing...'

'We were told Perkin Warbeck was convincing, yet he couldn't answer any of the questions when I tested him.'

Henry sat up in bed. 'When was this?'

'You don't imagine I could live under the same roof as one who said he was my brother without questioning him?'

'I worried once that you, of all people, might prove him right, Elizabeth. It would have been the worst for me, so I showed him to others he might have known. He recognised none of them.'

'And now you have him in the stocks, reading aloud his confession to the people who ridicule him...'

He was surprised she knew. 'It was only for a day or two, as punishment for trying to escape after I'd treated him so well.'

'Where is he now?' The note of challenge in her voice reminded him of her mother.

'I expect you know he's in the Tower—and there with good reason.' He took a deep breath. 'There is another thing I must confess to you, Elizabeth.'

'What is that?' Again she seemed to hold her breath.

'We are no longer as wealthy as I would have people

believe. In truth, our expenses exceed our income and we cannot continue to live on reserves.' He'd not planned to tell her yet now found it comforting to share the secret that troubled him so greatly.

'How can that be? What about the new taxes? Where has all the money gone, Henry?'

'Not through my gambling, if that is what you are thinking. The new taxes were used to pay for the army. The fire at Sheen cost us dearly. I paid men to salvage what they could from the ashes but we lost everything there. The rebuilding expenses have far exceeded the estimates.'

'Who knows of this?' She sounded shocked at his news.

'Only the Treasurer of the Chamber, Master John Heron, and of course our Chancellor, Sir Thomas Lovell, who knows everything. His advice is to continue as if there is not a problem. I must, Elizabeth, for the sake of the country.'

She was silent for a moment. 'My new gowns will hardly have helped—and you've even bought gowns for my ladies.'

Henry's brow furrowed in the darkness as he realised she was referring to his gifts to Lady Katheryn. 'I was anticipating payment of the dowry from King Ferdinand—or at least the first instalment. It would have tided us over...'

'I thought Rodrigo de Puebla met with you to agree the payment?'

'He told me King Ferdinand cannot make the payment while there remains a challenger to our throne.'

She looked him with a question in her eyes. 'Did you encourage Warbeck's escape, so you could lock him up in the Tower?'

'He escaped of his own free will and must accept the consequences.' Henry's tone was abrupt.

'Do you plan to have him executed?'

'That will not be necessary. I've already confirmed to King Ferdinand that our throne is now secure. Our son can marry his Aragon princess at last, God willing.'

Chapter Fifteen

February 1499

Henry and Elizabeth watched with great pride as their new son was held over the gleaming silver font brought all the way by wagon from Canterbury Cathedral. Named Edmund, after Henry's father, their fifth child howled through the blessing as cold, holy water was poured over his head.

Wrapped in a coverlet of lamb's wool to save him from the cold, a lit taper was put into his tiny hand by the bishop. Edmund stopped his crying to stare in fascination at the bright flame of the taper, a symbol of how the king's son would light the way.

The baptism, held like the others in the church of the Observant Friars at Greenwich, was a state occasion, with all the great and good of England in their finery, despite the recent fall of snow. As before, Henry's mother, the new Prince Edmund's godmother, presided over every detail of the service.

A choir gave a spirited performance of a song composed in honour of the new prince at the banquet in the great hall of Greenwich Palace. Wine flowed and musicians played as the first of twenty courses was served by servants in royal livery. The cost of entertaining so many guests seemed a small price to pay for a third healthy son.

Lady Margaret sat under a cloth of estate in place of Elizabeth, who'd retired early on her physician's advice.

Anyone new to Henry's court could be forgiven for mistaking Lady Margaret for the queen. Only fourteen years older than Henry, she looked unchanged since his coronation.

For Henry, the strain of his years on the throne and the sleepless nights had taken their toll. He knew he now looked older than his forty-two years, and that people said as much behind his back. As he watched his laughing guests he wondered how many he could count as true friends.

He relied on his mother's advice about who to trust. Devout, well-connected and respected by the nobility, she had a shrewd talent for seeing the truth of things and always considered his best interests.

'I was thinking my new son shall be made Duke of Somerset, in tribute to his Beaufort ancestors.' Henry told his mother. 'We could raise him as a scholar and champion of the arts.'

'Your father would be honoured to see his name remembered so well. He was proud of his title of Earl of Richmond.'

'What sort of man was my father?' He'd never asked her before and his question made her glance at him in surprise.

'He was part of God's plan for you, Henry, for us. He was loyal to his king and fought for what he believed in. He was taken before his time.' She surprised him by sounding wistful, the first time he'd heard her speak of his father with anything other than detachment.

'My Uncle Jasper told me my father always wished to make his mark on the world—and has, through our growing family.'

Lady Margaret agreed. 'Your uncle would never hear

anything said against his brother. I am certain your father would have been most proud of you, Henry, may the good Lord rest his soul.'

Henry raised his goblet of wine in agreement and wondered if it was her way of saying she was proud of him. Like any son, her praise would mean much to him, yet he'd become accustomed to not expect it.

He found it impossible to imagine what his mother must have been like as a fourteen-year-old girl, a wealthy heiress, married to a lusty young knight. Once, when a little drunk on wine, Jasper told him everyone had known his mother was too young to bear a child.

Jasper had said there was nothing he could do to stop his brother, who knew he would secure her fortune when she bore his child. Edmund Tudor was impatient and ambitious, a deadly combination for his young mother. Henry wished his father had lived long enough to have seen the result of his short marriage.

News of yet another new pretender sped through the court in London like a flat stone skimming across a tranquil lake. By the time word reached Henry at Richmond it was already common knowledge.

There to inspect the building works, he'd been in a good mood to see such promising progress. Although the fire destroyed his own apartments and the chapel, much of the remaining structures, including Henry V's massive tower, could be recovered without great expense.

His domed octagonal towers were already rising from the ashes under a complex network of scaffolding. The once peaceful grounds were a confusion of noise and activity. Kilns burned night and day to fire huge quantities of red bricks and men cursed as they sawed whole oak trees into massive beams. The air rang with the musical sound of stonemasons' hammers on chisels as they carved the pale stone brought from quarries in Dorset.

Henry was not about to repeat the mistake he'd made with Lambert Simnel or Perkin Warbeck and demanded the immediate arrest of the new impostor. Named Ralph Wilford, the young shoemaker's son claimed he was the escaped Earl of Warwick and said he'd had dreams where he'd seen visions of his coronation.

Henry summoned his old ally Sir John de Vere, who arrived with news that Wilford had already been captured.

'We must show a firm hand this time, Your Grace.' His gruff voice sounded uncompromising and his advice more like a command.

'At this rate we'll run out of space in the Tower, Sir John. I still have the Earl of Warwick there, as well as Warbeck.'

De Vere frowned. 'I was thinking we must make an example of this latest impostor. The people need a reminder of the punishment for treason—and should see it carried out.'

The ominous shadow of another death clouded Henry's conscience but he knew Sir John was right. It was easy enough to grant pardons and demand fines. There was a danger this could be seen as weakness. Now he must put a stop to further impostors.

'He must have a fair trial—but if he's found guilty of treason he is to be sentenced to death and hanged.'

'I understand there are two of them involved, Your Grace. The other is an Augustinian priest by the name of Patrick, who aided and encouraged him.'

'I cannot hang a priest, Sir John.'

'Yet men might listen to a friar who seems to have nothing to gain by his treason?'

'If the friar makes a full confession, he might plead the protection of his faith.'

'These plotters test our faith, Your Grace, yet if we act swiftly it will send a message no one can fail to understand.'

'I pray you are right, for all our sakes.'

'What do you plan to do about Warwick, Your Grace? I checked on him, to be sure he was still in his cell. I must say he seems more of a simpleton than I remember.'

'He is the cousin of the queen and means no harm, but this latest plot against us...'

De Vere scratched his beard. 'If either Warwick or Warbeck attempt to escape we'll be ready for them.'

'Be sure that you are, Sir John.' Henry gave him a knowing look.

He rode to visit Elizabeth at Eltham Palace and found her with Harry, who was writing with a large quill, his face a frown of concentration. Henry inspected his work, a Latin prayer.

'I would never have guessed this was your hand, Harry. I must say you have more skill with a pen than I did at your age.'

Although it was true, Harry's work was a little clumsy and lacked Arthur's graceful line. What impressed him was how Harry made up for lack of talent with sheer determination to impress. He smiled at his son's beam of pleasure at his encouragement.

Harry looked up at Elizabeth with admiration. 'I have the best of tutors, my lady Mother.

'We must reward your good efforts, Harry.' A

thought occurred to him. 'Would you like to come hunting? There are many stags in the parks. We can take the oldest—and have some fine venison for the table!'

Harry grinned. 'Thank you, Father. I'd like to go hunting.'

Henry turned to Elizabeth. 'You look well. Are you well enough now to come hunting with us?'

She laughed at the suggestion and shook her head. 'It will be good for the two of you to know each other better.'

Henry glanced down at his red-haired son and realised she was right. Harry would be eight years old at the end of June, yet he still treated him like an infant, leaving him in the nursery at Eltham with his sisters and tutors. His second son was growing up fast and he'd been too busy to notice.

Once they reached the forest the gamekeeper signalled them to stop and dismount. It could take all day to find a lone stag but the keepers knew the forests well. Henry could have brought his crossbow but decided this would be his son's day. He called for Harry's bow and checked the tension of the bowstring.

'A fine hunting bow, Harry. You practice every day?'

'As you asked, Father.'

'And you find your aim improved?'

'A little... although I've never killed a deer.'

Henry handed him the bow and they followed the keeper into the woods. Harry seemed at home in the dense woodland, his eyes scanning the trees. After an hour of tracking, the keeper raised a hand. He put a finger to his lips and pointed to the dark outline of a stag silhouetted in the late afternoon sun.

Henry stood back while the keeper beckoned Harry to approach. As Harry nocked a good broad head arrow something startled the deer. Harry drew to the head and shot. His arrow led the bounding animal by several yards as the stag reached cover.

The arrow struck, entering the muscular flank of the stag, which continued its run into the bush. As it did so the protruding arrow shaft snapped. The pursuing keeper bent and retrieved the broken piece.

'We cannot leave it now, Your Grace.'

They followed the sound of the stag crashing through thick undergrowth, and found him lying in a sunlit woodland clearing. The keeper drew his knife, ready to end the animal's suffering, then shook his head and sheathed it again.

'A heart shot, Your Grace, one of the finest I ever hope to see.'

Henry turned to his beaming son in surprise. He'd not expected Harry to hit the running stag at that distance. 'Your first kill, Harry. I could not be more proud of you.'

White doves fluttered from the dovecote of Tickenhall Palace, Prince Arthur's residence in Bewdley, Worcestershire. Henry walked with his son in the wooded grounds and explained the betrothal ceremony.

'It is important you are betrothed in the eyes of God, Arthur, even though your wedding will not take place for another two years.' He smiled. 'Our alliance with Spain makes us stronger—and means the new King of France will respect our treaty. You are only twelve years old, yet you already hold the key to the longest peace with the French anyone can remember.'

'I have been writing to the Princess Caterina, Father,

with the help of my Latin tutors, as she cannot yet speak English.'

'Your mastery of Latin is good enough to write such letters?'

Arthur gave him a shy glance that reminded Henry of Elizabeth. 'I do not know how to proclaim my love for her...'

'I must speak to your tutors. You are too young to be proclaiming love,' Henry laughed at the idea, 'although you will be blessed if you find love with this princess.'

'I can learn to love Princess Catalina, Father, God willing.'

For the first time Henry heard the note of confidence in his son's voice and had a glimpse of the man Arthur might become. They shared the same tall, lean build, which Jasper told him came from his noble Valois heritage. Arthur also had Elizabeth's amber eyes and her Plantagenet blood, yet he was a Tudor.

'You must call her Princess Catherine, Princess of Wales, from now on, Arthur. I will tell ambassador Puebla to make sure she is taught to speak our language before your wedding day.' He smiled at his son. 'She has plenty of time.'

They arrived back at the palace, where the Spanish ambassador waited with the priest and witnesses. Rodrigo de Puebla sweated under a black hat and a brocade robe with a thick leather belt emphasising his considerable girth.

'You make a poor substitute for a beautiful princess, Ambassador!'

De Puebla grinned at Henry's joke. 'It is a great honour for me to represent her Highness, Your Grace.'

'Well, we are grateful to you, Ambassador, for your part in making this betrothal possible.' Henry patted the portly Spaniard on the back. 'I'll confess there were times when I doubted this day would come.'

'I have reassured King Ferdinand, as you requested, that the throne of England has never been more secure.'

'And he has agreed to pay the dowry?'

'This betrothal will make certain of it, Your Grace.'

'Then we must proceed—without delay.'

Elizabeth had not been well enough to travel for the Easter pilgrimage, so, once again, his mother took her place. Accompanied by her chaplain and confessor John Fisher, Lady Margaret insisted on visiting every shrine and chapel on their route. This slowed their pace and meant several stops to complete the sixty-mile journey from her manor at Coldharbour.

The annual pilgrimage to Canterbury was a time away from the demands of Parliament and court, a chance to restore his faith. Henry enjoyed the anonymity of mingling with other pilgrims and dressed in simple clothes, preferring not to be recognised, although his yeomen were never far behind.

He found himself riding alongside his mother's confessor, a stern yet articulate and well-educated cleric. 'My mother speaks well of you, Master Fisher. I must congratulate you on your achievements as Proctor of Cambridge.'

'Thank you. It is a great honour to serve Lady Margaret,' Fisher spoke with the blunt Yorkshire accent of his birth, 'and to accompany Your Grace to the shrine of Saint Thomas. His life was an inspiration.'

Henry nodded. 'I cannot imagine my Mother has a great deal to occupy the services of a priest confessor.'

John Fisher glanced across at Henry as if making a

judgement. 'We all find our faith tested, Your Grace, and the most devout find the test the greatest.'

'I'll agree with you, Master Fisher.' He understood why his mother had chosen Fisher as her chaplain.

They rode in silence for a mile or so then Henry turned in the saddle. 'What do you say of the martyrdom of Thomas Becket?'

Fisher thought for a moment before replying. 'Like Archbishop John Morton, I understand as chancellor Thomas Becket enforced the king's taxes, including from the church—until he became archbishop. He was made a martyr for arguing the church was above the state.'

'I believe he was murdered by knights who misunderstood the wishes of their king, who faced a dilemma over what to do about him. Do you believe he was martyred, if it was through a misunderstanding?'

'He was a man of conscience, Your Grace.'

'My physician, Master Parron, holds the view that the life of one man can be weighed against the many who might suffer if he lives.'

'You are thinking of the present dilemma of the pretender in the Tower? The country waits to see the fate of Master Perkin Warbeck, and the Earl of Warwick.'

'And you, Master Fisher—do you have an opinion about what should be done with those who confess to treason against the crown?'

'Every life is sacred, Your Grace. Trust in the Lord, and he will guide your way.'

When Henry finally stood alone before the shrine of St Thomas, he recalled John Fisher's words and wondered if there was such a thing as a miracle.

Sit John de Vere, Earl of Oxford, presided over the trial of Perkin Warbeck in a crowded Westminster Hall. He listened as the list of charges were read out by the clerk of the court. Warbeck was accused of bribing his guards and attempting to escape, with the assistance of an Irishman named John Water, Mayor of the city of Cork.

De Vere eyed Warbeck for a moment. 'Do you have anything to say in your defence?'

Warbeck remained silent, staring at the floor. Chained and ragged, with bruises on his face, he was hardly recognisable.

Sir John de Vere ordered him to read out his confession then sentenced both him and John Water, as well as two of the hapless guards, to be taken to Tyburn and hanged.

Edward, Earl of Warwick, was next to be tried as a co-conspirator. He seemed to not understand the sentence and raised a hand to the curious onlookers as he was also led away to be executed before a jeering crowd at Tower Hill.

Henry paid twelve pounds for the burial of the last of the male Plantagenet line. Elizabeth said nothing about the death of her cousin, although he'd heard she cried when she heard the news.

Later, Henry attended a mass in Westminster Abbey and lit a candle for the twenty-four-year-old earl. As he watched the single yellow flame brighten, he doubted young Edward had known the consequences of Warbeck's daring plot.

As an afterthought he lit a second candle for the man

from Tournai who called himself Perkin Warbeck. He placed his hands together and prayed. He didn't move until both candles burned down to the end of their short wicks, flickered once and were extinguished.

Chapter Sixteen

April 1500

Henry felt relieved when Elizabeth agreed to sail with him to Calais to meet Archduke Philip of Burgundy. As well as an encouraging sign of her improving health, she would be good company. He'd also worried about the increasing number of deaths from the plague in London and prayed the pestilence would be over before they returned in two months.

As he watched the royal standards on the towers of Dover Castle vanish into the early morning mists, Elizabeth joined him on deck. Dressed in a warm fur hood and cape against the freshening breeze, she reached for the ship's rail with one gloved hand and took his arm to steady herself with the other.

'I shall miss our children, Henry, although I look forward to seeing Calais. I've heard so many stories.'

'The Channel crossing makes it feel much further yet Calais is half as far from London as York.' He studied the grey-green waves with an experienced sailor's eye. 'We're fortunate, as the seas look calm enough.'

She pulled him closer. 'We are not in danger there, from the French?'

Henry smiled her question. His old adversary, King Charles, died without an heir when he struck his head on a lintel. The threat now was from the new King of France, his cousin Louis XII. Five years younger than Henry, Louis had wasted no time in marrying Charles' widow, Anne of Brittany.

'Calais has our largest standing army—and King Louis campaigns far away with his army in Italy,' he reassured her. 'He shows more interest in seizing Milan than Calais. I pray for peace with France and will welcome King Louis when the time is right. In the meantime, I aim to make the Duke of Burgundy an important ally. His wife Duchess Joanna is sister to Princess Catherine, so we will soon be related by our son's marriage, God willing.'

'Will the duchess accompany him to Calais?'

'I doubt it, although if she does you would have the chance to learn something of our son's betrothed.'

Henry chose the old outpost of Guines Castle for their first meeting. On the furthest north-east border of Calais, it was close enough to be considered neutral ground. The great stone hall of the castle was being transformed from a soldiers' barracks in preparation for the grand banquet.

Women spread fine white linen over ancient tables, arranged around an open area, swept clean for entertainments and dancing. The air rang with the staccato sound of men on ladders hammering iron nails to support colourful tapestries and banners. Brought from Henry's London palaces, they brightened the bare walls and gave the castle an air of grandeur.

Wagons pulled by oxen ferried barrels of wine, fresh loaves, food and delicacies from the town. Cooks and servants worked from dawn, with blazing fires and great boiling cauldrons, preparing more than twenty courses for the feast. Musicians rehearsed with noisy drums and trumpets, their music sending fat pigeons flying from roosts in the high roof beams.

Henry made the short journey from the town riding at the head of a grand procession, escorted by his yeomen in royal livery of red, blue and gold. The queen and her ladies were followed by the knights of his court, lords and ladies and the mayor and men of the Staple of Calais. A hundred archers commanded by the Earl of Oxford marched at the rear, a precaution to reinforce the garrison of Guisnes.

The Duke of Burgundy lived up to his nickname of Philip the Handsome. Dressed in tight fitting velvet to show off his athletic build, he was also charming, kissing Elizabeth's hand and flattering her in soft-spoken French. Henry felt his years as he watched his wife's blushes at the attentions of the young duke.

'Duchess Joanna remains in Flanders with my newborn son Charles, Your Grace. She would be honoured to meet you yet is unable to travel.' He addressed Henry in accented English and shrugged his shoulders in apology.

Elizabeth smiled at the duke's news. 'Please convey our congratulations, Duke Philip, and our best wishes.'

'You can be sure that I will, my lady.'

Henry noticed the duke eyeing Elizabeth's attractive young ladies-in-waiting, as if trying to choose between them. It seemed he planned to enjoy the evening's entertainment.

'The banquet awaits, Archduke.'

The duke took his seat next to Henry and the Chancellor, Sir Thomas Lovell, proposed a toast to peace between their nations. Servants dressed in Tudor green and white brought trenchers of freshly baked bread, dishes of roasted meat, boiled fish and jugs of fine wine.

The duke turned to Henry. 'Our families are soon to be joined in marriage, Your Grace.'

'God willing. Have you met King Ferdinand and Queen Isabella, Duke Philip?'

'The marriage negotiations were conducted through their ambassadors, although I have since learnt a great deal of them through my wife, Joanna.' He leant over and spoke in a conspiratorial tone. 'I look forward to meeting her mother, Queen Isabella of Castile, her father King Ferdinand,' he pulled a face, 'less so.'

Henry laughed. 'They test my patience, Duke Philip, with their protracted deliberations. I must ask your opinion of what I should do if King Ferdinand does not pay the dowry due?'

The archduke looked puzzled. 'I am married to his daughter but would not presume to have great influence with the King of Aragon...'

'I was thinking of your sister, archduke.'

Understanding flashed in the quick-witted duke's eyes. 'My sister Margot married King Ferdinand's only son and heir, Prince John of Asturias. I cannot speak ill of my dearest sister, but they say her poor husband died from their... excess.'

'Excess?' Henry wondered if the duke struggled with his English.

The archduke gave Henry a knowing look. 'In bed.' He grinned. 'Of course, she says it is a lie!'

Henry sat back in his chair and took a drink of the sweet red wine, savouring the taste while he considered the implications. There was a possibility the young duke could inherit the wealthy kingdom of Castile through his wife, as well as Burgundy and the Low Countries.

The duke's sister was a few years older than Princess Catherine, yet he had hoped she might be a useful alternative if Arthur's betrothal came to nothing.

'Were there children of this marriage?'

'A girl was stillborn.' Duke Philip's voice was softer now. 'My sister was desolate and has returned to live with us.'

'She has had a full life for one so young,' Henry drained his goblet and mentally crossed the archduke's sister from his list. 'Please tell her we wish her better fortune in the future?'

'Of course, Your Grace.'

Henry glanced at the musicians, assembled and ready to accompany the dancing. 'My wife's ladies would be honoured to partner you, Duke Philip.'

The duke chose the most beautiful of all Elizabeth's ladies-in-waiting as his dancing partner. Lady Katheryn Gordon looked even more enchanting than usual in a tightly laced emerald green gown that complemented her slender figure. Henry guessed Duke Philip was already whispering his compliments. He felt an irrational jealousy to see them dancing together.

They sailed against the wind on the voyage home, in heavy, ashen seas. By the time the lights of Dover came into view Elizabeth and several of her ladies had taken to their pallet beds with seasickness. Henry counted their visit to Calais a success and had secured a promise from the young archduke to visit England with his wife.

He'd also been pleased to receive a delegation of ambassadors from King Louis, who presented him with a gift of fifty thousand francs. As well as covering the costs of his visit to Calais, the payment was welcome proof of French goodwill towards England.

Amongst the messages waiting when they docked was one from the chaplain to his old friend Archbishop

John Morton. The note explained that the bishop, now eighty years old, had suffered a palsy from which he was not expected to recover. Canterbury was on their route and at twenty miles a convenient stopping point. Henry decided to pay his respects to the man who helped plan the invasion from Brittany and officiated at their wedding.

Bishop Morton lay on an ornate carved bed with silk coverlets, in a dark, shuttered room lit by a single beeswax church candle. Henry detected the faint, sweet scent of precious incense and noted the deathly pallor of his old friend's face. The archbishop's voice wheezed as he spoke.

'God bless you, Your Grace. These physicians had me believe I might not see you again... yet here you are.'

Henry gestured for the bishop's attendants to leave. 'We owe you a debt, Bishop.' He moved a chair to the archbishop's bedside and sat in silence as he remembered. 'When you were in exile, you provided a letter of introduction to Duchess Anne, then Regent of France, who granted me and my men safe-conducts.'

'A small enough favour... for such a great reward...'

'You also gave me a small fortune to help raise my mercenary army. I don't recall that I ever repaid you.'

John Morton raised a withered, bony hand with some effort. 'You have repaid me a thousand times...' His rheumy eyes seemed to struggle to focus on Henry's face. 'You granted my tenure of this wonderful cathedral...' He struggled for his breath. 'I am also a cardinal of the holy mother church, my lifelong ambition.'

He closed his eyes. Henry watched the silk covering the archbishop's frail chest. It continued to rise and fall yet he knew the effort of their short conversation had exhausted his loyal friend. He placed his hands together and said a prayer for John Morton's soul.

His instinct told him something was wrong as soon as he returned to his temporary lodgings in the bishop's palace. His household servants, with eyes cast to the ground, stepped from his view. The yeomen guards, always ready with a polite nod, looked straight ahead as he passed.

A deep misgiving began to stir in his chest as he wondered in what way the world had changed. He'd been alone with the dying archbishop for less than an hour. He heard women's voices, loud sobbing, followed by a wail of anguish. Elizabeth.

Rushing through the dark hallway to her rooms, he found her surrounded by weeping ladies-in-waiting. As soon as he entered they vanished in a wordless rustle of silks. Elizabeth sat on her bed, her hair unpinned in disarray, shoulders heaving as she cried.

She looked up at him with reddened eyes. 'Our son...' She couldn't continue and stared at him with an uncomprehending look of despair.

His mind raced with the awful possibilities. Something might have happened to Harry, who'd always been a little too adventurous. Not Arthur, safe in Ludlow Castle, always so careful, watched over by his doting tutors. He sat next to her and took her hand.

'It is little Edmund?'

She nodded, a fresh tear falling down her cheek.

Henry knew he must be strong for her. He pictured the noisy infant at the christening, bawling so loud they'd had to halt the ceremony to calm him. He recalled the pride in his mother's face and wondered if she knew. He'd had three healthy sons. Now he only had two, the world seemed a bleaker place.

Henry put his arms around Elizabeth and held her tight while she sobbed. Fighting to control his own tears, he couldn't find any words to comfort her. Their kingdom, which seemed secure at last, now proved to be built on sand.

An endless line of marching men, dressed in black, carried burning torches ahead of the funeral procession, a slow-moving blaze of light that could be seen for miles. Sir Edward Stafford rode a black charger, escorting a fine chariot drawn by six horses, all caparisoned in black. Behind rode the mourners in pairs. Lords and ladies of Henry's court, bishops and priests, making the twenty-mile journey south to Westminster.

The men of the guilds and trades lined the streets, with the aldermen and Mayor of London, to greet the sad procession. At the abbey a crowd watched in reverent silence as Henry and Elizabeth arrived in deep blue mourning robes.

Four yeomen carried the small coffin, wrapped in white damask adorned with a red velvet cross. In keeping with tradition, an effigy of Prince Edmund Tudor, wearing a gold circlet, served to remind the mourners how he was in life.

Henry remained impassive until he spotted the little figure of his youngest son. The well-intended sculptor made it too lifelike, with knowing eyes which seemed to follow Henry with an inhuman gaze of unblinking accusation. He realised, yet again, he'd neglected his youngest child and now it was too late to make amends.

As he knelt in prayer in the stillness of the echoing abbey he struggled to keep his mind on the words of the service. If this was God's true purpose, it could only serve as the harshest of reminders not to take a single life, however young, for granted.

Henry found diversion from the air of misery which hung over his court by ordering the partial demolition of his palace at Greenwich. His mother, still in mourning for Edmund, was aghast.

'The work at the new Palace of Richmond is yet to be completed. Now you begin this?'

They watched as men climbed the rickety wooden scaffolding with the same agility as Henry's pet monkey. The once grand facade already looked a ruin, and the fine gardens were lost under an encampment of masons and labourers.

'It was Elizabeth's idea, as we've outgrown the old palace, but this location suits us well.' He pointed to the Thames, where black-painted sailing barges queued to unload bricks and materials. 'I shall make the main entrance opposite Queen Margaret's pier, with great windows of glass to make the best of the river views.'

His mother glanced back towards the old Norman church, scene of so many christenings. 'A covered gallery would reward the convent of the observant friars?'

Henry agreed. 'I have spoken to the prior. I plan to build a new chapel, as the present one is too small for our needs. I was thinking of commissioning a stained-glass window over the altar to celebrate our family.'

His mother studied his face for a moment. 'You should have another child, Henry, and soon, for the sake of Elizabeth. I know how the loss of Edmund has affected you both.'

'I wish it were so simple, lady Mother. Elizabeth has

become a recluse. I've hardly seen her...'

'Well, you would do well to listen to your mother. Another child will occupy her well,' she waved a gloved hand at the palace, 'as this work occupies you.'

Henry usually looked forward to the irreverence and disguisings of All Hallows Day at Richmond Palace, yet was in no mood for a banquet. He'd received word of the death of his old friend Bishop John Morton, his trusted advisor and Lord Chancellor.

Although he'd been expecting it, the news saddened him. Another of those who'd sailed with his intrepid invasion fleet, another of his inner circle, was now gone. Whoever he chose as the new Archbishop of Canterbury could never fill John Morton's shoes.

As he picked at his food, he realised he was lonely. His mother had invited Elizabeth to celebrate All Saints Day with her at Collyweston, her manor in Northamptonshire. Sir John de Vere had returned to Calais and Bishop Richard Foxe had resumed his negotiations in Scotland.

Henry glanced along the cluttered table at the young nobles and ladies laughing and drinking at his expense. Without realising, he'd surrounded himself with a new generation, the sons and daughters of the favoured members of his court, and at forty-three, he was starting to feel his age.

He held up his goblet for it to be refilled with wine and took a deep drink as the musicians struck up a lively dance. His courtiers had taken up the pagan theme of Samhain with their usual enthusiasm, dressing in colourful costumes, disguised as woodland fairies and spirits of the harvest.

One of the masked dancers caught his eye. She seemed familiar despite her disguise, then she was gone, hidden from his view. He watched as the dance brought her close again, until he could reach out and touch her.

Now he recognised her. Lady Katheryn Gordon. Elizabeth kept her close yet tonight she was here, dancing before him, dressed in a satin gown which flattered her slender figure. She wore a veil of gossamer as her disguise but he knew, in an unexpected frisson of arousal, it was Katheryn.

A servant refilled his goblet and he could feel the strong wine beginning to take effect. He remembered the first time he'd been entranced by the look of latent promise in her eyes. Despite his poor mood, he found improper thoughts swirling in his head.

He slept alone now. It would be easy enough to dismiss the guard outside his door on some pretext. He'd never been unfaithful to Elizabeth, except in his thoughts about the beautiful Scottish lady who now danced before him.

His personal physician, Thomas Linacre, had presented him with his translation of the New Testament from the Greek. He'd read of the seductive temptress Salome, who so entranced the king as she danced he offered her whatever she asked for, even up to half his kingdom.

The dance finished and their eyes met. Henry hardly realised he'd been staring at her. He'd not spoken to Katheryn Gordon since her husband's execution. It might have been the drink. Perhaps his eyesight failed him or her veiled eyes played tricks on his imagination.

In an instant he realised how easily she could have her revenge. He glanced at the bitter tasting goblet of wine in his hand. It would be easy for her to poison him and no one would suspect. She'd wormed her way into his wife's inner circle and had privileged access to his children.

His dark thoughts answered questions that lurked at the back of his mind. She'd bewitched him into showing her husband, his enemy, great favour. After his death, she could have returned to Scotland. He'd been glad she chose to remain at his court but now he wondered if he'd been too trusting.

The moment passed as the fiddle player struck up a lively tune. A handsome young courtier took her by the hand and led her back to the dancing. As Henry watched her pass from one partner in a complicated dance he'd never seen before. Then he understood what he'd seen in Katheryn Gordon's eyes. Worse than anger or even fear, she'd given him a look of pity.

Chapter Seventeen

August 1501

Henry tried to conceal his distrust of the flamboyant, self-important Don Pedro de Ayala, King Ferdinand's new ambassador. He knew from Bishop Foxe that Don Pedro had spent the past few years as ambassador in Scotland at the court of King James, although he now lived in a splendid London mansion.

It was rumoured he'd become close to Perkin Warbeck during his time in Scotland, yet he insisted he'd been instrumental in persuading King James to deport the impostor. Don Pedro also assisted Foxe to negotiate a seven-year truce with the Scots and would no doubt prove useful in discussions for Henry's daughter Margaret.

To show good faith and get the measure of the man, Henry invited the ambassador to come hunting in the forests of Eltham. As well as proving a skilled huntsman, he discovered the ambassador shared his passion for gambling at cards and dice. Although Henry continued to lose more often than he won, he found Don Pedro an engaging partner.

Summoned to explain the delay in the arrival of Princess Catherine, the ambassador arrived late for their meeting and seemed unapologetic, offering no explanation. To Henry's further annoyance he seemed to know little more about the arrival of Princess

Catherine than he'd already learnt from his old ally, Don Pedro's rival, Rodrigo de Puebla.

The two men could hardly be more different, as the rotund de Puebla was a self-made man from common stock, who'd worked his way up by his wits. Don Pedro was from a noble family in Toledo. Well-connected and persuasive, he enjoyed fine living and presented Henry with gifts of silks and Spanish velvet.

'I was informed the princess left the port of Corunna in May of this year.' Henry failed to keep the irritation from his voice. 'That was three months ago and there is still no word of when she might arrive in England.'

Don Pedro shook his head with exaggerated sympathy. 'There was a terrible storm in the Bay of Biscay, Your Grace.' He raised an eyebrow. 'I understand the princess was most alarmed when her ship began taking on water. She feared she might drown so her ships returned to Spain for her safety.'

'That was in the spring, Don Pedro. Even allowing for the ships to be repaired, I ask what delays her now?'

'The princess had to wait several weeks for favourable winds, Your Grace. Her captain was told not to sail until he was certain the storms had passed.'

'When will the princess arrive in England?'

'With a fair wind, I trust the princess will be here by the end of September.' Don Pedro looked at Henry. 'I will wait for her arrival and send a rider with word as soon as I know she is safe, Your Grace.'

Henry studied the ambassador, knowing he had little alternative. 'I shall pray for her safe voyage, Don Pedro. The arrival of the princess is eagerly anticipated, so it is good that I am a patient man.'

His patience had worn thin by October, when he

finally received word of Catherine's arrival. Instead of docking at Southampton as planned, her flotilla was blown off course and finally landed in Plymouth. He sent his heralds and messengers to meet her with his official letter of welcome. He also sent an escort to ensure her safe arrival in London, which included Prince Harry, representing him for the first time, to ride with her to the bishop's palace at Lambeth.

After more than a month had passed since the princess landed in Plymouth, Henry heard she was lodging at a manor house in Hampshire. Frustrated at the further delay, he rode to see her for himself, with a dozen lords and Prince Arthur at his side. They arrived late and unannounced and demanded to see the princess.

A woman wearing a high-necked gown covered with a shawl appeared. She scowled at Henry, reminding him of a ship in full sail, and spoke in French with a harsh Spanish accent.

'I am Doña Elvira Manuel, governess of the household of the Princess Catalina.' She fixed Henry with a stern gaze. 'The princess may not see you.'

'Tell her the King of England will see her, with his dear son, her betrothed, Arthur, Prince of Wales.' Henry, unused to being disobeyed, put as much authority into his voice as he could.

Doña Elvira didn't move. 'I cannot, Your Grace, it is not our custom.' She clasped her hands under her ample bosom as if the matter was closed.

'Well, it is our custom, my lady, to obey the command of the king. If needs be I'll go to her bedchamber and see her there!'

A black-garbed bishop, wearing a large silver crucifix on a chain around his neck, came to see what was going on. He spoke English and bowed to Henry. 'I am the Bishop of Malaga, Your Grace. It is my duty to inform you we are under orders from our Sovereign Lord. We are not to permit our lady princess any meeting or communication until the day of the marriage ceremony.'

Henry glowered at him in amazement. He'd not expected such a discourteous response. He turned and left, calling for his chancellor, Sir Thomas Lovell, who'd ridden with them to Hampshire. Sir Thomas listened to Henry's account of the situation.

'This is unprecedented, Your Grace. I would counsel you to find some compromise.'

Henry's frustration rose again. 'Must I allow these... foreigners to dictate to me?'

Sir Thomas glanced back at the manor house, now in darkness, except for candlelight flickering behind shuttered windows. 'The hour is drawing late. I imagine the princess has retired after her journey, so I suggest you allow her a little time to prepare for your meeting, Your Grace?'

Henry could see the sense of Lovell's suggestion. 'Please propose this to them—and see that they understand I will not leave without seeing the princess?'

'Of course, Your Grace.' Sir Thomas and several other lords left to tell the Bishop of Malaga.

Henry calmed a little as he waited with Arthur. 'We must learn to understand their Spanish ways, although they must in turn respect ours.'

'I am eager to see the princess, Father.' Arthur looked back at the house.

'As am I, Arthur, as am I.'

At last Sir Thomas and the other lords emerged. 'The princess will see you now, Your Grace.'

Henry followed them to Princess Catherine's rooms.

She stood as he entered and spoke in Spanish. Henry couldn't understand her but approved of what he saw. The candlelight turned her auburn hair to gold. Catherine wore a richly embroidered satin gown which showed a pleasant fullness of figure that promised fertility.

Her stern governess was right. In his eagerness he'd not shown the young princess proper courtesy. Henry knew he must look tired and dishevelled in his plain riding clothes, yet he was keen to make a good impression on the Princess.

He gave a slight bow. 'Bienvenida, Princesa.'

She looked surprised and spoke in Spanish, turning to the Bishop of Malaga to translate.

The bishop smiled. 'Princess Catherine is honoured to meet you, Your Grace.'

Rodrigo de Puebla had taught Henry only one more phrase. 'Este es el Príncipe Arthur.'

His son stepped forward and bowed. He spoke in French. 'Forgive our intrusion, Princess Catherine. We are pleased you are safely arrived in our country.'

Princess Catherine looked from Arthur to Henry. She studied him with questioning eyes, as if comparing him with what she had been told. She spoke again in rapid Spanish. She glanced at Henry once as she talked and he sensed the sincerity of her strange words, even though they had no meaning to him.

The bishop turned to Henry. 'The princess looks forward to her wedding with great gladness and joy. She asks if you would like to see her Spanish minstrels perform?'

For a moment Henry wondered if he'd misunderstood. 'If the princess is not too tired after her journey.'

As her answer Princess Catherine clapped her hands to summon servants to bring wine and clear the furniture, apart from chairs for her guests. A small group of musicians appeared and began to play rhythmic tunes with a lively beat that reminded Henry of music he'd heard in Brittany.

Princess Catherine entranced them with a Spanish dance with two of her ladies. To the beat of a drum, they swirled their silken dresses and stamped their feet in an exotic style he'd never seen before.

He discovered that the princess had a little French and Latin, which she spoke with a Spanish accent, although no effort had been made to teach her any English before she left Spain.

The hour was late by the time Henry decided he should leave. He turned to the bishop who'd acted as their interpreter. 'Please inform the princess my second son, Prince Henry, will be honoured to escort her to the bishop's palace at Lambeth, from where she will proceed to London for the wedding.'

He took one last look at his future daughter-in-law. He'd given little credence to Don Pedro's description of her as a paragon of virtue, an innocent young goddess. Once, after too much wine, Rodrigo de Puebla confessed she was in fact rather short. He'd drawn an exaggerated female shape in the air with his hands and laughed as he explained she was still blessed with the plumpness of her youth.

Henry knew Princess Catherine was yet to turn sixteen and had not even been born at the time of his coronation. He'd expected to see a shy girl, perhaps a little humbled by his unexpected visit. Princess Catherine was an exotic, confident and beautiful woman. Her dowry and the alliance with Spain would secure his throne and help ensure lasting peace. She was, he thought, the most perfect bride for his eldest son.

Princess Catherine of Aragon shivered in the wintry chill as she rode a mule to her wedding in the Spanish tradition. Beside her, dressed in a tunic of cloth of gold rode Prince Harry on his fine black destrier. Catherine wore a scarlet, long-sleeved gown, glistening with diamonds that reflected sunlight as she moved.

On her head she wore a braided coif and a wide-brimmed Spanish hat, held in place with gold lace. Her rich, reddish-gold hair, worn long to show her purity, reached below her waist and streamed loose over her shoulders.

Behind her rode her Spanish ladies, dressed in black, each with an English lady riding at her side. Their escort, of four hundred mounted soldiers in red-and-black livery, were led by the handsome young noble Sir Edward Stafford, Duke of Buckingham. Son of Lady Katheryn Woodville by her first husband, he was also to be the chief challenger at the grand wedding tournaments.

Royal heralds led them through gawping crowds to London Bridge, where the Mayor of London welcomed them to the city. At a signal, the bells of all the churches, St Paul's and Westminster began clanging. Colourful banners of welcome and celebration hung from windows and onlookers gathered in the streets.

Bands of musicians played on street corners and wine flowed freely in the conduits. High wooden stands, built by the London companies, groaned under the weight of their members, assembled to watch. Nobles thronged the main streets with their finely dressed wives, armed yeomen and liveried retainers.

Henry stood watching the procession with Elizabeth, Prince Arthur and his mother, from the high windows of a wealthy merchant's residence.

'I wonder what the princess makes of our mummers with their moral pageants?'

His mother answered. 'It takes little enough intelligence to understand them, even if she is unable to speak our language.'

Elizabeth pointed as the first of the fireworks flashed into the sky over London Bridge. More fireworks exploded high in the air to gasps from the watching crowds who'd not seen them since Elizabeth's coronation.

She took Henry's arm. 'I understand there are many Spanish nobles in her entourage who have never seen England before. They are certain to remember their first sight of our city.'

He watched as a large firework mounted high over the bridge began shooting great circles of crackling sparks into the air as a dramatic finale. 'I trust they will report to King Ferdinand that we've spared little expense. He has agreed to pay the first instalment of one hundred thousand crowns for her dowry—but I have yet to see one penny of it.'

'Have faith, Henry.' Elizabeth smiled. 'Enjoy our eldest son's wedding.'

The procession arrived at the great cathedral of St Paul's where the final pageant was held in the churchyard. The Mayor of London presented gifts to Catherine. A choir sang as she dismounted and entered the church, where she knelt in prayer before retiring to the archbishop's palace for the night.

The following afternoon, Catherine visited Elizabeth at Baynard's castle, Henry's mother's mansion overlooking the river. The conversation was difficult as Doña Elvira acted as interpreter, but Elizabeth's minstrels provided music. There was dancing well into the night, before Catherine returned to Lambeth.

On a bright, cold November morning Princess Catherine left the bishop's palace. A rosy-cheeked Prince Harry, dressed in silver embroidered with gold roses, walked at her side. Catherine looked magnificent in a white satin gown embroidered with a thousand pearls and pleated with gold thread in the Spanish style. A white silk veil, bordered with gold and precious stones, covered her face.

Henry had stayed the night at the well-appointed house of Lord Abergavenny, close to St Paul's Cathedral. On the morning of the wedding he rode in front of the procession on a white charger, wearing a silver breastplate studded with diamonds and rubies over his red velvet robes.

Behind him in an open carriage pulled by four fine horses rode Elizabeth with Princess Catherine. Elizabeth wore a gown of white satin with a long train of royal purple silk.

In keeping with tradition, Henry joined Elizabeth in a private room of the cathedral to watch the wedding ceremony from behind lattice windows. He took her hand in his.

'I can hardly believe this day has come.'

She smiled to see him happy at last. 'Once they are married, you must not leave them in that damp castle in Ludlow. Bring them to court, Henry. I have started trying to help Princess Catherine understand our ways and it will be good for Arthur to learn how to rule.'

'I plan they should make Ludlow Castle their home, Elizabeth. Arthur will learn to command the Welsh Marches. It is good for him to have the responsibility.'

Elizabeth looked doubtful. 'Do you remember yourself at his age, Henry?'

He smiled. 'Don't be concerned about Arthur. I have appointed Sir Richard Pole as his administrator, and we shall have them come to London as often as they are able to.'

The waiting crowds cheered as a deafening fanfare from the king's trumpeters announced the arrival of the princess at the Galilee porch. Prince Harry escorted Catherine through the west door of the cathedral along a raised wooden walkway, covered with red carpet, which led from the door to the altar. They walked down the long nave between pillars hung with the colourful standards of the great families of England.

Fifteen-year-old Prince Arthur waited at the altar, on a raised wooden stage. Dressed in white satin, he stood with the new Archbishop of Canterbury, Henry Deane, surrounded by another nineteen other bishops, the Spanish Legate and their attendants, all dressed in rich silks and cloth of gold.

The ceremony and mass lasted for three hours, before the newlyweds knelt to be blessed by Henry and Elizabeth. Princess Catherine and Prince Arthur returned to the west door to be greeted by a pageant representing King Arthur, flanked by the kings of Spain and France, all dressed in full armour.

Trumpets blasted fanfares as the crowds shouted 'Long live Prince Arthur,' and 'Long live King Henry.'

The entire wedding party made their way to Lambeth

Palace for the grand banquet served on gold plates which were decorated with precious jewels.

As she had done with each christening, Lady Margaret organised every detail of the young couple's first official night together. Henry applauded with the others as Prince Arthur was led in a grand procession of laughing young nobles, some already drunk, into his bride's bedroom.

The princess waited for him in their nuptial bed, where she was prepared by her ladies and blessed in readiness. Doña Elvira, her governess, had been tasked by Queen Isabella to ensure the consummation of her marriage observed the proper tradition.

Henry turned to Elizabeth. 'Our son is made a man at last.' He raised his goblet of wine. 'Here's to the next generation of Tudors!'

The next day a flotilla of more than forty barges carried the wedding party as they made their way upriver to Westminster, music playing as they went. A week of jousting and celebrations followed. Lady Margaret and her husband, the Earl of Derby, hosted a banquet for the Spanish guests at Coldharbour.

A splendid tournament was staged at Westminster, where the open area in front of the cathedral was paved with fine stones and sand for the horses. Princess Catherine sat and watched with the Queen, Lady Margaret and her two new sisters-in-law, the Princesses Margaret and Mary Tudor. Prince Arthur sat across from the ladies with Henry, his brother Harry, the Earl of Oxford and the Earl of Derby.

At the tournament Sir William Courtenay entered the lists disguised as a fire-breathing dragon, led by his squires walking on high stilts to give him the appearance of a giant. Others arrived in a large ship, which appeared to be propelled by oarsmen who sang lustily as they rowed.

After a week at Westminster the whole court sailed on barges to Richmond Palace. Henry knew his grand palace could not fail to impress the many members of the Spanish Court who had accompanied the Princess and would report back to her parents.

Chapter Eighteen

March 1502

Henry worked alone in his study, high in his tower at Richmond Palace overlooking the paved inner courtyard. Although the cold winter was coming to an end the paving glistened with a heavy frost. His grand Italian marble water fountain was still frozen solid, like some surreal sculpture carved from ice by nature. He suffered with the cold and wore his fur coat over his robes, despite a good fire burning in his hearth.

His study was also his library, with shelves of precious books lining the walls. It was impossible to replace many of the books destroyed in the fire. As with the rebuilding, Henry had taken it as a challenge and sent his agents to scour the country for copies of the older works, haggling for best prices.

The rising number of printing presses in London meant new English translations could be found to fill his shelves. In one section were his most precious books, original works in Greek and Latin. Bound in green and red leather, they had by some miracle survived the flames.

In the corner by the window sat his pet, Rodrigo, watching him with wide, lavender-blue eyes. Secured by a long chain, the little monkey groomed its fur, searching for fleas. Once he'd left it alone too long and it tore the pages of his precious diary into small pieces.

Henry's mother said he should keep the animal with

the others in the Tower, but he found the exotic pet worth the cost of the servant who cared for it. He sometimes spoke to it as he worked on his chamber accounts, checking the long list of expenses, initialling those he approved and making notes for those he wished to question.

He'd wished to make a good impression on the Spanish but it seemed he'd fed half the population of London at banquets which lasted for days. Even taking into account the first payment of the dowry from King Ferdinand, it was the most extravagant wedding the country had ever seen.

Henry took some comfort from the knowledge that his investment would secure public support of his son as the future King of England. King Ferdinand was also obliged to pay the balance of the dowry, a hundred thousand crowns, which would more than offset the costs of Princess Catherine's household.

He often found the neat records tiring to read and cursed his eyes, which continued to worsen despite the lotions of fennel and celandine prepared by his physician. He rarely wrote letters in his own hand now, even to his mother. His long-suffering scribe, a young cleric, was tasked to read his letters aloud and note Henry's dictated replies.

He tutted to himself as he made a marginal note to check the payments made to Elizabeth's household. His wife now had more than thirty noble ladies in attendance, as well as her nursery maids and other servants of her household. He'd encouraged her patronage and liked to see the bright young women at his court, but the costs of Arthur's wedding had eaten into his reserves.

Henry sat back in his chair as he recalled the

extravagance of the wedding banquet, the grandest ever seen in London. The Spanish delegation would return to tell King Ferdinand of celebrations, banquets and tournaments that lasted a month, long after Catherine and Arthur left for his castle in Ludlow.

He took the letter which lay opened on his desk and frowned as he held it close to read, although he already knew the contents. His son suffered with a fever and had taken to his bed in a weakened condition. He remembered how the sweating sickness could take young and old, rich or poor and prayed each morning for better news. So far this letter, now over a week old, was all he'd had.

Henry worried about his own health. He'd little appetite, despite the best efforts of his cooks to tempt him with choice dishes. He'd lost weight as a consequence and woke up in a sweat the previous night. He'd always taken to the country when he heard rumours of plague or the sweating sickness in London but feared one or the other would catch up with him in the end.

He resolved to visit Arthur in Ludlow with his own physician as soon as he could. First he must untangle the mess created by Edmund de la Pole. Grandson of Richard, Duke of York through his mother Elizabeth, Suffolk swore fealty to Henry. Despite his brother's treachery at Stoke Field, Henry allowed Edmund to keep his loyal father's title, although reduced it from duke to Earl of Suffolk.

Henry had taken the precaution of having agents within the Suffolk household. He'd been concerned when Edmund was reported to have sailed on a ship bound for Calais. As the last remaining York heir, there would always be the danger of a revolt.

Henry summoned the man he'd asked to help him and turned as he heard a servant knock at his door. Thomas Lovell wore a wolf fur riding cape over his tunic. He gave a look of disapproval at the monkey as he crossed to the fire to warm his frozen hands.

'I regret to tell you Suffolk has outwitted us a second time, Your Grace. He's reported to be in Austria at the court of Emperor Maximilian.'

'How could he have escaped to Austria? I thought we had him watched?' Henry heard the challenge in his voice, although he knew Sir Thomas was the bringer of bad news, not the cause of it.

'We did, Your Grace, and we obtained copies of Suffolk's letters, which is how we know his co-conspirators.' His shrewd eyes narrowed as he looked at Henry. 'Once he was in Guisnes, it was only too easy for him to make his escape through France, particularly as the captain of the garrison was sympathetic to his cause.'

'Sir James Tyrell, Governor of Guines?' Henry cursed at another Yorkist betraying his trust. He knew Tyrell was loyal to King Richard, and he had pardoned him against advice. Yet again, his leniency in those early days of power came back to haunt him.

'Tyrell put up a fight when we tried to arrest him. Even with all the men we could muster in Calais, he wouldn't surrender.'

'Yet you have him now?'

'We do, Your Grace. I had to promise him safe conduct.' He smirked. 'He had safe passage, directly to the Tower.'

Henry frowned. 'We must begin negotiations with Emperor Maximilian right away. He's always short of money, so I suggest we offer payment of ten thousand crowns. It would be a small enough price to see Edmund de la Pole in the Tower.'

'I agree, Your Grace, although I would be cautious about taking Maximilian on his word. He's not beyond taking our money and keeping Suffolk at his court.'

'That's a risk we must take.' Henry gestured for Sir Thomas to be seated.

'I've come from the Tower, where I've questioned Tyrell,' Sir Thomas sat heavily in the chair and stretched his legs. 'He confessed to helping Suffolk escape, Your Grace.'

Henry's eyes narrowed. 'Was this confession extracted by torture?'

'He's made a pleading for the life of his son Thomas, who was also arrested and brought to the Tower.'

Henry imagined how Tyrell might have seen his opportunity when Suffolk arrived in Guines. He must have known there were agents of the king within his own garrison, yet he'd risked his life to help the last York heir.

Sir Thomas looked across at Henry and took a deep breath. 'He has also confessed to his part in the murders of the two young princes.'

'What did he say?' Henry's mind raced. For sixteen years, even before Bosworth, the fate of Elizabeth's brothers had been a mystery. He'd invested a small fortune in searches of the Tower and its grounds. He'd had sleepless nights, worrying that the next impostor might prove to actually be either Edward or Richard of York returned from exile.

'He claims Sir Robert Brackenbury, the Constable of the Tower at the time, received orders from King Richard regarding the princes that his conscience caused him to refuse. Tyrell says he was sent to the

Tower with a letter commanding Brackenbury to surrender the keys.' He shook his head and produced a parchment note from which he read. 'He alleges that one of the prince's keepers, a man named Miles Forest, and Tyrell's groom, a John Dighton, whom he calls a strong knave, smothered the princes and buried them at the stair foot.'

'King Richard made James Tyrell a knight in reward?'

Sir Thomas shrugged. 'This could be false witness, Your Grace, although I cannot see what Tyrell would stand to gain—and his allegations further tarnish the name of York.'

Henry scowled as he considered the consequences. 'These men he names. Where are they now?'

'I have my agents looking for them, Your Grace. Rest assured we will find them—and when we do they'll be arrested and questioned.'

'Who else knows of this, Sir Thomas?'

'Only those who present in the Tower.'

'You are to return to the Tower of London and have them swear to keep this silent. I've waited sixteen years for any clue about what happened that night. This is to be done properly, with statements sworn before God.'

'Yes, Your Grace. I shall take care of it.'

Elizabeth stared at him in astonishment. 'You plan to have my sister Catherine's husband arrested?'

Her tone surprised Henry. 'I thought I should tell you—before you hear it from your gossiping ladies. I have no choice. William Courtenay is implicated in the conspiracy to support Edmund de la Pole...'

'By what evidence?' Her voice challenged him.

Henry held up a calming hand. 'He is named in correspondence obtained by Sir Thomas Lovell. It seems he dined with Suffolk and others shortly before he fled to Calais.'

'Is it now a crime to dine with my own first cousin?'

'He faces a serious charge of conspiracy. We have seen evidence that he supported Suffolk's plans to raise an army and invade from his estates in the west.' Henry shook his head. 'I thank God we have men such as Sir Thomas Lovell to protect our interests. If Sir William is found guilty...'

Elizabeth's eyes widened. 'What will happen to Catherine, Henry? Do you not care about their children?'

He remembered seeing Catherine's infant son, named Henry in his honour, with his brother and a baby sister. He cursed Edmund de la Pole's scheming. William Courtenay served him well when he prevented Perkin Warbeck from entering Exeter.

'You might support your sister with the children? You could bring them to one of your properties closer to London.'

'Catherine will be beside herself with worry.' Elizabeth wrung her hands together. 'Can I promise her... you will not allow Sir William to be executed?'

'You can assure your sister her husband will be well treated. He will be held in the Tower while the process of law takes its course. If he can prove his innocence...'

'And if he cannot?' She spoke with unexpected sharpness.

Henry frowned. He'd not expected Elizabeth to take the news so badly. 'It's not easy for us to accept that our own trusted family might be plotting behind our back.'

'You talk of your trusted family, yet you don't trust my own sisters. First you make my sister Cecily a pauper and banish her from court, now my sister Catherine...'

'Your sister Cecily married in secret!' Henry regretted raising his voice, even as he said the words.

Elizabeth's voice turned cold. 'Cecily knew what you would say if she sought your consent. She married for love...'

'Your sister chose her path—and should not be surprised to learn the consequences.'

'You've taken her dower lands and left her with no income.' The accusation in her voice was unmistakable now.

Henry tried to calm himself. 'I would have found her a good husband. A wealthy noble, with prospects, not some... commoner.'

Elizabeth glowered at him. 'You married my sister to your old uncle, Viscount Welles.'

'John Welles was a loyal, honest man. He served me well in Brittany....'

'And my younger sister was presented as his reward, just as my aunt Catherine was given to your Uncle Jasper.'

'Catherine was made a duchess...'

'He was thirty years older than her!'

Her words were like a slap in the face. Elizabeth had never raised her voice at him before and Henry could take no more. He stormed from the room without so much as a reply. Whatever he said would only widen the rift between them.

♔

In later years Henry would remember exactly how he received the dreadful news on the morning his life changed. Alone in his chambers at Greenwich Palace, he woke to a cautious knocking on his door and opened it to see the sombre face of the Observant Friar who served as his priest confessor.

'What brings you here so early in the morning, Father?' He gestured for the elderly friar to enter.

The friar bowed to him. 'If we receive good things by the hand of God, should we not also receive misfortune?'

'You must forgive me.' Henry frowned. 'I don't understand?'

His priest confessor handed him a folded letter and watched as he broke the dark wax seal. Henry struggled to read the handwriting and took it to the window to make the most of the early light. As he began to read, his legs grew weak and he sat down on his bed, letting the letter fall to the floor. Everything he'd worked for all his life unravelled in that moment.

The letter was from Sir Richard Pole, Henry's capable administrator of the Welsh Marches, based in Ludlow Castle. He'd kept the preamble brief and stated the facts in his usual businesslike, blunt manner. Henry sat in a stunned silence then stared up at the friar with tear filled eyes.

'Bring the queen to me, if you will, Father. Do not tell her your purpose, only that she must come at once.'

The priest slipped back out through the door and returned a short time later. Elizabeth wore a woollen shawl over her cotton shift. A plain lace coif looked as if it had been pinned over her plaited golden hair in haste and he guessed, like him, she'd been woken from her sleep.

She seemed to have a mother's intuition the moment she took in the shock on Henry's face and the letter, still lying on the floor. Henry waited until the priest closed the door and led her to the bed, then sat next to her. He took her hand in his and gave it a gentle squeeze as he tried to form the words.

'Our precious son Arthur is dead, and his Spanish princess is dying.'

Elizabeth stared at him in wide-eyed disbelief. She reached to pick the discarded letter from the floor. After reading it she folded it with great care and held it closed, as if the truth it contained could somehow be denied. She sat for a moment in silence as she thought through the consequences.

'Be strong for your noble person, for your realm. Be strong for me, Henry.' She brushed a tear from his face. 'Your good lady mother had no more children but you, and God by his grace has preserved and brought you to where you are.'

Henry stared into her bright amber eyes. They seemed to glow with a new strength he'd not seen before. Overwhelmed with love for her, he tried to focus on her words. He pictured Arthur, perhaps calling out for him as the sweating fever took hold. He'd been too busy dealing with plotters to visit his son. He knew he must be strong.

Elizabeth spoke softly. 'God has left us one fair prince—and two fair princesses.' She held his hand in hers. 'We are still young, Henry. Be strong for me?'

He pulled her close and found comfort in the warmth of her body as he tried to fight the despair breaking his heart.

A violent storm soaked the funeral procession as it made its slow journey to the ancient Benedictine Abbey at Worcester. Sir Thomas Howard, Earl of Surrey and Lord High Treasurer, representing the king, struggled to calm his startled horse as another thunderbolt crashed in a leaden sky.

The people of Worcester who braved the heavy rain bowed their heads as a hundred black-garbed mourners trudged past. Some looked in awe at the ornate wagon as it splashed through muddy puddles, hauled by a team of oxen. Carrying the cloth of gold draped coffin, for many it would be their first and only sight of the Prince of Wales.

Grim-faced lords and knights rode behind, led by a dark knight carrying the standard of the black raven. Prince Arthur's friend and ally, the Welsh lord Sir Gruffydd ap Rhys, was the eldest son of Sir Rhys ap Thomas, thought to have delivered the blow which felled King Richard at Bosworth Field.

In keeping with royal tradition, Henry withdrew into private mourning for his son, spending many hours praying alone in his chapel. His only contact with the world was through Bishop Foxe, who relayed to him every detail of the funeral.

Princess Catherine, married for less than four months, also by tradition stayed away and remained fighting the fever in her sickbed. Elizabeth collapsed and remained in her chambers, unable to face the world.

Chapter Nineteen

February 1503

Henry's mother told him the child, with typical Tudor impatience, had begun to arrive on Candlemas Day, a week too early. Elizabeth would never have chosen for the birth to be in the royal apartments of the Tower of London. In the depths of such a hard winter the rooms were always cold and damp, despite log fires kept burning by an army of servants.

Worse than the bone numbing cold was the atmosphere of sadness which hung over the Tower. Once a place of refuge for Elizabeth, it had always been a prison, haunted by ghosts. It was where her sister's husband languished in a cell, waiting for his fate to be decided. Others had been imprisoned so long they were forgotten by the world.

In the middle of the night they would be woken by the angry roars of leopards and lions, gifts from far away kings. It was no place to give birth to a prince, yet Elizabeth's physicians ordered that she was not to be moved, as to do so could risk the child's life and hers.

Lady Margaret did her best to ensure every detail of Elizabeth's confinement followed her ordinances, set out sixteen years before. The number and colours of silk cushions and even the size of coverlets were checked and noted.

Mistress Alice Massey, who served Elizabeth so well delivering her children in the past, was summoned. Two midwives took turns to watch over her all day and through each night. On Lady Margaret's instructions, Elizabeth's priest confessor slept in a nearby room, to be ready if needed.

Five times each day Lady Margaret said prayers for her in the Chapel of St Peter, built within the Tower walls by King Henry the third. As well as praying for Elizabeth, she knelt before the altar and prayed that her son's faith would be restored. Although he was still in mourning, she worried he'd lost more than his son. His mother prayed the new child would mean new hope, a new beginning.

His mother's messenger, an intelligent novice priest named Nicholas Aughton, found Henry already awake. He'd been unable to sleep, expecting news at any time. In no time he was dressed in his warmest coat and ready to leave, despite the early hour.

'How is the queen?'

'Lady Margaret requested that you are to come as soon as you are able to, Your Grace.'

'Does the child live?' Henry held his breath.

'I cannot say, Your Grace.' His eyes avoided Henry's.

'Tell me what you know!' Henry's impatience gave an edge to his voice, although he knew his mother would not have silenced her messenger without good reason.

Nicholas Aughton bowed to Henry's command. 'The child lives, Your Grace. The queen was sleeping when I left the Tower.'

Henry suspected Aughton knew more than he was saying. 'We'll take the royal barge and you shall see what else you can recall.'

The foul smelling river, an open sewer, offered the fastest way to reach the Tower, although the powerful tide would be against them for most of the way. Henry urged his sixteen strong oarsmen to row faster. The blades of their long oars splashed as they cut through the dark water, a rhythmic pulse as they battled against the outgoing flow. The helmsman began barking out the stroke and shouting words of encouragement in his deep London accent.

Henry said a silent prayer for Elizabeth and his new child. He glanced at the stony faced Nicholas Aughton, standing in the bows. It seemed his mother had shared little with her trusted messenger. It was unusual for her to summon him at such an hour and he feared Elizabeth must have suffered more than usual.

Arthur's death had changed them and fractured their already fragile relationship. They were both still mourning his loss and although she told him to be strong, Elizabeth became withdrawn, rarely even speaking to him.

He knew she blamed him for keeping Arthur and his young wife in the damp castle at Ludlow. He'd discovered that Elizabeth now kept her sister Catherine and her children, paying their expenses from her own purse. She'd also conspired with his mother to provide for her sister Cecily, although she never spoke of it.

Then, without even telling him, she'd gone on a progress, riding long distances despite being heavy with child. He'd finally tracked her down and joined her but instead of welcoming his company, it seemed she resented it. Now he prayed it wasn't too late to make amends. He had taken her for granted and the five miles from Westminster Palace never seemed so long.

When his mother finally met him in the royal apartments at the Tower he sensed that, like her messenger, she withheld more than she revealed. Her face tensed and her eyes avoided his. She held her prayer-book with both hands, as if it offered some security.

'How is Elizabeth?' He watched her impassive face

for any clue.

'She is disappointed the baby is a girl. She believed it would be a boy, another son...' Her voice sounded tired.

'It is no matter.' Henry interrupted. 'I trust to God they are both well?'

'The midwife has concerns, Henry. You should know it was... a difficult birth and the child is small.'

'I must see her.'

Lady Margaret held up a steadying hand. 'She sleeps now, Henry. I will send for you when she wakes.'

'I will see my new daughter.'

'You must keep silent, not wake her.'

He didn't promise but followed his mother into the darkened room. As his eyes became accustomed to the light he noticed the glance of concern on the face of the young nurse. His new baby slept in her arms, looking too small to be real. The nursemaid loosened the white linen swaddling for him to see as Henry bent to take a closer look.

'She seems pale?' It might have been the poor light but his daughter had an unnatural yellow pallor.

The nursemaid glanced down at the baby. 'We trust the colour will come to her soon enough, Your Grace.'

He heard the doubt in her young voice and began to prepare himself. He'd seen enough newborn babies to know there was something wrong. His daughter reminded him of the eerily lifelike dolls he'd seen her sisters playing with in the nursery at Eltham.

Henry decided to move to his own apartments in the Tower to be near Elizabeth. Two days passed before Henry's mother judged her well enough for him to visit. Elizabeth's white-bearded London physician, Doctor Lathis, waited to greet him in her antechamber. He studied the man's grave face. Like all of them, his expression gave nothing away.

'The queen is awake now, Your Grace.' The physician's cultured voice echoed in the cold, sparsely furnished room.

'What is her condition, Doctor?'

'She has eaten a little broth, an encouraging sign.'

Henry caught the misgiving in the elderly doctor's eye. His mother said they'd had concerns, although the last time they spoke she seemed to think Elizabeth was improving.

'It was a difficult birth?'

The physician nodded. 'The queen remains in a weakened condition.'

'Yet she is recovering now?'

'As the queen grows older the risk of complications increases, Your Grace, as does the toll each child takes on her body.'

'It will take her longer to regain her strength?'

'With God's grace she should be well again soon enough, but for now it is important she rests.'

'I should like the queen to be moved from this damp place to the Palace of Richmond.'

'My counsel is not to move the queen until her strength is recovered, Your Grace. The change of air might benefit her...' He glanced back at the closed door of Elizabeth's bedchamber as if afraid she might overhear. 'The queen is too weak to make the journey.'

'I wish her moved as soon as you deem it possible.' Henry frowned as he peered from the small window. His own apartments had views over the river but Elizabeth's opened onto a snow covered courtyard. A black raven pecked at the cold, hard earth, looking to Henry like a bad omen, a harbinger of dark times to come.

He consoled himself with the encouraging prediction of his own physician, William Parron. After a detailed study of the constellations, the Italian was confident Elizabeth would enjoy a prosperous year and live well to the age of eighty years and more. He turned to Elizabeth's Doctor, still waiting for instructions.

'I shall see the queen now.'

As he entered Elizabeth's darkened bedchamber the delicate scent of rose-water mixed with the heady aroma of incense. The fire smouldering in the hearth seemed about to burn out. The room was colder than her antechamber. Elizabeth lay in her opulent bed, swathed in dark red velvet and resting on silk cushions, set out according to his mother's ordinances.

Her servants bowed as they recognised Henry and he gestured for them to leave. He waited until the door shut behind them, then took one of the heavy gilded chairs and dragged it closer to sit at her bedside.

She gave a weak smile as she looked up at him. 'We have another daughter, Henry.'

'I've seen her.' He struggled to return her smile.

'I thought we might name her Katherine?'

'A good name. Katherine Tudor.' He'd not even given any thought to a name for his daughter, as if to do so would tempt providence.

He took her pale hand in his. It was hot to the touch. Feverish, despite the snow still falling outside. He raised her hand to his lips and kissed her gold-ringed fingers.

'I've missed you.'

She gave him a look of concern. 'Will our daughter live?'

'God willing.' He smiled as fleeting hope shone in her eyes. 'She's as small as a mouse, but she's also a

Tudor.'

He waited for her reply but she closed her eyes in pain, as if she'd already glimpsed the future.

Henry recognised the sharp knock on the door of his study. Bishop Foxe came as the bearer of news. He studied Henry's face for a moment without speaking, as if searching for the right words. Henry always found the dour faced bishop hard to read, yet now he knew the sad purpose of his loyal friend's visit.

'My daughter?'

'I am sorry, Your Grace.'

Henry crossed to the window and gazed out over the narrow, mired streets of London. So many people, going about their busy lives, oblivious to his personal tragedy. Any one of them would have envied his daughter. She would have been married into a royal family, bringing a new alliance and more peace to England. She had lived for little more than one week.

His heart hardened, like soft clay fired in a kiln, and stopped the tears he might have cried for his loss. He'd prepared himself as well as he could, yet now must let go of the slender thread of hope.

He turned to Bishop Foxe, one of the few men he could confide in. 'I struggle to understand God's purpose, in taking her life so soon.'

'Have faith, Your Grace.' He made the sign of the cross. 'Your daughter is with God now.'

'Yes... may God rest her innocent soul.'

Bishop Foxe took a deep breath. 'I must also tell you the queen is much weakened by a childbed fever, Your Grace.'

Henry cursed her incompetent physician. 'Will you summon Doctor Aylesworth? He must make haste, as it seems the queen's physician is failing in his duty.'

Bishop Foxe frowned with concern. 'I believe Doctor Aylesworth is in Kent, Your Grace, it will take some time for him to reach London.'

'My mother is with her now?'

'Lady Margaret sits with her night and day.'

'Then I shall sit with her also. Pray for us, Bishop Foxe. Pray for us.'

There was no mistaking the look on his mother's face. She wore a black mourning dress for the granddaughter she had not had a chance to know. Her starched white hood reflected the flickering light of tall candles arranged around Elizabeth's bed.

Elizabeth lay with her eyes closed, her hands clasped outside the velvet coverlet. Her long golden hair was combed over her shoulders and her head rested on a cushion of cloth of gold. She reminded Henry of icons he'd seen of angels.

Two of her ladies-in-waiting and her priest confessor stood in reverent silence as he crossed the room and sat at Elizabeth's bedside. His mother gestured to the others to leave and turned to Henry.

'We hoped to keep the loss of your daughter from her until she was stronger. She insisted on seeing her. I had to tell Elizabeth the truth and now... it is as if she has lost the will to live.'

'Her priest has provided absolution?' Henry fought the despair which clouded his mind.

'She has been blessed. I've sent word to the Archbishops of Canterbury and London, as well as York.' She glanced at Elizabeth. 'I shall see if there is news of their arrival.'

Alone with Elizabeth he took her hand in his. No

longer feverish, it felt cool to his touch. He leant over and kissed her. At first there was no response, then her eyes opened and she focused on his face.

Henry remembered how her eyes used to glow with some inner spirit. They would twinkle with humour as she made a joke at his expense or beat him again at a game of cards. The fever had taken her strength. The loss of their child had dimmed her spirit and her eyes filled with sadness as she recognised him.

'Henry...' She struggled to form the words. 'She was taken from us.'

'Our daughter is with God.'

'We are still young.'

Henry remembered it was what she said after the news of Arthur's death. She had wanted to give him another child. She must have known she was risking her life. She had not done it this time to please him or through some sense of duty. It had been her way to try to help them both overcome the pain of their grief.

'Today is your thirty-seventh birthday.'

'Too old?' Her eyes pleaded for him to disagree.

Henry shook his head. 'The first time I saw you, Elizabeth, was in St Paul's Cathedral. You wore a rich burgundy robe trimmed with black fur.'

She managed a smile at the memory. 'You looked more... handsome than I expected.' Her voice was a faint whisper of breath.

'I'd imagined your eyes would be bright blue, yet they shone... like gold.' He gave her hand a gentle squeeze. 'I love you, Elizabeth.'

She didn't respond to their secret signal and he saw her eyes were open. Lifeless. Something deep inside him hardened. He'd always believed he followed God's plan. Now he stared at the body of his beautiful dead queen and wished he could join her in Heaven.

The bells of St Paul's Cathedral rang out to tell the people of London the sad news and were soon joined by the clanging of bells in every church in the city. Elizabeth's body, dressed in her finest royal robes, lay on her bed as if she slept. Prince Harry led his sisters, Margaret and Mary, dressed in black mourning cloaks, and they wept as they came to say their farewells.

Elizabeth's coffin, wrapped in black velvet with a cross of white damask, was carried by four knights to the Chapel of St Peter. The queen's ladies-in-waiting followed in a sombre procession with every member of the queen's household following behind.

On the day of the funeral, a wooden effigy of the queen wearing her crown and golden robes, was placed on top of the coffin. Her lifelike long hair flowed in a golden cascade over her shoulders, as it had on the day of her wedding, and gold diamond rings adorned each of her fingers.

The procession wound its way on icy roads from the tower to Westminster Abbey, led by two hundred black-garbed paupers carrying burning torches. The queen's four sisters rode black palfreys behind the hearse, drawn by six fine horses led by grooms dressed in black hoods. Knights wearing armour, carrying standards on long lances, rode each side through streets thronged with mourners.

Thirty-seven virgins, dressed in white, represented each year of the queen's life. They held lit tapers that glowed orange in the cold air as they lined the route of the procession through Cheapside. The choirs of every parish church sang mournful anthems and priests called out their blessings as the procession passed.

The Ambassadors of France and Spain, Venice and Portugal rode horses trapped in black. Behind them marched their stewards, carrying torches and the colourful standards of their countries.

Eight bishops greeted the coffin at Westminster Abbey where it remained for the night surrounded by torchbearers. Elizabeth's ladies, knights, squires and heralds kept a vigil and the people of London filed past in slow procession to pay their respects.

Elizabeth was buried in a vault at the crossing of the Abbey, between the choir and the altar. Of the thousands who came to witness her funeral, one notable person was absent. Again, by royal tradition, Henry locked himself away from the world.

Alone in the royal chapel, he clasped his hands in prayer. He remembered his wife as a sweet golden girl, the York princess he married so long ago. Elizabeth had been his prize, the victor's reward, and legitimized his crown. He'd not expected to fall so deeply in love with her, to depend on her. Now she was gone, he wished he'd been kinder to her.

She'd never argued yet he'd banished her sisters, confined her mother in a convent and appropriated her fortune. For most of their last year she'd travelled on a progress without him and he'd been too busy being king to miss her.

Too late, he called out his apology and asked for her forgiveness. Her name echoed from the high-vaulted roof, and he heard the anguish in his voice. Henry prostrated himself on the cold stone floor of the chapel and wept until he could weep no more.

Chapter Twenty

June 1504

Henry dined with his mother at Coldharbour, her austere London mansion by the Thames. She'd saved him from the depths of despair and helped restore his faith. She also nursed him through a dangerous bout of quinsy brought on by his long vigils in cold chapels while he tried to deal with his grief.

The illness made his throat swell until he struggled to breathe or eat anything other than a thin soup. Then came the coughing—a dry, hacking cough, each day more painful than the last. His doctors seemed at a loss when his condition worsened, despite their remedy of celandine, fenugreek and hedgehog fat.

He'd fallen into a stupor by the time his mother intervened with her prayers for his recovery. She sent his physicians away. Confining Henry to his bed, she told him he would not recover his health until he recovered his faith. She sent her chaplain and confessor, John Fisher, to help him understand that his loss must all be part of God's plan, his destiny.

Henry had been tortured by the knowledge Elizabeth would be alive if not for his ambition. He'd gambled with her life as easily as he'd rolled the dice or bet on the turn of a card. John Fisher proved a patient man and, in time, Henry's faith was restored, although his life would never be the same.

Now his mother was determined to help him build

his strength and ordered her servants to set out her best plate and silver for his visit. Although Henry knew she had taken a vow of chastity, with her husband's consent, she'd not taken a vow of poverty. Her household still included over four hundred servants and her interest in his finances was as keen as ever.

His mother studied him with a look of concern. He was used to it now and knew he looked thin, his face pale, with grey stubble and forever lined with the burden of his grief. She sat with the sun behind her, casting her face into shadow and reflecting from her white cowl in a halo of light.

Henry washed his hands in the silver bowl of rose-water, trying not to spill any on his mother's polished table. A young serving-girl avoided his eyes as she stepped forward and dried them on a white linen towel. A simple ritual, yet he'd never become used to the intimate touch of servants. After she finished he looked across the table at his mother.

'I had a letter from my daughter Margaret in Scotland.'

'How is she?'

'In truth, her letter reveals little. She wishes she was back here with us. I must show it to you, as I am concerned for her.'

'You know my view on the marriage. Your daughter is too young.' There was an edge of disapproval to her voice.

He remembered the last time he'd seen his daughter was the day she left for Scotland. Small for her thirteen years, she'd worn a heavy brocade gown that hid her girlish curves. Around her neck glittered a ruby pendant on a gold chain, a farewell present he'd given her. He'd also recognised Elizabeth's diamond ring on Margaret's finger. He pushed away the memory of his dead wife's cold hand in his.

His mother had been forceful in her concern that Margaret was too young. He knew she was mindful of her own brush with death, as she'd been only a year older than Margaret when he'd been born. He'd agreed a compromise and delayed his daughter's departure by eighteen months, but the time soon passed.

He escorted Margaret on her way to Scotland as far as his mother's mansion at Collyweston in the North. Henry was unsurprised when she made one last attempt to persuade him to wait until Margaret was sixteen but by then it was too late. Even though he understood her concern he had to let Margaret go.

Now his daughter was married to King James, a man more than twice her age, with a reputation for taking mistresses. Margaret accepted her destiny in good faith and understood her duty. Their union had put the seal on the truce with Scotland, uniting their nations in blood. As her carriage disappeared into the distance he'd worried he might never see her again.

Henry tasted his Rhenish wine and found it a little sharp, although he would not say so to his mother. His remaining teeth ached and his throat still felt painful after the quinsy. His physician cautioned him the damage might be permanent and suggested he should thank the Lord to have recovered at all.

Another of his mother's servants, a middle-aged woman dressed in her Beaufort livery, brought a pie decorated with pastry stag antlers. Henry still found he had little appetite. He left the thick crust to the side of his plate but tasted the meat. The fine venison was cooked in herbs and lightly spiced with cloves.

'You know this is one of my favourite dishes?'

She nodded. 'I wish to see you eat again, Henry. I have never seen you look so thin.'

'Will you come with me on a progress to Scotland?' Henry changed the subject. 'I should like to see my daughter, now she is a queen in her own right.'

His mother waited while her servant filled her Venetian glass with the watery mead she now drank. 'Once the issue of your widowed daughter-in-law is resolved.' She watched his face, waiting to see his reaction. 'Prince Harry has been betrothed to Princess Catherine for a year now.'

'We wait for the papal dispensation—and it suits us to delay. King Ferdinand has only paid half of the dowry he agreed.'

Henry pushed his plate of pie to one side and the servant took it away, replacing it with a dish of larks cooked in mace and ginger. He picked at the tiny bones, searching for the succulent meat. 'I shall have the dowry paid in full.'

'And in the meantime you keep Princess Catherine as a hostage to her misfortune?'

His mother was right. He'd been so overtaken by grief and illness he'd forgotten how difficult the uncertainty must be for Princess Catherine. It was Elizabeth, not him, who moved her from Ludlow to Durham Manor, a bishop's palace overlooking the Thames.

Henry took another sip of his wine. 'We had to wait to see if she was with child. After that...' He didn't want to talk about what happened after that.

'I understand she has never said her marriage was not consummated, yet that is what we must accept.'

'What about Prince Arthur's reputation?' Henry felt the old wound reopen.

It was unfortunate that he'd first heard the news from the Spanish Ambassador. Doctor Rodrigo de Puebla informed Henry that Doña Elvira, governess of Princess Catherine's household, had already confirmed to King Ferdinand that his daughter remained a virgin. Henry reacted with outrage before he'd understood the game they all played.

De Puebla claimed to have done his best to defend Prince Arthur's honour. Henry recalled how the stubborn Doña Elvira had tried to prevent him even seeing the princess at their first meeting. This could be her act of revenge, to slight the name of Tudor and blacken his son's memory.

His mother's chair creaked as she leaned forward. 'If you question her word, it will mean returning the princess to Spain, as well as her dowry.'

Henry frowned. 'I shall keep my silence, although the world knows they lived as man and wife.'

'Then we will wait for the dispensation—and you must prepare Prince Harry.'

Prince Harry had hardly spoken with him since Elizabeth's death, a situation Henry wished to correct without further delay. Even when he'd decided to make Harry Prince of Wales there were few words exchanged between them. He'd always been close to Elizabeth and Henry suspected he blamed him for her death.

He decided he would not risk allowing his second son to be based in the doomed castle at Ludlow. Instead he would be moved from Eltham to Richmond Palace, where he should begin to learn the duties of a king. He summoned Harry to tell him the good news.

Harry was already taller than Henry, with the solid build and confidence of his maternal grandfather. He wore a fashionable doublet and had an iridescent feather in his cap. A silver dagger shone at his belt and he wore a thick gold chain around his neck.

He also had something his self-opinionated tutors might have taught him but Henry doubted it. Harry had a presence, a strength of character he'd never seen in Arthur. He was young, yet he had the makings of a king.

'Come out to the stables,' Henry grinned as he greeted his son, 'I have something for you.'

They crossed the cobble-stoned stable yard to where one of Henry's grooms held a lively black stallion by the bridle. Henry patted its neck. The horse was the finest he had ever seen and cost him a small fortune.

'It's yours, Harry, a present to celebrate your birthday.'

Harry grinned. 'You remembered.'

'Thirteen years.' Henry studied his son, much as he had the horse. 'You're big enough for this horse now— a destrier, a worthy mount for the joust.'

'Thank you, Father. It's the finest horse I've ever seen.' Harry ran a hand over its smooth flank. 'Does it have a name?'

'Draig.' Welsh for dragon. Like me, he was born in Wales.'

'Might I ride him,' Harry pleaded, 'in the tourney?'

'You may try him at the quintain first.' Henry grinned at his son's eagerness. 'You must have the measure of him before you try him in a joust.'

With a jolt he recalled the men he'd seen die jousting. He'd wished Arthur would ride at the joust but realised he could not afford to take such risks with his sole surviving heir. He would watch over Harry, keep him close, keep him safe.

Henry designed the royal apartments at Richmond Palace to allow for privacy. Before the fire at the old palace of Sheen, his rooms were connected to Elizabeth's by a long, narrow corridor. Poorly-lit, the floorboards used to creak. The passageway was also used by servants, who would scuttle back and forth like mice in the kitchens.

The rebuilding improved this arrangement with a private interconnecting door. Henry often used it to visit Elizabeth without the need to pass his guards and servants, who had their own door and stairway leading to the service accommodation.

He'd not been in the queen's apartments since her death, so it felt strange to open the door and step into her room. He lifted his hand to knock, as he once used to out of courtesy, as if he half expected to see her there, surrounded by her gossiping ladies. Her outer chamber was exactly as he remembered, with colourful tapestries to brighten the walls, and the low, silk covered chairs.

It had taken him more than a year to come to terms with his loss and he'd kept Elizabeth's room exactly as she left it, a shrine to her memory. His mother persuaded him the room should be used by Prince Harry, now he'd moved with his growing retinue of tutors and servants from Eltham Palace. It would give them the chance to know each other better and he'd be able to keep an eye on him.

He stood there, remembering Elizabeth. If he closed his eyes he could picture her, working on her embroidery by the light of the window, looking up at him with a twinkle in her eye. He imagined he could hear her in her bedchamber, singing in her soft, tuneful voice as she prepared for bed.

He opened his eyes and realised he wasn't imagining it. Someone was in Elizabeth's bedchamber. A woman, probably a servant. He frowned in annoyance, as he'd wanted a private moment in her room. Crossing to the closed door, he reached for the handle then hesitated. The singing stopped at the sound of his footsteps.

Henry pushed the door open and stared. Lady Katheryn Gordon's blue eyes held his for a moment. He'd not seen her for so long the sight of her brought back a confusion of repressed memories. While he'd aged with illness and grief, she looked as beautiful as ever. She sat at the elegant desk where Elizabeth once wrote her letters, with a quill in her hand.

She stopped her work and stood to curtsey as he entered. 'Your Grace.' Her voice still had the soft Scottish accent he'd found so attractive.

'I...' Henry struggled to think why she should be there. He'd not been alone with her since their first meeting, when she'd bewitched him into being lenient with her errant husband. He knew it wasn't right for them to have been alone together that first time and they should not be alone together now.

He realised she wore one of the dresses he'd given her, a rich black-and-crimson velvet gown with gold embroidery. A coif and formal hood hid her hair, making her look older. He guessed she must be about thirty now but she still retained her slender figure.

She seemed to understand his awkwardness. 'Lady Margaret asked me to note everything in the room, before we have the servants clear it.' She gestured to the desk where she'd been working on a list.

Henry realised it wasn't too late to change his mind.

There were other apartments that would suit Prince Harry, although none so close. A part of him wished to cling to Elizabeth's memory. It seemed as if by clearing her rooms all trace of her would be lost.

The lid of one of her wooden chests was open and there was a casket on the table, next to some leather bound books belonging to Elizabeth, including her precious book of hours.

He looked at Lady Katheryn. 'I thought you might return—to Scotland?' He'd given no thought to what became of Elizabeth's ladies-in-waiting. The year had passed in a dark emptiness of grief and illness, with his mother doing what she could to deal with matters in his prolonged absence.

'My life is here, Your Grace. Lady Margaret took me into her household and has shown me kindness.'

'I didn't know...'

'I was sorry... about the queen, Your Grace.' Her voice was soft. Hesitant to talk about his loss, she took one step closer to him then stopped, as if unsure what to say or do.

Henry spotted neat piles of Elizabeth's clothes behind her on the bed and crossed over to them. He picked up one of her white gloves. The fingers seemed too small, as if meant for a child. He wanted to remember her as the beautiful, intelligent woman she had once been, not the pale shadow, clinging to life on her deathbed.

'I wish these gloves as a keepsake. The rest of her clothes must go.' He glanced across at the desk. 'I'll also take her book of hours.'

'There is some jewellery, Your Grace.' Lady Katheryn took the casket from the table and opened the lid before handing it to him.

Henry examined the contents. Diamonds glinted in the light amidst gold broaches, rings and necklaces. He reached in and took out a pearl necklace. It had been a present from him, one of Elizabeth's favourites. He held it up to take a closer look. Each pearl was perfect and glowed with an incandescent light.

'I would like you to have this, for your service to the queen.' He handed her the necklace.

She hesitated, then stepped forward. 'I shall treasure her memory.'

Henry smiled. They had been an unlikely pairing. He would never have expected his wife to have befriended the wife of his adversary, but then Lady Katheryn was no ordinary lady-in-waiting. She was a cousin to the Scottish King, now linked to the Tudors through his daughter's marriage.

'Let me help you with it.'

'You want me to wear it now?'

He held it out in both hands and she turned so he could fasten it at the back of her neck. The gold clasp was a delicate test for his eyesight but he managed and stepped back. He'd been so close he felt the warmth of her neck.

She faced him and examined the pearls. 'They are exquisite, Your Grace.' her eyes sparkled. 'Thank you.'

Henry watched as she crossed to Elizabeth's table where she'd been working. Dipping her quill in ink she offered it to him. 'Might I ask you to initial the list, Your Grace.'

He crossed to the table and took the quill from her. 'I must confess my sight is not so perfect as it was for reading—although I see your writing is impeccable. She smiled and guided his hand to the item on the list. He breathed her delicate perfume as he wrote *gift to Lady*

Kateryn and initialled it. An idea occurred to him.

'I'm concerned about my daughter, Margaret. Since she married your cousin I've heard little from her. I will recommend you as her lady-in-waiting.' He studied her face, watching for her reaction. 'You could become my agent in the Scottish court and tell me how she is?'

Lady Katheryn's eyes widened at his suggestion. 'Your lady mother is in mourning for her late husband. She has little need for my company. If you wish me to return to Scotland, then...'

'Or you could assist me?' The thought had been forming at the back of his mind from the moment he'd seen her in Elizabeth's room. He felt as flustered as a young boy as he realised how his suggestion would sound. 'Bishop Foxe, my secretary, has his duties in Winchester. The cleric who helps with my letters is a worthy man yet poor company.'

She smiled again. 'I would be honoured, Your Grace. although...'

'You are concerned at what people might say?'

Katheryn nodded. 'Not for my reputation.'

'Let them say what they wish. I will speak to my mother, Lady Katheryn, and welcome you to my household.'

Chapter Twenty-One

June 1505

Henry decided to visit Princess Catherine. He'd heard disconcerting rumours about the growing number of Spanish courtiers now living at Durham House, the bishop's palace by the Thames. He had also received complaints from her about her allowance and decided to see her situation for himself.

Ambassador de Puebla, his trusted source of information on the health of the princess, had fallen ill. Instead, he had to rely on the arrogant Don Pedro de Ayala, who accompanied him as they rode from Westminster.

'I regret to tell you the princess is in great debt, Your Grace. She finds it difficult to manage her household on her current allowance.'

Henry glanced across at him, noting the implied criticism in the Spaniard's words. 'I've heard as much from Doctor Puebla, although I also know she brought a fortune in jewels from Spain as part of her dowry.'

Don Pedro shook his head. 'Princess Catherine had no choice but to sell some of her jewels. The rest are used as collateral for loans, which now become due.'

'I don't see why she has to maintain such a household. Many of those who arrived with her have returned to Spain?'

'They have, Your Grace, including Doña Elvira, who kept her household in order.'

'Her governess is gone?' Henry remembered the stern Doña Elvira and wasn't sorry he'd not see her again. Doctor Puebla disliked her and suggested she was a bad influence on the princess.

'Doña Elvira became blind in one eye, Your Grace, and retired back to her homeland. I've done what I can to support the princess and informed her father of her plight—yet I must confess you will find her in reduced circumstances.'

The news jolted a memory for Henry. His mother had told him to make proper provision for Princess Catherine. Grief and his own poor health had distracted him from attending to her welfare and now Don Pedro's words troubled him.

When they arrived at Durham House the scene was one of a hasty attempt to conceal disorder. Henry sensed that Don Pedro sent word ahead to prepare for his visit but he wasn't fooled. He knew the signs of a poorly run household. Well-trodden rushes crackled underfoot and cold ashes spilled over the neglected hearth. It seemed Princess Catherine was missing her formidable housekeeper.

Princess Catherine appeared wearing a long-sleeved mourning gown, her hair covered with a black Spanish hood. Born two months after his coronation, she would now be nineteen years old, a reminder of how long he'd been on the throne.

'Welcome, Your Grace.' She curtseyed but her face remained impassive.

Henry studied her for a moment. He noted a plain silver crucifix worn on a chain under a hint of a double chin. He also noted the neat repairs to the sleeves and hem of her gown. It seemed Don Pedro might be right about her hardship.

'Good day, Princess Catherine. I've not seen you since the loss of your mother and offer my condolences.' He replied in French, a language they shared.

'Thank you, Your Grace, it has been a difficult time for us all.' Her English was little improved since their last meeting. She stared back at him with sadness in her eyes. 'May I speak with you—in private?'

Henry glanced at Don Pedro. 'Of course.'

She led him into a room that smelt of cheap tallow candles, with views out over the gardens leading to the river. Again, he noted the old rushes under his feet. Her allowance should provide for such things. Henry realised Catherine was struggling to find the words as she clasped her hands together.

'Please do not abandon me, Your Grace.' She spoke again in French and the pleading in her voice was unmistakable.

Henry raised his eyebrows. 'I have not... abandoned you, Princess Catherine.' He glanced around the well-appointed room. 'You have a fine palace—and more people in attendance than I can count.'

'I have no money left. The allowance you provided has stopped and I've had to sell the jewellery and gold plate I brought with me from Spain to pay for food for myself and my household.' She spoke so fast her shrill voice sounded hysterical, with her Spanish accent returning.

Henry took a step back. He'd forgotten to renew her allowance and guessed she wished to ask him for more money. All the same, the passion of her outburst left him speechless for a moment. He should not have agreed to see her without the ambassador.

She stared at him with wild eyes. 'My good mother is

dead and my father refuses to send me money. He wrote that I am to depend on Your Grace for my maintenance. I am the widow of one of your sons and betrothed to another, yet I must dress in rags and eat pottage—like a servant?'

'I will increase your allowance to a hundred pounds, and will write to your father about your dowry, which remains an obstacle between us. In the meantime, you must reduce the number of your household to only those necessary.'

As he returned to Westminster, Henry resolved to keep a closer eye on Princess Catherine. It had been a mistake to leave her to her own devices. Without her governess, she had whittled away her fortune.

All he wished was to end the drawn-out wrangling over the dowry and make the best marriage he could for his son. Bishop Foxe devised a plan to break the deadlock, yet now Henry had to explain it, the whole idea troubled him.

Prince Harry appeared confused. 'So does that mean I will no longer marry Princess Catherine, Father?' He'd taken to pacing the room, as Henry did when he was agitated. He still wore his heavy riding boots and they clumped on the wooden floorboards. He also wore a short sword, hanging low at his belt.

Henry shook his head. 'The death of Queen Isabella means King Ferdinand no longer has the same importance as an ally.'

'I don't see what difference that makes, Father. I am old enough to marry now—and to start a family, if I wish to.'

He'd not expected Harry to object, although he had been told he'd marry Princess Catherine on the eve of his fourteenth birthday. Henry didn't want to compromise his relationship with his son yet had to listen to his advisors. Harry was young and impatient, so all Henry could do was hope he would learn the value of waiting until the time was right.

Queen Isabella's death was not completely unexpected. She'd been waning for some three years, since the death of her only son. Henry could identify with that and wished he'd taken the trouble to know her better. By all accounts she was a shrewd woman and could have encouraged her husband's scheming.

'We have to think about what is best for you, Harry. Her mother's death means Catherine is no longer a true princess, other than as your brother's widow.'

Harry stopped his pacing and turned to him in surprise. 'Does her father not inherit his wife's titles?'

'That would normally be the case, but Queen Isabella's titles in Castile are inherited by her daughter, Joanna, who is of course Catherine's sister—and wife of Duke Philip of Burgundy.'

Harry scowled as he tried to understand the politics. 'So why must I protest against the marriage? I wish to marry her.'

Henry raised an eyebrow. He'd encouraged his son to be forthright but he often overstepped the mark, as if testing him. Part of the problem was he'd grown up surrounded by servants and women, with tutors who were clerics and academics.

'Our advisors, Bishop Foxe and others, suggest a repudiation of your marriage will strengthen our hand in the dowry negotiations.'

'And when the remainder of the dowry is paid, then I will marry Princess Catherine?'

'In good time, once we have the papal dispensation.'

'My tutors told me the Borgia pope is dead, thought

to have been poisoned?' There was a boyish note of relish in his tone at the thought.

'They are right, although the pope was over seventy and in poor health. Whatever the cause of his death, we understand he sent a messenger with the dispensation to Queen Isabella on her deathbed, although we have not had sight of it. In truth, I expect it might be some time before they attend to our request.'

'What is to become of Princess Catherine in the meantime, Father?'

'The princess must wait, like us, for events to take their course.'

'Am I permitted to visit her?'

'Of course. I understand she likes to hunt with hawks—perhaps you could escort her to the forests at Eltham?'

'I should like to, Father.'

'Now if you'll come with me, you must make your renouncement.'

He led Harry to a poorly-lit room where Bishop Foxe waited with Lord Daubeney and the witnesses, James Read, the notary, and Henry's cleric, who held out a quill for Harry to sign the parchment.

Harry took the quill but challenged Henry before signing the document. 'Will Princess Catherine not be distressed when she learns of this, Father?'

'She will understand.' It troubled him that it suited his purposes for Catherine to react badly to the news. He was certain her Spanish entourage would waste no time in alerting King Ferdinand to the situation.

He watched as his son signed with a flourish. 'Now you must read it, aloud, in front of these witnesses.'

Harry picked up the parchment and studied it for a moment. He began reading, his voice, already deepening in the low-ceilinged room, sounding a little self-conscious.

'Being under age I was married to the Princess Catherine, yet now coming of age, I do not confirm that marriage...' He gave Henry a questioning glance. 'I retract and annul it, and will not proceed with it but intend to break it off, which I do freely and without compulsion.'

Henry ignored Harry's scowl and prayed it was not too late to build an understanding with his son. He could have allowed the marriage to proceed, as he had half the dowry and the rest would follow. At the same time, he had to listen to Bishop Foxe, who always took the long view.

He resolved to confide in Harry next time they were in private together. He'd told no one yet, but it might be best for Princess Catherine to return to Spain with her entourage. He could try to find a better match for his son, as whoever he chose would one day be Queen of England.

Sir Thomas Lovell cursed as he read the letter from Edmund de la Pole. The Earl of Suffolk had written to Henry from his exile requesting safe conduct for his return to England. He also wished for his confiscated lands to be returned.

'It seems things have not gone well for him, Your Grace!' Sir Thomas sounded pleased with the news.

Henry agreed. 'I confess to some satisfaction to know he is imprisoned in Hattem Castle by the Duke of Guelders—although I'd expect to be the last person he'd ask to intervene.'

'Suffolk has few enough options, Your Grace, to be making such demands.'

'He also asks to be restored to our favour, as if his disloyalty is to be rewarded!'

Sir Thomas grunted. 'These things are rarely what they seem. Do you think his hosts have put him up to this?'

'I do. Archduke Philip of Burgundy and Maximilian agreed to offer him no sanctuary—in return for my ten thousand pounds. Having him imprisoned allows them to appear to be keeping their word.' He smiled at his old friend. 'We are at peace with France, for now at least, and the Spanish would not wish to compromise Princess Catherine's marriage.'

'But we must not forget he is a Plantagenet...'

'No one would say Suffolk has a claim to the throne?' Henry felt the old stab of misgiving return. It seemed that whenever he began to feel secure, something like this happened to remind him of the fragile hold he had on his crown.

Sir Thomas shrugged. 'We must not underestimate our enemies, for that is what they are. Our agents report that Suffolk borrowed a fortune in his efforts to raise support for an invasion.'

Henry cursed. 'I suppose he thinks if I could do it...'

'We've tracked down as many of Suffolk's supporters and relations as we can find. It gave me no pleasure, Your Grace, but many are arrested and imprisoned.'

'How many?' Henry had been too preoccupied with his grief to worry at the time.

'Last year more than fifty were attainted.'

'I had no idea there were so many. I trust you've not been over zealous in your work, Sir Thomas?'

'There are no doubt more we have yet to uncover. You cannot afford to show leniency to Suffolk, Your Grace.'

'I do not intend to   but what do you suggest?'

'We must ensure he doesn't slip through our fingers again. I suggest we negotiate with Archduke Philip and this Duke of Guelders.' He gave Henry a knowing look. 'We might have to trick him into returning here—then he must be locked up in the Tower.'

'I shall leave it to your conscience, Sir Thomas, but keep me informed?'

'Of course, Your Grace. You may rely on it.'

♔

Henry's mother became a widow yet again at the end of July. He found her in her chapel, holding a vigil for her late husband, who died in his beloved Lancashire and was buried in the family tomb at Lathom.

He waited until she finished praying then laid his hand on her shoulder. 'I grieve for the loss of another of those who proved so loyal when I first came to the throne.'

His mother nodded. 'His passing serves as a reminder of our own mortality, Henry. I have paid for masses to be said for his soul. He was a good man— and will be missed.'

Henry agreed. 'He was the last of the great Lancastrians, one of a kind.'

'Yet he found it within his heart to be loyal to York when it suited him.' His mother allowed a rare smile. 'He fought on both sides but also built alliances.'

'I owe him a debt. We would not have found victory at Bosworth without him.'

'I thought he would be executed by King Richard. Those were dark times, Henry. It seemed I would lose everything, including my husband, yet he was spared, by God's grace.'

He took a taper and lit a candle for Sir Thomas Stanley, Earl of Derby, and prayed to the Holy Virgin that he had finally found peace.

Henry worked in his study in Westminster Palace, going through the pile of chamber accounts which had built up there. Lady Katheryn had become invaluable to him now, as she read out each page in her soft Scottish voice. He would then dictate any notes and he would initial the entry.

Katheryn soon learnt to spot items that needed checking and already knew more about his finances than she should. She'd also shown a talent for helping with his correspondence. Unlike his previous clerks, she often helped with ideas and suggestions for the wording of his replies.

It amused him to think his courtiers no doubt suspected they were having an affair, spending so much time alone together. In truth, she cared for him more like a mother than a wife. She worried about him eating properly and consigned his pet monkey to the menagerie at the Tower.

He knew his mother would disapprove. Even Elizabeth had less influence over matters of state and had never been allowed to see the court accounts. Henry knew he could rely on Lady Katheryn to keep her contributions confidential, along with the growing number of secrets they shared.

She held a letter for him to see. 'From Doctor de Puebla, ambassador to Spain, regarding the niece of King Ferdinand, Joanna of Naples.'

'What does he say?'

'He confirms she is still unmarried. He also adds that King Ferdinand has remarried, to Germaine de Foix, the seventeen-year-old niece of the French king.'

Henry twisted in his chair to see her better. 'Ferdinand is hoping for a new male heir to the crown of Castile—and now has an alliance with France.' He smiled at her. 'I've observed the proper time of mourning now—perhaps it's time I sought a wife.'

'Do you know they say you were planning to take Princess Catherine for yourself?'

Henry laughed at the thought.

'It was true?' She didn't share his amusement.

'My mother told me I was out of my mind. Perhaps I was, although it always was King Ferdinand's ambition for his daughter to be Queen of England.'

'Why would you choose this... Joanna?'

'Is that jealousy I hear?' He was surprised to see the colour rise to her cheeks.

'I am curious.'

'The suggestion came from Queen Isabela shortly before she died. I have her letter somewhere. Her niece Joanna is a wealthy widow.'

'How old is she?'

Henry did a quick calculation on his fingers. 'Twenty-seven now. I've never seen a portrait and de Puebla is a great flatterer, so whatever he says about her...'

'You must send an envoy, someone like Bishop Foxe, whose opinion you can trust.'

'You are right, Katheryn, although I cannot say the good bishop is much of an expert on the fairer sex.' He chuckled at the thought and rang for his servant.

Since Elizabeth's day, he valued his privacy more and instructed his servants to wait out of sight until he summoned them with a bell. Another change was he now drank wine while he was working and often shared it with Katheryn.

The young serving-girl curtseyed. 'Yes, Your Grace?'

'Bring the good wine, if you will—and two goblets.'

As she scuttled away he gave Katheryn a meaningful look. 'You know why I must remarry?'

Her reply was interrupted by the serving-girl returning with a carafe of red wine and two silver goblets. He watched in silence as she filled them and waited until she left and closed the door behind her.

Katheryn moved closer to Henry to reach for her drink. 'There is no better way to strengthen your alliances.'

'That's true enough, although sometimes I believe God's plan has a part in it.' Henry tasted the sweet wine, feeling it soothing his throat. She was so close he could feel her warmth. 'My mother made the match with Elizabeth to win over the Yorkists.'

'Yet you fell in love with her,' Katheryn's eyes never left his face as she sipped from her goblet, 'the daughter of your enemy?'

Henry shook his head. 'I never thought of her father as my enemy. He promised to treat me well if I returned from exile.'

'But you didn't trust him—and came with an army!'

'They tried to trick me into boarding a ship—who knows what would have become of me after King Edward died...'

'You managed to escape.'

'Yes, but nothing so heroic as it might sound. I pretended to be too ill to sail, then ran off as if my life depended on it.'

She laughed and refilled their goblets from the carafe. 'So... what will you look for in a wife?'

Henry took another deep drink as he thought. It seemed impossible that any wife could ever match

Elizabeth. For a moment he struggled with the deep sense of loss. He should have involved her more, confided in her, as he did so easily with Katheryn.

'She would have to be young enough to bear me another son.' He smiled. 'It would be easier for me if she was pretty.'

Katheryn gave him a look of mock disapproval. 'I thought this was to be a political marriage?'

'She would have to come from a noble family, although if she is wealthy...' He took another drink.

'We shall have to draw up a list of questions for your envoy to Naples.'

Henry laughed at the thought. 'I thank you for being so understanding, Lady Katheryn.'

She raised her goblet in pretend formality. 'A toast, Your Grace. To the perfect marriage.'

He raised his goblet in reply and smiled at the mischief twinkling in her eyes. 'To marriage, whatever destiny provides.'

'You sound doubtful?'

Henry nodded. 'I must confess my conscience is still troubled. I should have treated Elizabeth better. I didn't realise until it was too late.'

'I'm sorry.' Katheryn placed her hand on his arm. 'I spent much time with her, towards the end, and can tell you she bore you no ill feeling.'

He found her touch comforting. 'I should dedicate what remains of this life to preparing the way for my son.'

She smiled. 'Harry is grown into a fine young man now.'

'But do you think he has what it takes to be king?'

Chapter Twenty-Two

March 1506

Henry's court was at Windsor Castle when savage gales hit London. The brass eagle weather-vane from the highest spire of St Paul's Cathedral toppled with a crash into the churchyard. The more superstitious of his courtiers were agreeing this was a bad omen when a messenger arrived with news of another consequence of the storm.

The fleet of Archduke Philip had been caught in the tempest and sought refuge near Weymouth. It seemed to Henry that providence had brought the duke to him. As well as securing a stronger alliance, he hoped to negotiate the return of the exiled Edmund de la Pole. If necessary, he planned to hold Duke Philip hostage until he agreed terms.

Henry rode out to welcome him with Prince Harry riding at his side. He wore his new scarlet riding coat and was followed by five earls and a dozen armed knights with several hundred retainers, so they appeared like an advancing army.

The duke looked exhausted from his journey, with several day's growth of beard, but in good spirits as they met. 'Good day, Your Grace!' Duke Philip held up a hand in greeting. He studied Henry's entourage waiting on horses behind him. 'You seem to have brought half your household, Your Grace.'

Henry smiled. 'I understand you sailed with an army

of several thousand German mercenaries?'

The duke grinned with disarming charm. 'And I have left them, guarding my ships.'

'We give thanks God chose to bring you safely to our shores, Archduke Philip.'

'We were on our way to Spain in some of the worst seas I've ever encountered.' The duke shook his head at the memory. 'The storm raged for days. I lost three of my ships and the rest were taking on water. I thank God I was spared.'

Henry escorted the duke to Windsor and invited him into the warmth of his chamber, where a crackling log fire kept the unseasonable chill at bay. Magnificent tapestries of hunting scenes decorated the walls. Tall glazed windows flooded the room with light and provided views across the deer park.

He waited as the duke was served a cup of hot mulled wine. When they last met, he fitted his nickname of 'Philip the handsome' well. He'd even charmed Elizabeth, as well as her ladies. Duke Philip was still an impressive figure but had put on weight with fine food and easy living.

Henry already knew the reason the duke risked the long sea voyage without waiting for the storms to pass. He'd braved the Atlantic tempests because he wished to be crowned King of Castile. He couldn't wait to claim his wife's inheritance and had to act before his father-in-law turned the Castilians against him.

'Did your lady wife sail with you, Duke Philip?'

'She insisted on it,' the duke gave Henry a meaningful look, 'although after the storms I expect she might have regretted her decision.'

'We must bring her here to Windsor. I will have her sister Catherine sent for and we shall have a banquet in their honour.'

The duke hesitated before replying. 'I must confess that my wife is not well, Your Grace, which is why she remains in the west.'

Henry took a step backwards despite himself. Harry was with him at Windsor Castle. He lived in constant fear of his son falling ill. Although the duke looked well enough, he knew how easily he could lose a healthy son.

'Not a fever, I trust?'

The duke shook his head. 'She is strong enough to fight off a fever.' He glanced around to see if they could be overheard and his tone became conspiratorial. 'Since the loss of her mother she has been afflicted by a madness. Sometimes she seems as she always was— then she becomes... a mad woman.' He frowned. 'I regret she might have to be placed in a nunnery for her own protection.'

Henry heard the coldness in the duke's voice. 'I am sorry to hear that, Duke Philip.'

The duke nodded. 'It has been difficult for us both, although with God's grace we will find a way.

'I shall still have her brought here. I wish to honour the Queen of Castile.'

Henry sat in a high-backed gilded chair on the raised stage, under a cloth of gold canopy of estate, for the welcoming festivities in the great hall of Windsor Castle. Duke Philip, as guest of honour, sat to his right with the ambassador, Don Pedro and his senior nobles. Henry's mother sat to his left, with Prince Harry and his daughter Mary, who would soon be celebrating her tenth birthday.

Unlike Harry, who grew more like a Plantagenet each day, Mary already had the willowy beauty of the

Woodville women. She'd inherited Henry's love of music and often reminded him of her mother. Mary had also become a great favourite of her grandmother and sometimes showed signs of Lady Margaret's Beaufort steel.

As well as providing them with the best view of the entertainments, the red carpeted stage meant they looked down on the other guests. These were seated around the walls of the long hall, leaving an open dance floor in the centre.

Musicians tuned their instruments and played a few lively bars on fiddles and flutes, creating an air of anticipation as the guests assembled. Henry turned to his mother, who'd been responsible for arranging the evening's entertainments.

'What have you planned for us tonight, lady Mother?'

'You will not be disappointed.' Lady Margaret glanced at Duke Philip, who had already emptied one goblet of wine and was eyeing young ladies as he started on the next. 'And neither will your guest.' The note of disapproval in her voice was only heard by Henry.

Heads turned as the herald announced the arrival of Princess Catherine of Aragon. He'd expected Catherine to be resentful following the delays to her marriage to Harry. Instead, she'd flourished since being presented at court.

She wore a magnificent gown of scarlet velvet with a row of gold scallop shells decorating the square neckline. In place of the plain silver crucifix she wore a gold collar studded with diamonds, which sparkled in the light.

Flanked by two attractive Spanish ladies-in-waiting, Catherine looked ready to become a queen. She stared up at Henry and glanced once at Harry, seated at his side, before her elegant curtsey.

'Good evening, Your Grace,' she turned her head towards Harry, 'and to you, my lord prince.' She spoke in passable English.

'Your understanding of English improves, Princess Catherine.'

'I've had some,' she struggled for the right word, '*tuition* from your daughter, Princess Mary, Your Grace.'

'Good.' Henry gestured towards the duke. 'May I present Duke Philip, soon to be crowned King of Castile.'

Princess Catherine curtseyed to the duke. 'It is a pleasure to meet you, Duke Philip. I should like to see my sister Joanna?' She spoke to him in rapid Spanish.

The duke glanced at Henry. 'My wife has been sent for. She should arrive in a day or so.' He replied in Spanish.

After she left the duke turned to Henry. 'She wishes to see her sister,' he explained. 'You would do well to watch her. You know she tells her father everything?'

The musicians struck up a traditional dance before Henry could reply. He turned to watch. Harry had already joined in and danced with an attractive lady Henry had never seen before. He glanced around for Lady Katheryn to ask her who it was and spotted her dancing with a handsome young courtier. He felt a flicker of jealousy and made a mental note to find out who the young man was.

Princess Catherine approached the duke and spoke to him in Spanish. Henry didn't understand what they said but Duke Philip was shaking his head. Curious, Henry leant across.

'She asked you to dance with her?'

The duke gave him a wry look. 'I told her I'm a

mariner—not a dancer.'

Henry grinned. 'That's not what I recall from our last meeting at Guisnes Castle.'

The duke gave him a knowing look and glanced across at Catherine. 'Her father would claim the throne of Castile if he could.'

'I consider her father an important ally...'

'Yet you recognise my right to Castile?'

Henry nodded. 'I would feel obliged to—if you return the traitor, Edmund de la Pole.'

Duke Philip sat back in his chair. 'I promised not to support him—but not to send him to his death.' There was an arrogant edge to his voice, suggesting he had no idea he'd be held in England until he agreed.

The dance floor cleared except for Henry's daughter Mary, who prepared to play her lute. She wore a blue silk gown, trimmed with gold lace, which Henry had bought for her. She looked up at him with shining eyes. He felt a flutter of concern for her as a group of young courtiers laughed at some shared joke. It would be difficult for Mary to hold the attention of her audience.

Then she began to play, her slender young fingers moving with amazing skill. Henry recognised the piece immediately as Elizabeth's favourite. Seeing Princess Mary dressed like her mother, Henry's heart filled with pride and sadness. Elizabeth would have loved to see her daughter play with such confidence in tribute to her.

When she finished to a thunder of applause, two servants carried her clavichord onto the dance floor. Although intended more for practice than for concerts, as she began to sing the room fell silent, spellbound by her clear young voice.

Princess Mary stood and gave a graceful curtsey after

her performance to more rapturous applause. The servants carried away her instruments and she was joined by Catherine and one of her Spanish ladies, with the ambassador Don Pedro and two handsome young Spanish nobles as partners.

Henry's minstrels were replaced with Princess Catherine's musicians, who began playing a haunting Spanish dance, accompanied by drummers who struck up a rhythmic, hypnotic beat.

With their partners kneeling on one knee, Catherine, Mary and the Spanish lady swirled around them in circles, their long gowns billowing out as they spun. Henry watched in amazement to see how well his daughter had learnt the formal Spanish dance. He also noticed Prince Harry catch Catherine's eye, grinning and applauding with the others.

Looking beautiful in her scarlet gown, Princess Catherine took the central role in the dance. Mary and her lady deferred to her as she danced with each of the men in turn, and even Don Pedro bowed to her when their dance ended.

Henry knew this was no spontaneous act on Catherine's part. She must have taught Mary and rehearsed every move, as their dancing was striking and accomplished, arranged to display her importance to Duke Philip and also to attract Prince Harry. His mother must have helped her bring her own musicians to Windsor. Henry realised he must not under estimate Princess Catherine.

He was alone in his private apartments in the new three-storey tower he'd had built when his servant announced that Princess Catherine wished to see him. He was about to turn her away, mindful of her outburst at the bishop's palace, then his curiosity got the better of him. He suspected she wished to warn him about Duke Philip, her father's rival.

'Thank you for seeing me, Your Grace.'

He could see concern in her eyes and realised something important had happened. 'What is it?'

'Might we speak in French, Your Grace?' Her face reddened. 'I am still finding English a difficult language.'

'Of course.' Henry replied in French.

'My sister... Joanna has arrived here in Windsor.'

'Good. I look forward to meeting her.'

'That's why I've asked to see you. Her husband is telling everyone she is mad and should be locked away.' Her Spanish accent returned. 'My sister told me he plans to rule Castile without her, Your Grace. He has treated her without respect and takes mistresses to dishonour her.'

Henry shook his head. 'Duke Philip said your father wishes to rule in her place. Is that true?'

Princess Catherine's eyes widened in surprise. 'He would not wish my sister to be treated like this.' She studied his face, as if trying to make a judgement. 'Will you see my sister Joanna, in private, to hear her side?'

Henry nodded. 'I had her brought here for exactly that reason. Bring her to me.'

Catherine curtseyed. 'Thank you, Your Grace.'

After she left, Henry reflected on the implications of what she'd told him. He recalled his Uncle Jasper telling him about the madness of his own stepbrother, King Henry VI. Once, in his grief, he'd thought he was going mad. If what Catherine told him was true, it would be the cruellest trick Duke Philip could play on his wife. At the same time, he would expect Catherine to protect her sister's interests.

A knock on the door announced their arrival and his servant showed them in. Queen Joanna wore a blue gown so dark it made her look as if she was in mourning. She had the same round face, blue eyes and reddish-gold hair as Catherine, showing under an embroidered Spanish coif. They both curtseyed and he invited them to come in and take a seat.

Joanna spoke first, in accented but fluent French. 'I am honoured to meet you, Your Grace.' She attempted a smile. 'You will forgive me but I speak little English.'

Henry returned her smile and replied in French. 'The honour is mine, Queen Joanna. I have heard much about you.'

He felt pity for Catherine's attractive elder sister and her plight appealed to his sense of chivalry. Although she was one of the richest women in Spain and a queen in her own right, he sensed her deep despair.

Princess Catherine turned to her sister. 'King Henry wishes you to speak the truth about your situation. You must speak freely.'

Joanna took a deep breath. 'I am not mad, although my husband and my father conspire to drive me insane.'

'Your father?'

Joanna nodded. 'My father declared I am unfit to rule. He persuaded the Castilian nobles he should rule in my place—and even had coins minted, naming him as king. Now we fear my husband will go to war with him for the crown of Castile....'

'Which is why he sails with so many German mercenaries?' Henry understood now, although he didn't see what he could do about it.

He sat between his mother and the duke at the

banquet. The Bishop of London said a long grace, then Henry's liveried servants carried in the first course, civet of hare, venison from the king's herd and a loin of veal, covered with saffron and flavoured with cloves. Henry tore a chunk of bread and dipped it in the rich sauce.

He turned to the duke. 'I have a proposal for you regarding Edmund de la Pole.' Henry studied the man and realised he was already a little the worse for drink.

The duke held up his empty goblet for a servant to refill. 'With respect, Your Grace, I've already told you I'll not return him to have you cut off his head.' As if to make his point, he cut a trencher of bread from a loaf with his knife.

'I'm prepared to give you my word he'll not be executed. I need you to order his transfer to Calais. He would have to face trial for treason—but I can exercise my prerogative if he is found guilty.' Henry could see the duke was wavering now, and it might be his best chance.

A servant brought a sturgeon cooked in parsley and covered with powdered ginger, as well as a fierce pike with savage teeth, which appeared to be snarling from its silver platter, surrounded by small silver eels to represent the water.

Duke Philip chose the sturgeon. 'Perhaps it was destiny that blew us onto your shores, King Henry, as I would be happy to agree such an arrangement.' He cut a chunk of pale flesh from the sturgeon and tasted it. 'I have a proposal of my own.'

'What's that?'

'Duke Philip leant across. Your daughter, Princess Mary, is most talented.' He grinned. 'She would make a fine wife for my son Charles.'

Henry picked at a plate of fried whitebait. He liked

the tiny fish although his teeth were giving him trouble again. He knew the duke's son would be about six years old and would one day inherit not only the crown of Castile but also the duke's other lands in Burgundy and perhaps even Aragon.

He called for more wine and raised his silver goblet in the air. 'To our children, Duke Philip, and prosperity.'

As he drank the wine he glanced at his mother. She sat in silence at his side, missing nothing. He glimpsed a look of satisfaction on her face and realised the whole thing had been part of her plan.

The two last dishes were exotic fruits, gilt sugar-plums and pomegranates, in tribute to their Spanish guests. Henry turned to his mother.

'What do you think of the prospect of this marriage of Princess Mary, lady Mother?'

'After the days of his grandfather Maximilian, young Charles could become Emperor of Rome, with Mary at his side.'

Henry nodded. Such a marriage would bind their alliance against Ferdinand, as well as placing the Tudors at the centre of the world stage.

Henry decided to return to Richmond Palace as the leaves began to fall from the trees. Elizabeth's greyhound sprawled in front of the fire in his study as Lady Katheryn helped him deal with his letters.

'The pope has finally granted the dispensation for Prince Harry to marry Princess Catherine.' She held up the parchment with a large wax seal for Henry to see.

'I know. It was delivered by a papal emissary but I have been... too busy to acknowledge it.' He sat back in his chair. 'I have still not heard from Catherine's father. He plays games with us, Katheryn.'

'I doubt he ever intended to pay the dowry.' She lay the parchment down on the desk and stroked the greyhound, which raised its head, alerted by the tone of her voice.

For a moment it seemed to Henry as if Elizabeth was back in the room. With a jolt he realised Katheryn was wearing one of Elizabeth's gowns. She must have altered it to fit. He remembered the dress now, as he watched her stroke the dog's head, just as his wife used to.

He still didn't understand why Katheryn showed him such kindness, but he'd grown fond of her and relied on her every day now. He listened to her advice yet she never asked for favours for herself or others.

He realised she was waiting for his response. 'Perhaps you are right—but it's a matter of principle, despite all that has changed.'

Katheryn broke the seal on another letter and scanned the contents. 'Doctor Puebla says he has news of great importance that he must deliver in person.'

Henry sat up, intrigued. 'The ambassador has a taste for the theatrical—but send for him, if you will?'

'Do you think it concerns your daughter Mary's marriage?'

'God willing, Katheryn, God willing.'

The Spanish ambassador, Doctor Rodrigo de Puebla, was now only able to walk with the aid of a stick. His once jet-black hair showed ashen grey under his wide-brimmed Spanish hat, making him look even older than his advancing years. He sat heavily in one of Henry's chairs and explained the important news from Spain.

'It regards Archduke Philip, Your Grace, and I regret it is not good.'

'He is ill?' Henry had heard little from the duke since his visit to Windsor, although he had kept his word and Edmund de la Pole was now locked up in the Tower of London.

'He is dead, Your Grace.' De Puebla lowered his voice. 'They say from too much drink and womanizing, although he was a relatively young man—and well used to drinking.' He gave Henry a knowing look.

'You think he might have been poisoned?'

Henry guessed who might be the culprit. He was prepared to bet it would not be long before Ferdinand was crowned King of Castile. A thought occurred to him.

'What has become of Queen Joanna?'

'She tries to rule,' the ambassador shook his head, 'although she does not have the support of the noble families, who think she suffers with madness.'

'Nonsense!' Henry's chivalric instinct rose to protect her again, as it had when he met Joanna at Windsor Castle.

'I regret, Your Grace, it seems she has refused to permit the burial of her husband's body. I understand she has his coffin carried around with her... and keeps it in her chambers.'

True or not, Henry knew the story would have been enough for Ferdinand to have his daughter locked away. He would insist on it for her own good. He felt his plans unravelling in an instant. Ferdinand had won after all, and he would no doubt oppose the marriage of Princess Mary.

Chapter Twenty-Three

April 1507

Henry gasped for a drink. His throat was as dry as parchment and he could hardly speak. The dreaded quinsy had returned, causing a painful swelling in his throat that made it impossible to swallow. He'd taken to his bed in a weakened state and would only see his mother and physicians.

His mother stood at his bedside with a silver cup in her hand and a frown of concern on her face. 'You must take a sip, Henry.' Her voice carried stern authority, as if she was speaking to a small child.

He tried to reply. 'Pray for me...' His words rasped like the growl of old dog. He could see she struggled to understand. Leaning forward in his bed, he sipped the milk with sweet mead, warmed so it soothed his raw throat. Henry tried to swallow and choked, spluttering the drink over his embroidered silk coverlet.

He lay back and closed his eyes as he heard his mother calling in a shrill voice for the physician. She was always so controlled, particularly when dealing with physicians. To hear her note of panic could only mean she suspected the worst. He'd seen it in her eyes, the dreadful fear of a parent that they might outlive their child.

Henry slipped back into one of his favourite dreams, of the day he would be reunited in Heaven with his beloved Elizabeth and Arthur. Somewhere at the back of his mind doubt at the possibility of ever seeing them again lingered. Margaret's confessor, John Fisher, spent long hours at his bedside to ensure he didn't lose his faith in God's providence.

His fiftieth birthday had passed without celebration in January. When he failed to appear on St George's Day, a time when he would be seen by his people, rumours began to spread through the taverns of London. Some even suggested he was dead, those closest to him keeping up a pretence.

'He must eat soon.' Henry heard the worry in his mother's voice and could imagine the look she gave the physician. They spoke as if he wasn't there.

'Has the king been able to drink?'

'A little—but if he doesn't have some sustenance soon...' His mother's words tailed off, as if to say them would tempt fate.

'We should bleed him again, to see if he improves, my lady.' The physician sounded as if he thought it unlikely.

'I will visit the chapel. Be sure to summon me when he wakes?' Again, Henry heard the note of anguish, so rare in his mother's voice.

A fitful sleep offered the only relief from the pain in his throat. He drifted off into an elusive memory of feeling Elizabeth's protective warmth shielding him from the harsh reality of the world. It troubled Henry that he found it harder to recall exactly how it felt to hold his wife close.

He opened his eyes in time to see the light glint on the doctor's knife as it pierced his vein. Bright red blood spurted into the bowl. He closed his eyes again and tried to swallow. His throat burned.

An angel sang, her voice pure and clear. Henry listened. The tune sounded familiar, one of Elizabeth's favourites. His eyes focused on his daughter, seated by his bedside with her lute. She wore a gown of cornflower blue with a white coif over her golden hair, reminding him of her mother. Radiant, as if glowing with some inner power, she smiled when she noticed he'd woken.

'Mary...'

'Don't try to speak, Father.' A flicker of worry passed over her innocent face. 'Nod if you would like to drink?'

Henry nodded. Their roles had reversed. Now he'd become the child. He watched as Mary called for servants to bring his drink of milk. Unlike his mother she didn't ask him to sip from the cup. Instead, she fed him with a small silver spoon, showing great patience. A little spilled from his lips and she dried it with a clean white linen cloth.

'Thank you.' He managed to say the words as his mother entered the room. She stood behind his daughter, her hand on Mary's shoulder, a sign of reassurance and solidarity in their shared task.

She gestured to the servant carrying a steaming bowl and a platter of bread. 'If you sit you might find it easier to swallow?'

Henry sat up and his mother placed cushions at his back to support him. Mary exchanged the cup of milk for the bowl and offered him a small spoonful. The lukewarm, watery soup tasted good and didn't cause him to choke as it slid down his throat.

Mary tore a morsel of the bread and soaked it in the soup before offering it to Henry on the spoon. He somehow managed to swallow, although he felt a twinge of pain as it passed down his swollen throat, a small victory. He longed to talk, to thank them both properly, but knew he needed to rest.

Henry felt weak yet was determined to attend the May tournament in the grounds of Kennington Palace. As well as the most influential people in London, the guests included ambassadors of many foreign countries, so the tournament offered an ideal way to end the rumours and reassure his subjects.

His throne, under a cloth of gold canopy high on the royal grandstand, was padded with cushions and a physician stood ready with a soothing potion if needed. Henry's mother sat to one side, wearing a deep crimson gown, with his daughter Princess Mary to the other.

Mary dressed as Queen of the May, in a rich green gown on a throne decorated with bright spring flowers, surrounded by servants also dressed in livery of matching green. She'd only turned eleven the previous month yet Henry noticed how his daughter turned heads with her natural grace and Woodville beauty.

Her patient care might have saved his life, or at least hastened his recovery, although she made light of it. Henry made her the lady of honour, to present the prizes for the tournament, as her sister Margaret had done in the past.

In contrast he'd refused Prince Harry's request to take part in the jousting. Instead, Harry had to content himself with competing in the archery contest and the sport of running at the ring. Although still a great challenge and a chance to show his skill, both events lacked any element of danger. Henry's decision created a rift between them and he'd hardly seen his son since.

Royal heralds in Tudor green and white announced the parade of competitors with a fanfare of trumpets. Henry raised a hand in acknowledgement as the knights each held up a gauntleted hand in salute. As the long procession passed he turned to his daughter.

'Who is the knight riding behind your brother in black armour?'

'Charles Brandon, Father, he rides as the challenger. Do you not recognise him?' She giggled at her own joke, as Brandon could hardly be better disguised.

Henry recalled Charles Brandon's father, Sir William Brandon, who'd been his standard-bearer at the Battle of Bosworth. In a cruel twist of fate, Sir William was one of the few men slain by King Richard. He could have defended himself but stood his ground to hold Henry's standard high before the fatal blow.

Sir William's only surviving son had been in Henry's household since he was a boy. Handsome and quick to learn, he'd become a good companion for Harry, one of the few now permitted to lodge with him in Richmond Palace.

'Charles Brandon has become an experienced jouster by all accounts.' Henry's brow furrowed in a frown as he searched the field for Prince Harry. 'I trust your brother will learn to understand why I couldn't let him compete in the joust.'

'I doubt it, Father.' Mary placed her white-gloved hand on Henry's arm. 'I can tell you Harry and Charles practised in secret for this tournament for many weeks.'

'I cannot allow him to joust, Mary. The tiltyard is a dangerous place. I've seen good men maimed and even killed.'

'You need not worry for Harry, Father.' She smiled. 'Harry and Charles both have great skill with a lance.'

Henry heard the pride in her voice and wondered if it was for her brother or for young Charles Brandon. Although Brandon was twice Mary's age, she spoke most highly of him. He hoped she would be so enamoured of Charles of Ghent, Ferdinand's seven-year-old son and heir.

As he watched the cheering crowds he wondered if it was time he relaxed his control over Harry. Some part of him wished his son to become a warrior king but in his heart he feared the consequences. Henry turned to his mother.

'I refused Harry's request to ride in the joust, for his own safety. Do you think I was right to do so?'

'Of course you are right, Henry. If he were killed or severely wounded, what hope would there be for the succession, for the future of the Tudors?'

Henry cursed his dilemma. He'd done everything he could to protect Harry at the cost of their relationship. Harry had not visited him once when he'd been on his sickbed and had become surly and remote. Henry knew his mother was right yet his decision to stop him riding only made this worse.

Another cheer from the crowd meant the combats were about to begin with an archery contest. Drummers beating taborins led a parade of archers from all over the country, chosen to compete for the honour to shoot at targets before the king. Henry's poor eyesight meant he could no longer take part, although it cheered him to know Prince Harry made it to the final rounds.

Shooting from twenty paces, arrows swooshed through the air as the archers all fired at the targets. On command of the master archer, they moved back three paces before firing a second time. Henry appreciated the practiced ease with which Prince Harry handled the powerful longbow, drawing it with no effort.

His son stared up at the grandstand to make sure they were watching. Henry had encouraged him to use a bow as soon as he was able to, and paid for the finest tutors, yet Harry had a natural ability. He also had a strong competitive instinct, which may have come from his Tudor grandfather but was more likely from his Plantagenet bloodline.

The crowd cheered and applauded as the winner was announced and came forward for his prize. It was not Harry, although he'd come a close second. Princess Mary presented the purse of gold to the handsome young archer, who beamed with pride at the honour and bowed to Henry.

Next came the tourneying on foot, where knights fought with great broadswords and maces. The jarring sound of steel blades clanging against armour took Henry's mind back to the horrific slaughter in his name at Bosworth Field. He was glad Harry was not taking part, as one of the knights was felled by a savage blow to his helmet and lay still until carried off by his stewards.

Before the jousting Prince Harry gave a demonstration of riding at the ring. With his black destrier caparisoned in the royal colours of red, blue and gold, he raised his lance high in the air and thundered towards the suspended ring. In a show of well-rehearsed bravado, he lowered the heavy lance at the last moment, spearing the ring with apparent ease.

At last, the Master of the Joust announced the main event, a combat with lances on horseback. A number of competitors met in pairs. The first two failed to score as their wavering lances didn't even make contact.

Henry grew tired and struggled to see into the far

distance, so relied on Mary to tell him it was the final contest, between a Burgundian knight in blue-enameled plate armour and the challenger, Charles Brandon. Resplendent in black armour, Brandon raised his lance in the air to show he was ready at the far end of the tourney.

The crowd jostled for the best view and shouted as they began to place bets on who would win, although all knew it would be a close match. At the signal from the tournament master both horses lurched into a charge and closed in front of Henry's royal grandstand. Henry held his breath and felt a sense of foreboding as they began the charge. Hooves pounded, raising clouds of dust from the hard packed ground. The crowd gasped as Brandon's lance shattered against his rival's shoulder and cheered as a section of the lance broke off and spun in the air before thumping to the ground.

The Burgundian knight toppled back in the saddle. For a moment it looked as if he would recover, then he fell with a crash to the ground and lay still. Henry stared down from his high vantage-point. His mother was right. If Harry had suffered a serious injury he would never forgive himself. Whatever the cost of protecting Harry, it was the price he had to pay.

Princess Catherine wore a new gown of shimmering blue silk and a hood decorated with pearls for her meeting with Henry. After many refusals due to his poor health, he'd decided he should summon her and listen to her complaints. She looked well enough to Henry, despite another bout of her recurring illness.

'Thank you for agreeing to see me, Your Grace.' Catherine spoke in French and curtseyed yet failed to conceal the resentment in her words.

Henry waved towards the empty chair. 'I regret I have been... indisposed.' He replied in French. 'I understand there are matters you wish to discuss?'

Catherine nodded. 'I've not been able to learn what is to become of me.' She began her habit of speaking too fast, her Spanish accent returning. 'I am betrothed to Prince Harry yet he also refuses to see me for more than four months now, although I know he is here at Richmond. I write to him many times, asking for a reply to my letters...'

Henry held up a hand to silence her. 'It is not any slight to you, Princess Catherine. I had a condition that made it difficult to talk. I was able to see no one.'

She bowed her head. 'I am sorry... I felt as if I'd been forgotten.' She looked up at Henry. 'It has been a difficult time for us all, Your Grace.'

'You know your father has not paid the remaining portion of your dowry, as promised when we agreed your betrothal to Prince Harry?'

Princess Catherine stared at the toes of her blue silk slippers. 'I understand, Your Grace, and have written several times, begging for the matter to be resolved.'

Henry nodded. 'I proposed part payment in diamonds and gold plate but have received nothing since your marriage to Prince Arthur.' His voice wavered at the memory and he struggled to compose himself.

'A hundred thousand crowns is a great deal of money...' She sounded as if she finally understood their shared dilemma.

'I shall be honest with you, Princess Catherine. I have decided to break your engagement to my son.'

'You cannot. We are united before God, betrothed in the eyes of the church!' Her voice was raised and her eyes flared with anger.

Henry ignored her outburst and took a deep breath as he tried to remain calm. 'Prince Harry has been advised to repudiate the betrothal and free himself of obligation, which is why he's not been able to discuss a date for your marriage.'

'What is to become of me, Your Grace?' Her tone changed completely now.

'You might take the matter into your own hands by becoming Spain's Ambassador to England?' Henry watched for her reaction. Doctor Puebla was now too unwell to continue as ambassador and had to be carried in a litter. At their last meeting he revealed Ferdinand had suggested Catherine as his replacement, although she'd yet to respond to the offer.

She gave him a questioning look. 'There are already several ambassadors yet none have resolved this...'

Henry interrupted. 'Our hope is that you might have more success in persuading your father of his obligations.'

'And if I cannot?'

'Have faith, Catherine.'

'My faith is *not* the problem. I pray every day for an end to this waiting, Your Grace.' Again, the note of reproach sounded in her voice.

Henry cleared his throat. 'I also need to ask you about the rumours regarding your confessor.'

'Friar Diego Fernández is without question the best confessor any woman in my position could have.' Her reply sounded defensive. 'I mean, with respect to his devout life as well as his holy doctrine and proficiency in letters.'

Henry wished he'd thought to have his mother present before raising such a delicate issue. 'Is it true that this friar makes you kneel before him?'

Catherine's eyes flashed with defiance. 'It is the custom. My mother knelt at confession.'

Henry shook his head. 'You are an English princess now. You should learn to speak English—and it is not the English custom to show such deference to your confessor.' A thought occurred to him. 'I do not recall approving the engagement of this Spanish friar?'

'I am free to choose my own confessor, Your Grace. He serves me faithfully, giving me good advice and a good example. He asks for nothing—and nothing grieves me more than that my poverty does not permit me to reward him as he deserves.'

'I am told he is... unsuitable. It is said he is arrogant, with a high opinion of himself and a low opinion of women.' He studied her face. 'I am concerned because I promised to treat you as my own daughter.'

'De Puebla has been poisoning your mind against my loyal confessor, who has warned me about the ambassador's disloyalty to Spain.' Her strong Spanish accent returned.

Henry frowned but kept his voice calm. 'It was not from Rodrigo de Puebla, but it has come to my attention that staff of your own household say your confessor has such a hold over you that you obey him in everything.'

'Lies!'

He glared at her. 'You must take care, Princess Catherine, not to provide the gossipers at court with opportunity.'

Chapter Twenty-Four

May 1508

Henry worried about his health as he waited with his mother to receive yet another senior envoy from Spain. In February he'd suffered with swelling and tenderness in his joints, which his doctors told him was gout. They prescribed a potion of smelly boar's grease but it did little to alleviate the pain.

His vision had diminished still further, despite daily use of the lotion purported to make bright his sight. He also worried about the recurring soreness in his throat. His physicians warned his recovery might be temporary. They were reluctant to say as much but he knew he might be too weakened to survive another attack of the quinsy. The problem was he had no idea how he could avoid it.

He viewed the world differently as a consequence of his poor health and awareness of his own mortality. He'd become more devout, never missing mass and paying for prayers to be said. He'd also abandoned thoughts of remarriage or fathering another son and heir. Instead he planned to put his remaining energy into ensuring his children married well.

The new envoy, Commander Gutierre de Fuensalida, was a Knight of the Order of Santiago and Mayor of Granada. Tanned and well built, he wore a wide-brimmed hat and a scarlet cape trimmed with gold braid. His good English suggested an excellent education yet he lacked the flattering charm of his predecessors.

Fuensalida bowed and studied Henry with a soldier's eye, as if noting his weaknesses. 'King Ferdinand asks me to convey his most sincere best wishes, Your Grace.'

Henry glanced at his mother, who had cautioned him to remain civil towards their guest. 'You're a military man...' There was still a slight rasp to his voice. 'May we speak frankly?'

'Of course, Your Grace.'

'You should know I've grown tired of promises from King Ferdinand. When does he intend to pay the balance of the dowry?'

'King Ferdinand asked me to see that the princess is in good health and to reassure you of his good intentions, Your Grace.'

'I need more than good intentions, Commander Fuensalida. Have you met with Princess Catherine?'

'I have, Your Grace, and am concerned to find her illness has returned.'

Henry's mother replied. 'Princess Catherine has a cold. She will recover soon enough, with God's grace.'

Fuensalida frowned at Lady Margaret's intervention and continued to address Henry. 'I will do what I can to progress payment of the remaining dowry, Your Grace, but I need you to confirm your intention for her to marry your son, Prince Henry.'

Henry heard the hint of a threat. He looked at the commander. The man's grey hair and lined face suggested he must be close to sixty, yet he appeared as fit as a much younger man. Unlike other envoys from Spain he had an arrogance Henry found unsettling.

'I had an agreement with your master that remains

binding—despite the tragic loss of my eldest son.'

'All we ask, Your Grace, is your acknowledgement that the betrothal of Princess Catherine to Prince Henry is equally binding.'

Henry felt his anger rising and nodded to his servants to open the doors. These meetings were not good for his health or his temper. It was becoming obvious why King Ferdinand had chosen Fuensalida as his envoy. The Spaniard gaped in astonishment that the meeting was over so soon.

'There are still matters to discuss, Your Grace.'

'I will therefore ask you to meet with my counsellors.' He waved a hand. 'Good day to you, Commander.'

After he'd gone Henry's mother turned to him. 'You could have indulged him for a little longer, out of courtesy.'

Henry shook his head. 'I've had enough of their posturing, Mother. It irks me to allow Fuensalida to think he's been responsible for letting Ferdinand off the hook.'

With Bishop Foxe away on other duties, Henry summoned the bishop's secretary, an ambitious young cleric named Thomas Wolsey. It amused him to know Wolsey tried to keep secret his humble origins, although his father was a butcher and cattle farmer.

Establishing a reputation as a skilled administrator of both church and state, Wolsey was an Oxford graduate before his ordination. He'd been chaplain to the Archbishop of Canterbury and now acted as one of Henry's chaplains, as well as supporting Bishop Foxe. He dressed in the sombre robes of a priest and carried a leather bag from which he produced several letters.

'I thought these should be brought to your attention,

Your Grace.' He unfolded one and pointed a stubby finger. 'It is from King Ferdinand to his daughter, Princess Catherine, and has been written in some form of code.'

'Have you been able to decipher this, Master Wolsey?' Henry squinted at the contents, frustrated by his poor eyesight before realising he could read none of the coded Spanish words.

Thomas Wolsey shook his head. 'We managed to read his instruction to the princess to do everything in her power to preserve your goodwill, Your Grace, as well as the love of the Prince of Wales and the esteem of the people of England.'

'That is all?'

'He suggests you have no better chance of securing the succession of your son than by marrying him to Princess Catherine. I can only suggest that the other contents were intended to be kept secret.' He produced a second letter and held it up for Henry to see. 'Although it is in Spanish, we can learn more from Princess Catherine's coded reply.'

'You've intercepted her letters?' Henry frowned.

'All letters from the princess to Spain are checked as a routine precaution, Your Grace.'

'Were they not sealed?'

Thomas Wolsey's face reddened at the challenge. 'There are ways of dealing with the seals.' He gave Henry a knowing glance.

'What does she say?' Henry felt uncomfortable with the idea of intercepting Catherine's messages yet was intrigued. He doubted young Wolsey would have bothered him with them if they were of no consequence.

'The codes use strange symbols, as well as Latin

numerals and keywords in place of names.' Wolsey frowned. 'We have been able to see she places the blame for her situation on Doctor de Puebla and asks for him to be removed from his post as Ambassador.'

'That comes as little surprise. The two of them have always distrusted each other, although it seems unfair to blame Puebla now he is infirm—and has little influence over her situation.'

Wolsey consulted his notes of the decoded letters. 'The princess also complains to her father, forgive me, Your Grace, of your... cruelty in not permitting her to see your son, the Prince of Wales.'

'I allow her to live in the same house!' Henry heard the defensive note in his voice, although he knew what she said was true and he must do something about it before too long.

Wolsey pointed out another line in the coded letter. 'We think she says you wish to marry her sister—and hopes to use your interest to her advantage.'

'I once considered the possibility of marriage to Queen Joanna. She is an attractive woman, Master Wolsey, still of childbearing age.'

'It is no longer your intention?' Wolsey's dark eyes watched him with the same sharp interest as he showed in the letters.

Henry grew wistful as he recalled how entranced he'd been at his first meeting with Joanna. 'I asked Doctor de Puebla to make enquiries. He informed me she is in mourning for her late husband and her excessive grief means she is unfit to marry anyone.' He looked at Wolsey. 'I do not accept that she is insane—but I no longer have any intention of marriage, to her or anyone.'

Wolsey hesitated to reply and studied Henry as if

deciding not to comment. 'What do you wish to do about this correspondence, Your Grace?'

Henry scratched the grey stubble on his chin. 'I wish to meet one last time with Ambassador Fuensalida. We must put an end to King Ferdinand's games—and I would like you to attend as a witness, Master Wolsey, to note whatever is agreed.'

Later he shared a flagon of his best wine with Lady Katheryn in the privacy of his study. One of the few he felt he could trust, she knew him better than anyone now and had become his confidante, closer even than his mother.

'Prince Harry resents my efforts to keep him safe. He hardly speaks since I broke off his engagement to Princess Catherine.' Henry lowered his voice. 'He takes his meals alone and spends more time sparring with his friends than studying to become king.'

Katheryn sipped her wine before replying. She wore a gown of azure blue satin that shimmered when she moved, and sat close enough for Henry to know she'd used the intoxicating French perfume he'd given her.

'Harry is young and will understand in time.'

'Time is the one resource I do not have in abundance.' Henry frowned. 'All I wish is the best for him, which might be to marry Princess Catherine, but first I must be sure.' He took a deep drink of his wine, enjoying the rich taste and the soothing effect on his throat.

Lady Katheryn gave him a questioning look. 'What do you have in mind?'

'I plan to begin discreet negotiations for a marriage between my son and Catherine's niece, Princess Eleanor of Austria.'

'The daughter of Queen Joanna of Castile—and you would marry your daughter to her son.'

'What do you think of it?'

'Do you want to hear the truth?' She took another sip of her wine.

'Of course.' He drained his glass.

'If I didn't know better, I would think you were doing this to spite King Ferdinand for playing games with Catherine's dowry. Princess Eleanor is not yet ten years old.' She studied him with a twinkle in her eye. 'Prince Harry is not noted for his patience. He won't thank you for making him wait another six years before he is allowed to... consummate a marriage.'

Henry examined his empty glass. Of the finest quality, it had been a gift from the Venetian ambassador and engraved with a lion wearing a crown. The slender stem had a spiral twist and the bowl sparkled in the light as he turned it. He frowned as he noticed it had suffered a chip on the rim.

'You are right, as usual. Although I feel obliged to explore all the possibilities, I wonder if I will be around by the time this... marriage could be agreed.'

Her eyes narrowed with concern. 'You feel unwell again?'

Henry massaged his knee. 'My joints ache with this gout. The doctors have no idea of a cure—and warn me the quinsy could return at any time.'

'I'm sorry.' She placed a comforting hand on his arm. 'I forget how you suffer.'

'All I can do is pray, Katheryn—which seems to be my solution for most things these days!' He liked the warmth of her touch. He missed the intimacy he enjoyed with Elizabeth. Lady Katheryn was an attractive woman and he might be in love with her, yet he would never take it further for fear of losing her as a companion.

Thomas Wolsey wasted no time arranging Henry's meeting with Fuensalida. This time they met in the Palace of Westminster and the Spaniard strutted in with an air of arrogance. Henry could imagine what Princess Catherine had been telling him.

'Commander Fuensalida, I trust you bring me better news?'

'I regret, Your Grace, that since our last meeting I have discovered your son is no longer engaged to Princess Catherine.'

Henry studied the Spaniard, trying to work out what game he played. 'You must know there are many eligible princesses, with greater dowry prospects, yet I have not favoured any over Catherine.'

Fuensalida continued undaunted., 'It is proposed that you agree to forgo the balance of the dowry. King Ferdinand also advises that he refuses to sign the declaration confirming the marriage of his grandson, Prince Charles and your daughter, Princess Mary.'

'You insult us, Commander Fuensalida.' Henry raised his voice and scowled as new pain flared in his throat. 'It is no secret that we are negotiating the payment of a generous dowry to the Holy Roman Emperor Maximilian, Prince Charles' *paternal* grandfather.'

Henry could see the information was news to him. They both knew Emperor Maximilian needed the money and the payment would unite him in an alliance against King Ferdinand. Henry glanced across at Thomas Wolsey.

'You will inform King Ferdinand that I consider

Princess Catherine as my own daughter. My son is free from the marriage contract because the dowry has not been paid within the time agreed.'

'Forgive me, Your Grace, I am only the messenger.' Fuensalida avoided Henry's eye.

'You may also inform your master that he has incurred my displeasure for refusing to support the marriage of Prince Charles and Princess Mary.' Henry's tone sounded harsher than he intended because of the soreness of his throat but it was clear Fuensalida understood.

The queen's presence chamber at Richmond Palace, with its priceless tapestries and polished oak floor, held many poignant memories for Henry. Kept as a memorial to Elizabeth, it was the only place he could go to feel a sense of her, as her chambers had long since been occupied by Prince Harry.

Now he decided it would be the ideal place for the betrothal of his daughter Mary. In a treaty signed in Calais it was agreed the marriage would take place in six years, when Prince Charles reached the age of fourteen. In the meantime, Henry wished to bind Charles to Mary in the eyes of God.

The shutters were opened for the first time since Elizabeth's death and the windows polished until they shone. A fire had been lit to ward off the December damp and rows of seats arranged for the guests, with a long red carpet down the middle to represent the nave of a church. Princess Mary sat alone on a low throne under a grand canopy of cloth of gold.

The Lord of Bergues, stand-in for young Charles at the ceremony, arrived with an impressive entourage of

Flemish and Spanish nobles. Tall and thin, with a hat too large for his head, he bowed to Henry and presented him with a velvet covered box containing a gold fleur-de-lis glittering with fine diamonds.

Henry thanked him in French and introduced his daughter. The Lord of Bergues bowed again and presented her with another wedding present, a large diamond brooch set in a circle of perfect pearls. He then read aloud in French a letter from Charles, an unconvincing speech about how devoted Charles was towards his new bride. Princess Mary, dressed in her bridal gown, stared at the Flemish lord, her face reddening with embarrassment at his earnest words.

The sour-faced Lord Chancellor, Archbishop of Canterbury William Warham, gave an overlong sermon in his booming voice on the sanctity of marriage. He then blessed them both and asked Mary to repeat her marriage vows before God and the assembled witnesses.

Her voice lacked conviction as she promised her life to an eight-year-old prince she had never met, while staring at the thin-faced Lord of Bergues. At one point she stumbled over her words and Archbishop Warham had to prompt her.

After repeating his vows on behalf of Prince Charles, the Lord of Bergues kissed her on the lips with more enthusiasm than required. He then reached into a pocket in his doublet and took out a heavy gold ring, which he placed on her slender finger.

Henry breathed a sigh of relief to see another of his children married well. He'd grown close to Mary when she helped nurse him through his illness, and was glad it had not been her duty to marry a man much older than herself.

At the banquet that followed, Henry sat with Prince Harry and the Lord of Bergues, while the ladies were at a separate table. Later there would be dancing but for now the musicians played tunes chosen for the occasion by Mary.

Harry turned to Henry after the grace was said by Archbishop Warham. 'I see Princess Catherine is seated at the far end of the table, Father. Has she offended you in some way?'

Henry shook his head. 'We thought to avoid causing awkwardness to your sister.'

'You know they are still close, Father? Mary has been helping Catherine with her English, in return for tuition in Spanish.'

'I'm glad to hear it, Harry. It is well past time when we could converse with the princess in English.'

He glanced across the room and caught his daughter's eye. He was surprised to see a glimpse of sadness before she composed herself, rather than the joy he'd expected. He decided it must be due to the stress of the occasion, although he guessed there might be another reason.

He knew she'd been seen with Charles Brandon on more than one occasion. Brandon had proved himself an unsuitable companion for Mary. He'd fathered a child with an attractive young courtier, Lady Anne Brown, then married her wealthy widowed aunt, Lady Margaret Neville, eighteen years his senior.

Henry suspected Harry's involvement when Brandon divorced his new wife and married Anne in a secret ceremony. He should be banished from court, yet was a great favourite of Prince Harry, and Henry felt reluctant to further antagonize his son.

Chapter Twenty-Five

April 1509

Henry lay in his canopied bed in Richmond Palace, propped up with silk pillows and exhausted by his aches and pains. The quinsy had returned with a vengeance and he struggled to eat or speak. He'd lost track of the days and slept restlessly, waking in the night with a raging thirst.

His most frequent visitor was his mother. Approaching her sixty-sixth year, she looked thin and pale in her black gown, another concern to add to Henry's list. Although she sometimes stayed in her apartments in Richmond, she'd moved her household to Coldharbour so she could visit him every day.

'My dearly beloved son,' she studied him, as if making a judgement, 'I pray for you, yet in my heart I know this will not be so easily recovered from.'

He replied in a hoarse whisper, so she needed to lean closer to hear. 'I have learnt to read the faces of our physicians, lady Mother. I know to ignore their reassuring words...' He coughed, doubling up in pain with each contraction of his throat. 'They do not expect me to last long and there is much to do—while there is still breath in my body.'

Lady Margaret wiped a tear from her eye then regained her composure. 'I understand you have appointed me as executor of your will.'

'Who better?' His voice rasped, each word an effort.

'Master Wolsey read it to me, as my own eyesight is not as sharp as it once was.' A flicker of concern passed over her face. 'You make no mention of the succession?'

'Prince Harry will succeed me, Mother.' He coughed again and grimaced as he tried to control the pain. 'I regret he has not been well enough prepared...'

Lady Margaret shook her head. 'He is too young at seventeen for such responsibility.'

'I appoint you as Regent until he is of age. Will you speak with Harry, to assure him of my intention?' He suppressed another cough.

His Mother held his cup of mead while he took a sip. 'Has he not visited you?'

Henry was unable to reply. It saddened him that Harry found better things to do than comfort his ailing father. His mother would deal with it, as she always had. His Uncle Jasper used to say it was Beaufort steel that gave her such strength in adversity.

Bishop Foxe came to administer a special mass and blessing while Henry remained in his bed to receive communion. He couldn't manage the wafer of bread but he sipped a little holy wine. The familiar rituals gave him a certain inner strength and provided order in his waking and sleeping hours. Afterwards, Foxe sat to keep him company by reading from the scriptures.

'I owe you a debt, Richard.' Henry wheezed when he had finished.

'Your Grace?'

'I learnt from Wolsey it was you who secured the betrothal of my daughter Mary.'

'It was not difficult, Your Grace.' Foxe was dismissive. 'Once Emperor Maximilian knew it would be to his advantage he could not wait to agree.'

'Accept my gratitude, Bishop, while I can still speak.'

Foxe nodded, concern written on his lined face. 'Two thousand masses have been said, Your Grace, and Thomas Wolsey is arranging for all the parishes to pray for you.'

'Convey my thanks to Master Wolsey. He is thorough in his work.'

Foxe stood, holding his precious Vulgate Bible. 'I shall, Your Grace, and will return once I've dealt with matters at Winchester.'

'Before you go, as my confessor, you must help redeem my sins.' Henry's voice reduced to a wheezing whisper. 'I've been... too ready to jail those who offend me and too slow to release them, for fear of what they might do.'

Bishop Foxe thought for a moment. 'You could proclaim a general pardon, Your Grace. Free all those held in jails except for murder and treason. They might pray for you in gratitude for your mercy?'

Henry nodded. 'Make it so.' His voice was failing now and he held up a hand in farewell. 'Thank you, Richard.'

After Foxe had gone Henry reflected on the men such as him who'd shown such loyalty over the years. It saddened him to know people said he'd appointed bishops such as Foxe and Fisher out of patronage.

Henry woke from a troubled sleep to see his precious Elizabeth seated at his bedside. For a moment he thought he might still be dreaming. She looked as young and beautiful as ever, golden hair showing under a white coif with a border of dazzling pearls.

'How are you, Father?' She reached out and placed

her cool hand on his feverish forehead. 'Can you speak?'

Betrothal had changed Mary. Like a butterfly emerging from its chrysalis, she had bloomed from a girl into a woman. She dressed like a queen and wore the diamond and pearl brooch, her wedding gift from Charles.

She studied his face with the look of one who knows a poorly kept secret. Henry couldn't fail to notice the way they all looked at him now. He'd grown skeletal from lack of nourishment. His grey hair was lank and his chin rough with stubble but he knew the look of pity.

'Mary...' The words formed in his mind yet none came from his mouth. Before the quinsy he'd always taken being able to speak for granted. Now it had become elusive, something to be worked at.

'Don't try to talk, Father.' She brightened as she produced a folded parchment. 'I have had a reply to my letter to Prince Charles.'

Henry tried again. 'Charles will have many enemies when he... becomes Emperor of Rome.' His voice sounded hoarse. 'As his empress... you can help him make peace with France.'

'I should like to see the world beyond these shores.' Mary's face lit up at the thought. 'It will be a great adventure, Father.'

Henry struggled to suppress a cough. The burning pain of coughing was the worst of the quinsy. He pointed to his cup of warmed mead. Mary understood and held it to his lips. He focused his mind on swallowing a little of the sweet liquid.

She placed the cup back on his side table. 'Would you like me to read his letter to you?'

Henry nodded his head. She would make Charles a fine wife, a credit to the Tudors. He remembered the first time he held her in his arms. Mary entered the world without fuss after the sad death of their daughter Elizabeth. Now he could picture her as queen of an empire, surrounded by her ladies-in-waiting. Her mother would have been so proud.

Mary began to read in French. Henry thought the words sounded far too mannered and formal for a nine-year-old. He suspected it had been composed by his advisors but Mary seemed pleased with it. When she'd finished reading she folded the letter as if it was of great value to her.

'I would like to ask you a favour—or for you to at least consider it, Father.' Her face was serious and he glimpsed what she might look like when she was older.

'Whatever you wish, Mary. How could I refuse you?'

'It is not for myself, Father. I ask on behalf of Princess Catherine. She has been gracious company for me, teaching me Spanish in return for lessons in English.'

Henry nodded. 'Your brother told me. What is it you ask?'

Mary took a deep breath. 'She is in despair about her future. I would like to ask that you permit her marriage to Harry.'

Henry lay back on his soft pillows and closed his eyes. 'I confess I've not... treated her as my own daughter, as I promised.' His voice was a whisper, as if he spoke to himself.

He didn't hear her reply and opened his eyes as Mary left, pulling the door closed behind her. He should have agreed with good grace, yet his old enmity against Ferdinand lingered. He would see her again when his throat recovered a little. In the meantime, he would give the matter thought. He was in no condition to meet with Princess Catherine, although his conscience told him he should.

Lady Katheryn's eyes were full of sadness, despite her forced smile of greeting. She had not been to visit him for over a week and he suspected he knew the reason. She dressed as if already in mourning, and took his frail hand in hers, as Elizabeth had once done, a sign of her affection.

Henry managed a smile. 'I hoped you would come to see me soon.' He sounded hoarse yet was determined to speak.

'I... wanted to remember you as you were—then I realised it would be selfish.' She stared into his eyes, as if trying to read his thoughts.

'If you hadn't come, I would have summoned you, Katheryn...' Henry closed his eyes as he dealt with the pain then continued. 'There is something I want to tell you.'

'I already know.' Her soft voice was a whisper. 'I know you too well, Henry, so of course I am aware of your feelings towards me.'

'I could never tell you, no matter how I wanted to.'

'I was the wife of your enemy...'

Henry nodded as he remembered. 'Love your enemies and pray for those who persecute you...' He noticed her smile at his translation of the Vulgate. 'I've had more than my share of enemies yet few were as easy to love.'

She gripped his thin fingers in her hand. 'I never was your enemy.'

He realised she was on the brink of tears. 'I've often

wondered why you show me such affection, risking your reputation, after your husband...' His words tailed off. He could not remind her he'd had her husband executed.

'Queen Elizabeth showed me great kindness.' Her voice sounded wistful at the memory. 'On her deathbed she asked me to promise to watch over you.'

Henry wished he hadn't asked but remembered the many times she'd shown him true affection. He doubted it had been much hardship to keep her promise to Elizabeth. He decided to use the little voice he had left for something of greater importance and gave her hand a squeeze.

'I wish you to marry again, Katheryn.'

'Who would you have me marry?' Her eyebrows raised in surprise at his suggestion.

'The most eligible nobles of my court would fight each other for your hand.' He managed a smile. 'You are a beautiful woman. I've seen the way they look at you.'

'I have been married once—and am in no hurry to do so again.'

'You are still young. You are as clever as any of my advisors. All I ask is that you live your life to the fullest.'

'I will think on it, Henry,' she returned the squeeze of his hand, 'while I pray for your recovery.'

Harry had not visited until summoned and arrived late. The chair scraped on the tiled floor as he sat. Henry stared at his son, as if seeing him for the first time. His fashionable clothes emphasised his athletic build and the gold clasp with large ruby adorning his cap looked familiar.

Henry raised a hand and pointed to the precious

jewel. 'I remember... that belonged to your mother.'

'I wear it as a keepsake.' His tone softened for a moment. 'I miss her, Father.'

Henry nodded. 'As do I, Harry.'

'You sent for me, Father?' He glanced back towards the door, as if he would rather not be there.

'We have... important matters to discuss, Harry.' He studied his son's serious face. 'You are to succeed me, yet I've failed to prepare you well enough.'

Harry remained silent for a moment. 'I have spoken with my grandmother. She recommends Bishop Fisher to help me select advisors.'

'Good. Listen to John Fisher, Harry, he offers good counsel.' Henry took a deep breath. 'There is another matter... regarding Princess Catherine. I wish you to set aside the dowry and marry her.' He paused to recover his breath. 'I have wronged her and wish to make amends.'

Harry nodded. 'I will do so gladly, Father. May I inform her now?' His youthful energy and enthusiasm shone in his eyes.

'You may, Harry,' he felt his voice failing, 'and inform the princess that I... regret—no, tell her I'm sorry she has been made to wait so long.'

He knew Harry wished to go. 'Take care of your sisters...'

Harry stood. 'I shall write to Margaret in Scotland and invite her to visit you.'

Henry winced with pain. He would never see his daughter Margaret again, even if she made the long journey from Edinburgh. He pictured her anguished face the last time he'd seen her and wondered if he'd been right to marry her to King James. He stared at his son, straining at the leash like one of Elizabeth's greyhounds.

'Look after Mary... she seems older than her years but needs you to watch over her.' He gasped for breath now.

Harry was gone without a farewell. He felt a pang of sadness that his son seemed to care so little for him. If he had his time over again it would be different, as would many things.

They surrounded his bed on three sides, hands clasped together as Bishop Fisher said a prayer. The hour was late and stumps of candles flickered, casting long shadows on the tapestried walls. The last embers of a fire glowed bright amber in the hearth, offering little warmth, yet no one bothered to throw fresh logs on the fire.

'By the sacred mysteries of man's redemption may almighty God remit to you all penalties of the present life and of the life to come. May he open to you the gates of paradise and lead you to joys everlasting.' Bishop Fisher anointed his head with oil. 'May almighty God bless you, Father and Son, and Holy Spirit... Amen.'

Henry heard John Fisher's words and knew what they meant. Blessed relief from the pains that troubled him. He would never again have to worry about usurpers, no longer make decisions of life and death.

He couldn't speak and found it difficult to breathe, so closed his eyes and surrendered to his destiny. He'd ensured the succession of the Tudor line and overseen the longest peace anyone could remember. His children would marry well and he'd made his mother proud. Now he reached out towards the light, for Elizabeth and Arthur, waiting for him.

Author's Note

Henry Tudor died on 21 April 1509. There has been speculation about the probable cause, including tuberculosis, gout and asthma. Having spent over three years researching every detail of his life, I decided a fitting end to the final book of the trilogy would be to visit his tomb in Westminster and pay my respects to Henry, his wife Elizabeth and his mother, Lady Margaret Beaufort.

There is something surreal about making your way through Westminster Abbey to the Lady Chapel at the far end. There are many distractions, as you pass the tombs of earlier kings and queens and see Henry's granddaughter Elizabeth I in a side chapel.

Henry's towering tomb dominates the centre of the Lady Chapel. Surrounded by a blackened bronze grille, his effigy is raised too high to see. I climbed a step and peered through the holes in the grille and finally saw Henry. His effigy lies at the side of his wife, Elizabeth of York. Their faces have been burnished by the touch of countless hands over the centuries and their hands are clasped in prayer.

Designed by Italian sculptor Pietro Torrigiano the black marble base has gilded medallions representing the Virgin Mary and Henry's patron saints. At either end of his tomb cherubs support coats of arms and at each corner are Henry's badges of the Welsh dragon and the greyhound of Richmond.

The inscriptions on the tomb are translated as:

Here lies Henry the Seventh of that name, formerly King of England, son of Edmund, Earl of Richmond. He was created King on August 22 and immediately afterwards, on October 30, he was crowned at Westminster in the year of Our Lord 1485. He died subsequently on April 21 in the 53rd year of his age. He reigned 23 years eight months, less one day.

At Henry's funeral Bishop John Fisher said:

'His politic wisdom in government was singular; his reason pithy and substantial, his memory fresh and holding, his experience notable, his counsels fortunate and taken with wise deliberation, his speech gracious in diverse languages. His dealings in time of peril and dangers was cold and sober with great hardiness. If any treason was conspired against him it came out most wonderfully.'

Tony Riches
Pembrokeshire, Wales
www.tonyriches.com

Also by Tony Riches

Owen - Book One of the Tudor Trilogy

England 1422: Owen Tudor, a Welsh servant, waits in Windsor Castle to meet his new mistress, the beautiful and lonely Queen Catherine of Valois, widow of the warrior king, Henry V. Her infant son is crowned King of England and France, and while the country simmers on the brink of civil war, Owen becomes her protector.

They fall in love, risking Owen's life and Queen Catherine's reputation, but how do they found the dynasty which changes British history – the Tudors?

This is the first historical novel to fully explore the amazing life of Owen Tudor, grandfather of King Henry VII and the great-grandfather of King Henry VIII. Set against a background of the conflict between the Houses of Lancaster and York, which develops into what have become known as the Wars of the Roses, Owen's story deserves to be told.

Available as paperback, audiobook and eBook

Jasper - Book Two of the Tudor Trilogy

England 1461: The young King Edward of York has taken the country by force from King Henry VI of Lancaster. Sir Jasper Tudor, Earl of Pembroke, flees the massacre of his Welsh army at the Battle of Mortimer's Cross and plans a rebellion to return his half-brother King Henry to the throne.

When King Henry is imprisoned by Edward in the Tower of London and murdered, Jasper escapes to Brittany with his young nephew, Henry Tudor. Then after the sudden death of King Edward and the mysterious disappearance of his sons, a new king, Edward's brother Richard III takes the English throne. With nothing but his wits and charm, Jasper sees his chance to make young Henry Tudor king with a daring and reckless invasion of England.

Set in the often brutal world of fifteenth century England, Wales, Scotland, France, Burgundy and Brittany, during the Wars of the Roses, this fast-paced story is one of courage and adventure, love and belief in the destiny of the Tudors.

Available as paperback, audiobook and eBook

The Secret Diary of Eleanor Cobham

England 1441: Lady Eleanor Cobham, Duchess of Gloucester, hopes to become Queen of England before her interest in astrology and her husband's ambition leads their enemies to accuse her of a plot against the king. Eleanor is found guilty of sorcery and witchcraft. Rather than have her executed, King Henry VI orders Eleanor to be imprisoned for life.

More than a century after her death, carpenters restoring one of the towers of Beaumaris Castle discover a sealed box hidden under the wooden boards. Thinking they have found treasure, they break the ancient box open, disappointed to find it only contains a book, with hand-sewn pages of yellowed parchment.

Written in a code no one could understand, the mysterious book changed hands many times for more than five centuries, between antiquarian book collectors, until it came to me. After years of frustrating failure to break the code, I discover it is based on a long-forgotten medieval dialect and am at last able to decipher the secret diary of Eleanor Cobham.

Available as paperback, audiobook and eBook

Warwick - The Man behind
the Wars of the Roses

Richard Neville, Earl of Warwick, the 'Kingmaker', is the wealthiest noble in England. He becomes a warrior knight, bravely protecting the North against invasion by the Scots. A key figure in what have become known as 'the Wars of the Roses,' he fought in most of the important battles. As Captain of Calais, he turns privateer, daring to take on the might of the Spanish fleet and becoming Admiral of England. The friend of kings, he is the sworn enemy of Queen Margaret of Anjou. Then, in an amazing change of heart, why does he risk everything to fight for her cause?

Writers from William Shakespeare to best-selling modern authors have tried to show what sort of man Richard Neville must have been, with quite different results. Sometimes Warwick is portrayed as the skilled political manipulator behind the throne, shaping events for his own advantage. Others describe him as the 'last of the barons', ruling his fiefdom like an uncrowned king. Whatever the truth, his story is one of adventure, power and influence at the heart of one of the most dangerous times in the history of England.

Available as paperback and eBook

Made in the USA
Lexington, KY
07 July 2017